THE STORM KILLINGS

A twisty serial killer thriller

IAIN HENN

Published by The Book Folks

London, 2024

ISBN 978-1-80462-152-3

www.thebookfolks.com

THE STORM KILLINGS is the third standalone book in a series by Iain Henn about a special FBI unit set up to investigate seemingly unsolvable mysteries. Look out for the other titles, THE PIPER'S CHILDREN, THE WHISTLER'S OMEN, and THE DEVIL'S ARTIST!

Details about Iain's other novels, the mystery DEAD SET ON MURDER and the romantic thriller THE GREATEST BETRAYAL, can be found at the back of this book.

"The thunder beings are the Great Spirits, and they have the power to give life, as well as take it away. They send rain to refresh the earth and nurture life, but they also send destructive winds, floods, and droughts, and burn with their bolts of lightning."

Algonquian legend

Prologue

The girl heard the distant roar, a sound like the freight train she often heard thundering along the far-off track. Only this was no train, and the roar grew louder as though magnifying a thousand times and then a thousand times again with each passing second.

She watched as her aunt drew back the front window drapes, gasping as she did, "Oh, dear Lord—"

"What is it, Auntie Lizzie?" The girl ran to her aunt's side. Her breath caught in her throat as she looked outside, her gaze transfixed. The sky was alive with twisting shapes that seemed to leap and hiss, dark formations that were etched into mountains of fast-moving clouds. At its center, dominating everything, was a towering column of sheer fury that whirled toward their farmhouse.

"Auntie, I'm scared." The walls shook and it seemed to her that creatures were slamming in fury against the windows.

The woman clasped her niece's hand and pulled her toward the door. "We need to get to the shelter, darling, now."

"But what about Goldie?" the girl protested.

"No time, honey—"

The five-year-old yanked her hand free and ran toward her bedroom, screaming, "Goldie! Goldie!" As she ran, she heard a booming, banging knocking at the front door. It was as though the wind was forcing its way in.

"Cassie," her aunt called after her.

Cassie ran into the room and took hold of the chubby-faced, blonde-haired Goldie. The doll was where she'd left it, propped up on the bed.

With the doll tucked firmly under her arm, Cassie turned back to the door, just as it slammed shut from the force of the wind.

She heard crashing sounds, shattering glass from exploding windows, and she heard her aunt scream. "Aunt Lizzie!" the girl called out. And then she heard her aunt's voice. It was muffled by the deafening roar and the girl couldn't make out what she was saying. Was she talking to someone? Then her aunt screamed again but as quickly as it began, the scream faded beneath the thunderous blasts of the storm.

The house rocked, shifting and sliding like a fun-park tilting house, and the girl fell to the floor.

She crawled under the bed, grabbing hold of the iron leg, with Goldie still pressed tightly against her. She closed her eyes tightly, willing the horror to pass. This had all happened so quickly. It had been cloudy and rainy but quiet just a short while ago, a day like so many others, and she'd hoped the sun would come out. The winds had erupted suddenly, and the darkness had rushed in just as the night sometimes did but Cassie knew it was only the middle of the afternoon.

There was another powerful blast and this time the bedroom door was ripped from its hinges. Cassie opened her eyes, sobbing now, and she peered through to the hallway, dark and misted over with debris. She saw a shape, not her aunt, but someone or something else, brandishing a long stick with curving shapes that reminded her of something, but she couldn't remember where she'd seen it before. She wished her mom would come, but instead a beam of light shone, illuminating a patch of the darkness around her.

A deep voice. The shadow beyond the door was calling out to her, the voice strangely calm. "The thunder beings will look after you." And then this dark figure, with light emanating from its eyes, was gone.

PART ONE

Chapter One

Day One

Spawned from thunderstorms, tornadoes are the most powerful of nature's tempests. They appear suddenly, funnels descending from dark clouds. Savage whirlwinds that hit the ground and roar across the landscape at speeds that can reach two hundred miles per hour.

I sat in the Seattle field office and watched the video footage of the twister, imagining it as the embodiment of all the unleashed energy in the world's weather systems. It reminded me of my own pent-up anxiety, released when I indulged in the secret that I knew was an unhealthy obsession. And just like the destructive nature of that twister, I knew that with one mistake my hidden life could cause my death. Or if discovered, would bring about the destruction of the career that meant everything to me.

And yet I hadn't been able to stop.

"What's this about, Zoe?" I asked.

"Ilona, this footage shows a tornado that touched down three days ago in Oklahoma," Zoe said. "The farmhouse in its path was occupied by a woman named Liz Markus. The house belonged to her sister. Liz Markus was staying there, minding her sister's daughter while her sister was at work."

I knew that tornadoes came in all shapes and sizes and this one was a monolithic tower that whirled like an out-of-control spinning top, its direction shifting suddenly so that it narrowly missed the farmhouse. As it thundered by, its fierce winds ripped away part of the roof as portions of the walls rippled and swayed.

Zoe shifted in her chair, tugging as she sometimes did at her springy, dark afro-style curls, her gaze wandering over Will, Marcia, and myself. "Liz Markus was killed but miraculously her five-year-old niece survived. Unharmed. Cause of the woman's death, severe blunt-force trauma to the head."

Less than an hour earlier, as I'd been leaving my apartment, I had received a text alert from the FBI Special Agent in Charge, Will McCord. It simply stated that as soon as I arrived, there would be a meeting in the main command area of the UCU, or Unsolvable Crimes Unit. The team's tech guru, Zoe Marshall, had urgently highlighted one of the overnight reports from the predictive artificial intelligence software named Themis.

My arrival coincided with that of our team's coordinator and analyst, Marcia Kendall, and together with Will, we were grouped around the expansive horseshoe-shaped console and bank of monitors that comprised part of the Themis hardware.

The video footage had no sooner stopped when rows of data scrolled across the screen. "Themis compiled this list of storm-related US deaths from blunt-force head trauma over the past ten years." Zoe's gaze flipped from us to the screen and back again and she raised her hand, her fingers splayed toward the monitor. "What you're seeing is that deaths with that specific description are few and far between for the first seven years. *But*" – her voice lifted as she glanced at each of us – "in the past three years there have been nine of these storm-inflicted fatal head injuries, all remarkably similar in the position and extent of the wounds. All of these victims were women, living alone, except for this last one, who was minding her niece in her sister's home."

"That's not so unusual, is it," Marcia wondered aloud, "where the tornado victim has suffered a head blow from a fall or flying debris?" Bespectacled, middle-aged Marcia was a Bureau languages expert who'd advised the newly formed UCU on its first case. Since then, alongside her official role as Bureau translator, Marcia had stayed with the UCU part-time.

Will weighed in. "Head wounds, multiple bruises, broken bones, all would be common."

Zoe was quiet for a moment. "But I'm seeing something else."

Marcia frowned. "Seeing what?"

"A pattern."

My eyes were glued to the data. I tried to dismiss the idea I sensed was in Zoe's mind, it seemed outlandish, but as fast as I pushed it away, it pushed back. "You think there's more to those deaths than storm injuries."

"Themis is implying it, Ilona," Zoe said, glancing at me. "Someone seeking out destructive storms. Committing murders that appear to all intents and purposes to be deaths caused by tornadoes."

"Undetectable killings?" My inflection implied a question. The workings of Zoe Marshall's mind fascinated me, even more so than the artificial intelligence software that Zoe had created.

"That's a hell of a long shot," Will said.

"Yes," Zoe conceded, "however, drilling down on the detail in each of the nine cases shown here, these injuries could have been caused by the same blunt instrument, based on the size and indent of the blows. And yes, *blows* plural." Her words were short and sharp. "All in states that are considered part of Tornado Alley, all during the tornado season, and all could be explained away as coincidental. But it's not the only marker."

I raised an eyebrow, flicking aside a strand of my hair. "What's the other marker?"

"There's more than just one," said Zoe. "Take a look at the police report for Liz Markus's death." She zoomed in on one of the documents on the screen. "The woman's niece is just five years old. Her account to the emergency rescue team has an unexpected comment. Separated from her aunt, the little girl saw a stranger in the house."

She watched as we scanned the report. And then she navigated to another document. "Searching all storm-death reports for the past several years, Themis detected two others with a near-identical story. This is one of them. A surviving eyewitness in Texas reported a stranger fleeing from the home of a neighbor. That neighbor was later found to have died at the scene from head injuries."

"Analyzing accidental deaths as possible murders," Will said, "that's not part of Themis's programming."

Zoe pursed her lips, a wrinkle rippling across the otherwise smooth, dark skin of her forehead. "You're right. *She* doesn't analyze accidental deaths," Zoe emphasized the gender she attributed to her AI creation, "but the young girl's comment meant this report was placed with detectives for possible further action. They've since dismissed the child's account as imagination under stress, but the report was in the system and got included in Themis's daily intake of newly reported cases. That's how Themis came to draw parallels with the other storm deaths where a stranger was seen." She took a breath, her expression betraying for just a second that she, too, was grappling with this development. "Themis identified strong similarities in the coroners' findings. It's why she then identified these as crimes."

"Potentially unsolvable," I said, "because they've never been identified as murders."

Zoe nodded, highlighting a specific paragraph as the others moved closer. "This is the Texan eyewitness's statement. From a distance, she caught a glimpse of a stranger running out of the side entrance of her neighbor's house. That house was destroyed. The eyewitness was unharmed, but her neighbor, a young woman who was still in the house before the tornado hit, was killed."

"A stranger breaking into a home during a tornado event?" Marcia questioned.

Zoe turned toward her. "The police didn't take it further, assumed the stranger was probably someone seeking shelter. Their theory was that this person realized the house he'd chosen was directly in the tornado's path, so he fled, too, without encountering the house's occupant."

"Do we know for certain it was a *he*?" I asked.

"No. The neighbor's glimpse meant she only saw a blur. Couldn't give a description. But these reports are not the only reports of a break-in during a severe weather event."

"You said there were more markers?" I said.

"In each of the eight previous cases, the victim was a woman, on her own. There was a storm shelter or basement on the property that she would normally have retreated to before the twister hit. Each death was from a massive head injury, but, in each case, Themis highlighted that the victim had extensive multiple bruising, including to the neck and throat, bruises consistent with attempted strangulation."

Will gave an exasperated sigh. "Okay, but the injuries are consistent with tornado fatalities, Zoe. And the stranger seeking shelter theory makes perfect sense."

"By targeting someone in the path of a tornado, a killer would be placing himself in mortal danger," Marcia pointed out. "That's crazy."

"Totally nuts," Zoe agreed.

Silence hung in the air and then Will said, "Seems like a long bow."

"Themis doesn't draw long bows," Zoe said with an irritation that flared from time to time, an edge she often kept easily masked. But right now, I could see she was fired up. "Themis draws parallels and provides informed, educated possible outcomes. From those, we make operational decisions, as we did with our first two cases."

I suppressed a grin. I liked Zoe's grit.

"That may be so, Zoe," Will responded, "but a healthy dose of skepticism is also part of our process. We're dealing, after all, with intangibles, and it's essential we take on the right cases. As you know, every move we make during our trial period is under scrutiny, even more so now with the internal audit that's underway."

I knew that despite being one of the champions of Zoe's program, Will was also a textbook example of pragmatism, a stickler for procedure and common sense who needed hard facts and figures to convince him of… well, anything. A trait that could also be extremely annoying and no one knew that better than me.

He continued, "Okay, so you support the notion there are a series of undetected crimes taking place?"

"Something isn't right about these deaths." Zoe then allowed herself to relax a little, the trace of a grin forming around her lips, her kooky side breaking through the intensity, even if just for a moment. The mood in the room lightened. "Maybe it's my sixth sense, checking in."

I knew, as did Zoe, that Will didn't believe in sixth sense or anything of the sort.

"Can you give us some more detail on all the cases?" I asked.

"Each time, the victim was found face down, either lying across or under the edge of a table, or against the sharp corner of a wall, where the impact caused damage to the larynx as well as the head. But I think they were strangled to the point of passing out and were then struck a fatal blow to the side of the head."

I turned to Will. "No harm in speaking with this young girl, and the local coroner. I'd like to know more before we make a call on whether this is a coincidence or we take it further." I flashed a look at Zoe. "Maybe Themis has a sixth sense, as well."

"Okay, but we need strong physical evidence of a crime," Will warned. "Zoe, why don't you accompany Ilona? You wanted to get experience in the real world. Perfect chance."

Zoe was already directing her next comment to me, as she brought up a meteorological map of the Tornado Alley region on her monitor. "We're at the start of the storm season in these states," she pointed out, always more comfortable when she was interacting with her tech. "This area traditionally gets close to a thousand tornadoes over the next three months and thousands more severe thunderstorms with destructive winds. And this is the period and the region, each year, in which all of those nine deaths occurred."

"That's what – an average of around ten tornadoes a day for that period," Marcia observed.

"Sure is," said Zoe.

I stepped closer to the screen. The map, from the National Oceanic and Atmospheric Administration, or NOAA, showed the storm sequence from the previous year's season. I scanned the red dots that represented the nine-hundred-and-fifty tornadoes that had occurred across the Midwest and the Great Plains. Many of those would be brief and cause only limited damage. Identifying the monster tornadoes with enough warning time was always a challenge for meteorologists.

"A smorgasbord of thunderstorms," Zoe said. "There are generally over seventy deaths from tornadoes across the US each year, most of those in the regions shown. Perfect cover for a killer who knows how to be on the spot at just the right moment."

How anyone could do that – and why – brought up a huge question mark. But Themis had identified a pattern, and Zoe was convinced there was a killer out there. Was she right?

Chapter Two

Ilona Farris stuck her head through the open doorway to Will McCord's office. "I don't know how she does it, but Marcia's got Zoe and me on a flight within the hour."

"Good. The sooner we have clarity on this the better."

Will could tell from the concern in her expression that she'd sensed his unease in the meeting.

"Something else going on?" she asked, raking her fingers through her chestnut-brown hair.

"This internal audit is taking a deep look, not just at integrity, but also budgeting, particularly with regard to specially created units – like us."

"For God's sake, Will, we're the dream team that exposed the corruption that led to this audit."

He shrugged. "I'll have a better take on all this when I meet with John Stafford, the Acting Assistant Director, later."

He sensed that Ilona wanted to probe his unease further but glancing at her watch, she said, "I don't have much time to make the airport."

"Then go and get some answers."

* * *

I dashed home, packed an overnight duffel bag, and then raced to meet Zoe at the airport in time for departure.

Five hours later, the Delta Airlines flight touched down at Will Rogers World Airport in Oklahoma City. I hadn't been here before, but the airport held the same bustling sense of urgency and expectation as every other major US airport I'd visited.

From the lower-level baggage claim area I could gaze at the outdoor garden. A touch of glamor. A bronze statue stood there; it depicted the iconic cowboy actor of yesteryear, Will Rogers, throwing a rope while astride his favorite horse. He was the state's most famous citizen, buried in the nearby town of Claremore.

Although recruited specifically for the creation of Themis, Zoe had insisted on being a fully-fledged agent and had completed her training at Quantico. "We're on a case but I feel a bit like a tourist," she remarked, grabbing her bag as it rounded the carousel.

I knew something about this, having been on the road several times since becoming a special agent. "The feeling doesn't last," I assured her.

It was a half-hour drive to the farming sector of El Reno, where Carol Gainsbury and her daughter Cassie were staying with a friend on a neighboring property while their home was undergoing repairs.

The neighbor, an elderly woman, ushered Zoe and me to the large closed-in deck at the rear of the property, its easy, rustic charm holding an immediate appeal. I imagined this was the kind of place to which you could retreat for a vacation, and it was without question the best place for Carol to be as she dealt with the loss of her sister. A brisk wind was flattening the long grasses in the surrounding field and away in the distance, the propeller-like blades of a windmill were spinning furiously.

"I can't believe she's gone." Carol Gainsbury was choked by tears, her voice hoarse. "She was more than a sister. We were… besties." She looked up, staring at me, but I knew she wasn't really seeing what was in front of her. "We invented our own term. Sisties. Oh, God…" Her voice trailed. "And Liz wouldn't have been in the house with Cassie. My daughter was meant to be spending the week with her father in Texas, but he came down with the flu…"

I glanced at the notes in the open folder that sat on my knee. Carol Gainsbury and her husband had divorced twelve months earlier. As he lived and worked across the border in northern Texas, the arrangement was that Cassie would spend a weekend with him, every four or five weeks. Carol and Cassie had remained in the farmhouse in Oklahoma, and Carol continued running her interior design business in Oklahoma City.

My eyes were drawn to the pendant that Carol was holding, rubbing her thumb across its shiny surface. "So ironic, isn't it, that she died wearing this."

"It's striking," I said.

"She loved her jewelry," Carol reflected. "Always buying a new trinket of some sort. And this one…." She choked up.

I leaned in for a closer look as she continued to rub the surface, as though trying to rub out the past and enable everything to return to how it had been before the storm.

I saw that the pendant was a series of tornado spirals, and a lightning bolt, fashioned from metal and enclosed in a circular shape. The pendant was attached to a necklace chain. "Had your sister owned this piece for long?"

"I haven't seen this one before, but as I said she was often buying up something new." She glanced down at the image. "It's beautiful but I don't think I can keep it. Liz was wearing it when she died. In a way, I might've felt close to her hanging onto it, but… the image." She shrugged, staring off.

"Give yourself time to think about it, to see how you feel in a week or a month or so," I said softly.

"Yes, I suppose you're right."

"Mrs. Gainsbury, would you mind if my colleague and I spoke with Cassie about the man she believes she saw in the house?"

Confusion worked its way into the woman's face. "The police believe that was her imagination. Why would you…?" She didn't finish, her head dropping, emotion overcoming her, a sob rising from deep within.

"Just procedure," I said in as comforting a tone as I could.

The woman's eyes, glistening with tears, wandered. "I suppose so."

The little girl had been sitting at a table on the far side of the room, intently working on the pictures in her coloring-in book, displaying a child's concentrated focus on blocking out the horrors of the real world.

As gently as I knew how, I rose and walked across to where Cassie was seated. Zoe followed, keeping her distance, pulling up a chair a little further back from where I now knelt beside the girl. "Hi, Cassie." I held out my hand, but the girl ignored it. "My name is Ilona and I work with the police and with the rescue people. I'm so glad you're all right."

Cassie's eyes remained focused on the page as she studiously applied her coloring pencils to the image.

"Do you like coloring-in books?" I asked.

"Yes," Cassie said without diverting her attention from her task.

"She likes to draw, as well," Carol called across the room.

"Sounds like you're very artistic," I said to the girl. "This is my friend, Zoe." I waved, indicating the spot where Zoe was seated. "She works with me."

There was no response and, after a beat, I pressed on. But gently. Ever so gently. "Would you be okay, Cassie, if I asked you some questions about the tornado? I know it must have been awfully scary, but it would be a great help to Zoe and me and all those brave rescue workers if you could answer."

The girl shrugged as she continued applying her colors.

"You said you'd gone to get your doll when the door slammed," I said.

"She's not a doll," Cassie objected. "She's Goldie and she's my sistie."

My eyes were drawn to the flaxen-haired doll that lay on the chair alongside Cassie. "I'll bet you and Goldie are really, really good friends."

"Goldie is the best friend ever."

"It must have been very scary when your bedroom door fell in," I said. "You told the policewoman that was when you saw a man in the house."

No answer.

Zoe and I exchanged a glance and Zoe, sensing an opening, simply and quietly said, "You and Goldie are such brave sisties, Cassie."

Cassie stopped her coloring and picked up her doll, drawing it close as she looked across at Zoe. She nodded her head up and down.

"And the man just looked in at you from the hallway and then he was gone, is that right, Cassie?" I asked.

"He said they would look after me."

I shot a glance at Zoe. This was not in the report. "He spoke to you?" I said.

"Yes."

"What exactly did he say, honey? Can you remember?"

"I told you. He said they would look after me."

"Did he say who 'they' are?" I asked.

Cassie scrunched up her face, thinking.

I waited. And then I saw a note of remembrance light up in the little girl's eyes.

"The thunder beings."

"Is that what the man said?"

"Yes. The thunder beings will look after me."

I pushed my tongue against the inside of my cheek, my mind racing. I chose my words carefully. If the girl had imagined the man, then I needed to determine if this was an extension of that. At the same time, it was important not to load her up with too many questions all at once. A change of subject was needed.

My eyes wandered over the table where the girl was seated, and I saw a pile of papers with sketches. "Are those some of your drawings, Cassie?"

"Yes."

"Could I have a look at them?"

The girl shrugged. She reached for the papers without speaking and pushed them toward me.

I spread them out as Zoe leaned in for a closer look, all the time throwing smiles in the little girl's direction.

Our eyes were drawn immediately to the first two drawings on top of the pile. The first was of the twister and the farmhouse, crudely fashioned in the style you would expect from a child. The second depicted the man Cassie had seen, sketched by her as a stick figure with a long coat and a misshapen head and with a wavery red shape in front of his face. He was holding a stick-like shape in his hand, with a protrusion at either end, one larger than the other, a childlike depiction perhaps of a zig-zag lightning bolt. *The weapon?*

"Cassie, is this the man you saw?" I asked.

"Yes. The storm man."

"I can see that you've drawn something in his hand. What is that, Cassie?"

"His thunderbolt," she proclaimed.

"He was carrying his thunderbolt when you saw him, was he?"

"Yes."

I motioned to the drawing of the shimmery circle in the man's face. "And what is this circle here?"

"The big burny hole," the girl stated.

"Cassie, honey, do you know what the man meant when he said thunder beings?" I asked.

"No."

"Is it a name you've heard before, in a story, or maybe in a movie?"

The little girl shook her head, her eyes wide, her lower lip trembling. I placed my arm around her shoulder, a calming gesture. "It's okay, sweetie. You and Goldie are being such a great help."

The girl nodded rapidly as she clutched her doll tightly to her chest.

"They're such good drawings, Cassie. Would I be able to keep these two?"

She thought it over for a moment and then said, "Okay."

"And thunder being is not a name your mom or dad or your teachers might have told you about?"

"I said *no*." Emotion was overcoming her.

"Okay, that is so helpful, Cassie," I said. "Let's call your mom over, eh?" I nodded to Carol Gainsbury, who'd been watching and listening.

Her confusion growing, Cassie's mother gave me a bewildered glance. As she came and sat beside her daughter, Zoe and I stepped outside the room to confer.

"None of that was in the police statement," Zoe said.

"They didn't question her as we have, they had no reason to."

"What do you make of it?"

I brandished the drawings. "As you're aware, drawings are a child's way of expressing memories."

"The strongest indicator that she did see an intruder," Zoe said. "She describes a bright burning hole in his face, I'm not sure what to make of that. And while she might not know what the item he carried was, it could be the murder weapon."

I held the drawing of the coated man out in front of me so that we both had a clear view. The coat, or perhaps it was a robe, the odd shape of the head which could have been a hood, the stick-shape held aloft. "What do you think this looks like?" I asked.

Zoe's eyes widened and she shrugged. "Some kind of mythical storm man."

Chapter Three

"Thank you for taking the time to see us, Dr. Simpson," I said, extending my hand.

"It's Warren, please." The coroner shook my hand. "And it's no problem at all. Not every day I have a visit from the Feds. How can I help?"

"We have some questions about Liz Markus."

"Poor woman. So young. Just thirty-eight."

His moment of reflection was heartfelt, I thought; despite dealing with death every day, he was still affected by it, not desensitized as so many became.

"So senseless," he added. The moment of reflection morphed into a questioning glance. "Why would the FBI be interested in a storm victim?"

Zoe responded. "Looking through your medical examination, Warren, I see the cause of death as head trauma, and your report also listed multiple bruising – to the legs, arms, and throat – but no broken bones."

"That's correct."

"And your report states the bruising is consistent with other storm-related fatalities," said Zoe.

"Absolutely."

He adjusted the glasses on the bridge of his nose. It was more a nervous tic than an actual need, I expected, sensing this man was more comfortable around the corpses on his morgue slabs than he was with visiting FBI agents.

"Victims of tornadoes are often lifted off the ground and flung through the air," he continued. "Hurled against walls and trees and then dropped back to earth, slamming into the ground. Severe bruising, head injury, broken limbs, all par for the course, I'm afraid to say. But those things are far from being the only cause of death from twisters. Not so well known is the simple fact that tornado winds are densely packed with small particles that sandblast off clothing and skin and can penetrate cavities like eye sockets and ears with fungus and dirt, causing internal damage and infections. That's why it's so important to get into sheltered places of safety."

"Liz Markus didn't have any broken bones," Zoe commented. "Is that unusual?"

"No. Not at all. She was, after all, inside the farmhouse. Her injuries are consistent with being buffeted by the wind and thrown against hard objects. Just one massive smash of the head can cause instant death, and it's one of the most common causes of death in these cases."

I shifted my eyes to meet Zoe's and then back again to the medical examiner.

Time to get down to the nitty-gritty.

"Liz Markus's bruising included her throat. Is that out of the ordinary?"

"When a person is flung against walls or furniture, every part of the body is prone to damage," Simpson explained. "From the state of this woman's injuries, I'd say her throat has come into contact with a corner of a wall, or the sharp edge of a piece of furniture. Part of the roof had lifted away; the rest of the house and all of the household items had been pulverized, so extensive bruising is the very least you would expect. It's a miracle the young girl survived without injury, but, once again, not unique."

"I noticed the damage to the larynx was also consistent with strangulation or attempted strangulation," I stated.

Simpson looked perplexed. "Well, yes, certainly there are similarities and if it wasn't for the fatal head blow and the fact that she was a tornado victim, it would appear suspicious, but–"

"But it's not the cause of death," Zoe completed the sentence for him.

"No. And, of course, she wasn't the victim of an assault…" His voice trailed off as another thought came to him. "Are these inquiries related to the young girl's statement that she saw a stranger in the house?"

"The police believe that was the girl's imagination," I said.

"Yes, that would be expected in a child who has suffered trauma."

"There are two tornado survivor reports from the past couple of years, one in Texas and another one from Oklahoma," I elaborated. "Women fleeing from twisters who saw a stranger exiting a neighbor's house."

"Those neighbors died. Head trauma," Zoe added. "We've accessed the reports and there was bruising to all parts of the bodies, including their throats."

The coroner frowned. "Really?"

"We're crossing 'T's and dotting 'I's to establish there are no suspicious connections between these reports," I told him.

"These previous deaths," the coroner probed, "how similar were the injuries specific to the larynxes?"

"The examinations didn't go as deeply into that detail," I said. I allowed him a moment to absorb that fact. "But perhaps you could confirm for me, Warren, whether the bruising to Liz Markus's larynx and vocal cords and neck, whilst not the cause of death, could be the result of attempted or partial strangulation. And whether the fatal blow to her head could have been delivered by someone wielding an item of furniture or a blunt weapon?"

"You would need a full autopsy to give more clarity on that, and of course, autopsies aren't routinely undertaken unless there's a need to establish cause of death." I could see from the expression in the man's eyes that his next words were not words he'd expected to say. "But in answer to your question, yes." A haunted expression crossed his face. "The injuries are consistent with attempted strangulation and a blow from a blunt weapon."

Chapter Four

I didn't want to be in a motel room tonight but that was life when you were an agent on an out-of-state investigation.

I needed to eat but I also needed to make two phone calls. The first was a video call to Professor Zach Silverstein, a college lecturer in criminology, history, and forensics. His encyclopedic knowledge of mythology and strange phenomena was an oddball combination for a professor, but even more so for a consultant to the Bureau.

The familiar head of longish curls, rounded glasses, and rubbery face, constantly either fixed with a mischievous grin or screwed up in intense concentration, appeared on the screen. "Zach, does the term 'thunder beings' mean anything to you?"

"Thunder beings?"

"Yes. I won't go into details right now, but I've spoken with a young girl, a tornado survivor who said there was a stranger in her home as the tornado was rushing in." I filled him in on my visit to Cassie Gainsbury, the drawings, and the stranger's words.

"The girl isn't Native American?"

"No. Why?"

"Thunder beings are what the Algonquian people call their ancient spiritual beings, the creators of storms."

"Algonquian," I repeated. "One of the Native American language groups."

"One of the most widespread of the native language groups across the country. Is the girl familiar with American Indian mythology?"

"Not that I'm aware of. I'll probe further. But it was clear from speaking with her that she hadn't heard this term before."

"That suggests, then," Zach said, "that the encounter wasn't imaginary, as does her drawing. 'Thunder beings' is not a term anyone is likely to use without knowing that it comes from Native American folklore. And it's fascinating stuff, a treasure trove of beautiful storytelling and spirituality. Right in my wheelhouse. Where are you calling from?"

"Oklahoma." I knew there were Native Americans indigenous to the Great Plains, including the Algonquians, but I needed to know more. "Zach, I'm aware that there is an Algonquian presence in these parts–"

"Yes, right there in Oklahoma. The Lenni Lenape people. Also known as the Delaware Tribe. But why are you there, talking to tornado survivors?"

"Pay a visit to the UCU," I suggested. "Marcia will bring you up to date. And I need you to send me whatever you can on the Algonquian legends."

"I thought you'd never ask. Looks like you've managed to do it once again."

"Do what?"

"Get me very, very intrigued," he said.

* * *

I checked my watch. Late but not too late for the second call I wanted to make. This time, to Marcia. It was a call I could have left until the morning, but I was afraid that if I did, I'd have a change of heart and the call wouldn't be made.

Marcia answered. "Ilona, hi. Everything okay?"

"All good. Sorry for the late hour–"

"Don't be ridiculous, you can call me anytime day or night, you know that. Provided it's not to ask if there's anything good on Netflix." She paused for humorous effect. "Okay, that's probably all right as well. And it's not like you're calling a normal household anyhow, we're the original night owls around here."

I laughed. "I thought I held that title."

"Not even close, honey."

I had known Marcia only a short while, since the formation of this team, but we'd quickly bonded in a daughter/mother kind of way.

"Could you run a check for me tomorrow?" I asked.

"Of course I can."

"That list of nine women, including the latest one in Oklahoma, I want you to look at their histories and check for any connection with one specific name."

"Sure. But you don't want to just add it to the search parameters Themis is crunching?"

"Not this. This is strictly between you and me."

There was a moment's silence. Marcia's response shouldn't have come as any surprise to me, but it did. "I think I know what you're going to ask."

* * *

Zoe jolted awake from her recurring nightmare and sat up, shaking, wiping cold sweat from her brow. She hadn't had it for a long time, but it was no surprise that it had returned now.

She rolled out from under the covers, pulled on a robe and slipped her feet into her slippers, and wandered out to the motel room's kitchenette. She boiled water and poured coffee, sat on the two-seater couch with her laptop, and fired up her remote access to Themis.

Her gaze flittered to the clock in the kitchen. She'd thought it was later, but it wasn't far past midnight.

Themis didn't sleep and continued through the night to survey the crime reports, filed the previous day from police precincts and both state and federal law enforcement operations across the country. It was constantly updating data and search results for Zoe to log, which covered most of her interactions with the machine.

But Themis could also respond verbally if Zoe chose to speak to it and ask a question directly. In a matter of minutes, it could accomplish what would take dozens of hours for hundreds of agents.

She was just filling in time, hoping to get tired enough to attempt sleep again.

She'd barely begun scanning the updates when she saw the highlighted information of another tornado head-injury death, once again a lone woman, just hours earlier in Texas.

Zoe picked up her phone, wondered whether to ring Ilona who was in one of the nearby rooms, but she didn't want to wake her. There wasn't anything else to be done until the morning anyway. She decided to send a text so that Ilona would see it first thing. She was tapping out her message when she heard the sound of footsteps on the outer stairwell that led to the first-floor landing, and she instinctively peered through the curtained window at who was returning to a room so late – just idle curiosity. She caught just a momentary glimpse of a figure in a dark-blue tracksuit, a flash of movement at the far end of the landing. She didn't see anything further, just heard the sound of a door opening and closing.

Zoe didn't think anything further of it as she returned to typing and sent her text to Ilona.

Chapter Five

Day Two

It was a one-hour-five-minute flight from the Will Rogers World Airport to Dallas Fort Worth International in Texas. Once again it required a last-minute, mad dash to make the flight that Marcia had managed to get us on.

Only this time, we arrived at the terminal to discover there was a delay to the departure.

I had read Zoe's text the night before when I'd returned to my motel room. I hadn't responded, waiting until I woke early to discuss it with her, and then to contact Marcia to arrange both a flight and a meeting with the local sheriff at the storm site.

Boarding for our flight was announced over the loudspeakers.

"Thank God," Zoe said, stooping to pick up her travel case. "Waiting around is not my strong suit. Let's go check out this death in Texas." She strode away ahead of me toward the boarding gate.

* * *

From Dallas airport, it was a half-hour drive north in our hire car to Denton County.

Coming off the expressway, we drove through the historic, picturesque main town center, and then followed the GPS out to the open country known for its hundreds of lush green horse-breeding ranches and centuries-old farmhouses. The local sheriff was a grizzly bear kind of man – large, whiskery, around fifty. His large blue eyes were particularly soulful in appearance, perhaps not what I expected of a northern Texas lawman but then, as I never stopped learning, we live in a world of infinite types. That was one thing about the world of which I would never grow tired.

If he was curious as to why the FBI was interested in a tornado death, he didn't show it. As we walked into the ruins of the farmhouse, he pointed to the spot where the first responders had found the woman's body. "From the position she was found in," the sheriff said, "the coroner believes she was flung against the wall, smashing her skull, and then bounced back, dropping to the floor."

"You saw the body?" I asked.

"Yes. I was on the scene not long after the forensics boys."

"The fatal injury was to the forehead, left side?"

"Crushed in." He shook his head. "Terrible what these blasted twisters can do to people. It's one thing to see a house shattered, but a human being…" He swallowed. "Whole other thing."

"What do you know about the young woman who lived here?"

"Carly Talbot. Twenty-eight. Single. No children, no siblings. She inherited this property from her parents; she lived here alone and ran her own small business from the premises – organic foodstuffs, sold directly from a website as well as distributing to local markets."

Mental alarm bells sounded in my mind. The house in which Liz Markus died belonged to her sister, Carol Gainsbury. And Carol was also the owner of her own business.

The sheriff looked at me as though he was going to ask what this was all about. Instead, his expression morphed into something of an acceptance that it wasn't worth pursuing. I guessed he'd been down a similar road before with federal authorities. "Not sure why the FBI is interested in tornado deaths, but if that's your interest then you've come to the right place. Texas gets around a hundred and thirty tornadoes every year, more than most states," he said. "Anyhow, you ladies let me know if there's anything else I can help you with."

"You said you could bring the medical examiner's photos with you," I reminded him.

"Oh, sure. In my car."

We walked out to the sheriff's Dodge Charger; he retrieved the pictures from a folder on the passenger seat and handed them to me as Zoe looked on.

My attention was immediately drawn to the photo taken at the scene, with the young woman's body lying askew alongside a partly crushed wall. She wore a necklace, and it was difficult to be certain due to the angle of the body but the pendant hanging from the chain appeared to be the same design as the one Liz Markus had been wearing.

I squinted as I focused on the necklace. "Are the deceased's personal effects still with the medical examiner?"

He gave it a moment's thought. "Yes. They wouldn't have been released this early."

I turned the photo so that the sheriff could see the image. "I need to take a look at this pendant."

Chapter Six

At the medical examiner's premises, in the neighboring Tarrant County, I turned the pendant over, examining it in a way I hadn't when looking at Liz Markus's necklace. On the back of the pendant, there was a middle section where the tornado spirals had been smoothed out so that there was less of an indent. In that area, there was a very light engraving, a stylized motif of a bird with its head and beak facing forwards and its wings folded in across itself in an X shape. It was subtle, camouflaged to some extent by the engraved swirly lines around it depicting clouds, but on close examination, the image revealed itself to the eye. I had seen this image before. A thunderbird, one of the legendary creatures of the Native Americans.

"I'm afraid I can't go into specifics, sheriff, but this pendant is of interest to the FBI for an ongoing investigation," I said.

Once again, his expression was one of puzzlement, but he didn't object. "If that's what you need, I'll get the papers so you can sign it out."

* * *

Zach Silverstein phoned as we returned to the hired, deep-blue Nissan Versa outside the Medical Examiner's building.

"Did you get that info from me about the Native American legends?" he asked.

"Yes, thanks. I'll take a look at it later. Zoe and I are in Texas at the moment."

"Marcia's brought me up to speed on what you're doing down there. What's happening?"

I filled him in on what we'd learned that morning.

"It sounds like that pendant is the clincher," Zach said.

"We'll get Themis pulling up ME photos from those other storm deaths to see if the victims all wore the same item."

"So, a killer is targeting lone women who are in the path of tornadoes?"

"Yes."

"What's the plan?"

"Working on that."

"You need to figure out how they're doing this," Zach said, assuming his professor of criminology voice, "and then you'll need to get on the same path they're on, follow the same storm patterns and alerts."

"You're on the money." It was no surprise to me that the professor was immediately right up to speed.

"And storm chasers can help with that," Zach said.

"Already figured they could prove very useful."

"Ilona, I hear you've got a conference call coming up with Will. Use those persuasive powers of yours and have him arrange transport for me to meet you down there."

"Why?"

"Because you need to choose the best storm chaser and I know just the man for that."

Ending the call, I held up the palm of my hand, motioning to Zoe to wait a moment before getting into the vehicle. I had one more call to make and I wanted Zoe listening in.

I tapped in the number and flicked the mode to loudspeaker. Seconds later, Carol Gainsbury answered. "Sorry to bother you again, Carol," I said, "but could I trouble you to take another look at your sister's pendant."

The woman's reply was tentative. "Yes."

"Could you turn it over and take a close look at the image?"

I waited a moment and then Carol said, "Okay."

"Could you describe what you see?"

"The same tornado-like swirls."

"Is there a smoother, finer indented area in the center?"

"Yes." There was a hint of surprise in Carol's response.

"If you could just examine that spot—"

"There's an engraving there…"

"Is it a bird with its beak facing forward and its wings folded in an *X*?"

"Yes." Now the woman's tone had taken on a grave tone.

"Carol, I need to arrange for that pendant to be picked up."

"What is going on, Agent Farris?"

"At this point, it's simply a line of inquiry that could assist us with a case."

"Okay." Carol Gainsbury didn't sound convinced.

I ended the call and said to Zoe, "That confirms there are at least two storm victims, both with the same pendant."

Zoe was leaning against the side of the car, engrossed in the tablet that was gripped tightly in her hands. "Not just two," she said. She held up the screen for me to view. "Themis has pulled up those county ME photos." There was a gallery of all the photos displayed. "All nine wore the same pendant."

"Let's give Themis a very select set of parameters for a search." The AI could be programmed to seek out and collect specific information as it related to an investigation.

"Shoot."

"Have her list the owners of every farmhouse with or without storm shelters in all of the Tornado Alley states. We need the program to pull out every female who is a single resident and who is a business owner. Then we'll scan for tornado alerts in the vicinity of those women's homes."

"Got it."

"And Zach sent me info on the thunder beings of Algonquian legend. Not sure how it fits in—"

"I'll have Themis pull up any references to thunder beings, specifically in the Midwest or the Great Plains."

"Good."

"What about the pendant?" Zoe wondered.

"I'll have Marcia seek out the manufacturer of that pendant and where they can be bought. Maybe those women had an interest in that specific design. Or maybe the killer brought those necklaces with him, something personal, part of his MO. We'll run prints and DNA on the pendants we have. Anything that helps determine who this man is before he strikes again."

Zoe drew a ragged breath, glancing at the horizon. A clear day, a smattering of clouds, a strong sun. "Trying to find him once he's out there on the road will be like trying to find a needle in a tornado."

* * *

The call from Agent Ilona Farris had ended but Carol Gainsbury's eyes were still focused on the motif on the back of the pendant. She hadn't asked what this other case was, she assumed it may be something to do with jewelry thefts, but she was too weighed down with grief to care. She wasn't sorry that the FBI would be having it picked up. It was a reminder of the way her sister had died. She wanted to scream and go on screaming until she had no energy left but then she was suddenly jolted by the sound of her daughter screaming.

She ran into the adjoining room where Cassie had been seated at the long table, drawing. The little girl had fallen asleep while sketching, her head laying flat on the tabletop. She was having another nightmare, screaming, calling out, her words unintelligible, her head shaking.

Carol rocked her gently. "Wake up, Cassie, darling, you're having a bad dream."

Her daughter opened her eyes and threw herself into her arms. "There's a bad storm."

"You're just having a bad dream, Cassie. There's no storm and everything's okay."

The girl shuddered. "Why are dreams so real, Mommy?"

"They just seem that way, honey."

"I miss Aunt Lizzie."

"So do I, sweet pea, so do I."

"Why didn't the thunder beings save Aunt Lizzie?"

Carol felt a stab in her heart. She opened her mouth, but no words came. How could she answer that? She simply hugged her daughter even tighter, and as she did her eyes fell on the drawing Cassie had been doing when she'd fallen asleep. Another stick-like figure of the man she thought she'd seen in the house. A figure with a misshapen head. A figure holding a curved, zigzag-type bolt. Why did Cassie think she'd seen such a man? Where had she heard this term, 'The thunder beings?'

For just a moment, as she stared at the drawing, Carol imagined that the man in the storm was real.

Why didn't you save my sister?

Chapter Seven

I drove into the parking station of the Dallas field office. Zoe had been quiet for most of the journey, her eyes glued to the tablet screen. "Anything on thunder beings?" I asked.

"Just one thing that sticks out. Back in Oklahoma, there's an Algonquian community—"

"The Delaware Tribe?" I said, recalling my earlier conversation with Zach.

"Associated with them, but this is a separate, smaller group. The Elders are co-founders with other local organizations in running community services. Among other things, they've assisted children orphaned as a result of storms throughout the Midwest and the Great Plains. And families who've been left homeless due to natural disasters. They provide short-term care and temporary homes, counseling, social activities, that sort of thing. They are called the Little Bear community but their motto states that for spiritual guidance they draw on the ancient wisdom of the great thunder beings."

"Then we definitely need to talk to them once we're done here."

We stepped from the Nissan and made our way to the front lobby where we were greeted by the field office chief, an intense, bespectacled, pocket-rocket of a woman. We were shown to one of the communication rooms that had been designated for our use and the woman departed, closing the door behind her. Zoe and I pulled up seats, facing the wide wall-appointed video screen with which we could teleconference with Seattle, and I operated the remote.

The system booted up, establishing the video link. Will, Marcia, and Zach appeared on the screen, seated around the broad UCU conference table back in Seattle.

Will kicked the session off. "What have we got?"

No fanfare, straight down to business. Classic Will.

"A whole lot more than I'd anticipated," I said. I held up the pendant. "Starting with this." I told them what we'd discovered both that morning and the previous afternoon with the Oklahoma ME and the young girl, Cassie.

"Incredible," Will said. "The prediction from Themis was beyond what was ever expected from the program."

It was clear from Will's response that he didn't require any further convincing that there was a killer out there. None of us did.

"And it was on the money," Zoe said. Under her breath, she remarked as an aside to me, "He's never going to call her 'she', is he?"

My raised eyebrow was the only response needed.

"This killer will have hundreds of severe storms he can seek out in the weeks ahead," Zach said, adopting his law enforcement persona.

I had become accustomed to how he rapidly switched from one of his fields of expertise to another.

"He'll be watching for certain prevailing conditions most likely to have a twister form, providing him with his hunting ground," he added.

Zoe tugged on the ends of her hair. "I'm getting Themis hot-wired to focus on reports of break-ins or suspected intruders across those states. And we'll get hourly storm activity updates from the NOAA," she said.

"He'd have to be online with the weather systems 24/7," I said. "Ready to pounce when there's a major storm near his chosen target."

"There are a lot of weather-watchers out there," Marcia added, "nerds with an obsession for storms. Not to mention those adrenaline-junkie storm chasers."

"He may very well be one of those," Will said. "Skilled at moving around a storm center without getting himself killed."

"He could also be a front-line worker," Marcia offered.

"First responders, fire and rescue units, paramedics," Zoe elaborated. "Someone moving in those circles without raising suspicion."

"And yet there's a specific pattern," I said. "Women on their own, or whom he expects to be alone, in the path of a tornado. How can he expect that all his intended victims will at some stage be hit by a twister?"

"He doesn't," Zoe explained. "One of those nine victims' homes suffered a direct hit by an EF4 tornado; another two, which includes the house Liz Markus was in, had a near-hit; with the other seven, the twisters – EF2s, 3s, and 4s – rolled through within a mile of the victim's home. But those twisters had a wide radius of destructive winds, and that's enough to give him the cover he needs."

I knew that the wind speed of a tornado was measured by the Enhanced Fujita scale and that EF3s and 4s, and the exceedingly rare EF5, were the most destructive. "So, a tornado always makes landfall nearby. He has to have the freedom to travel where and when it suits at a moment's notice, matching tornado alerts to one of his targets. It can't be random. Everything we know suggests he's already staked out the intended target, knows their address and their routine, but he can't direct a tornado to the victim of his choice."

"Unless he can," Zach ventured. "In Algonquian mythology, the thunder beings are the spirits that create thunder and lightning. They control the storms."

Marcia shook her head, throwing him one of her maybe-this-is-a-leap-too-far looks. "Really? You're going to go *there*?"

"The killer spoke to Cassie, letting her know she'd be looked after by these beings, and then moved on as though her safety wouldn't be a problem. That implies to me he either believed the beings were real, or he was able to draw on those same abilities himself. And the motif on the pendants is of the thunderbird, one of those beings."

"This is a stretch, even for you," Zoe said, a mischievous glint in her eye, wagging her finger at the screen.

Zach ignored the comments, expounding further on the thought, his speech speeding up as he became more enthused. "In Native American folklore, the thunderbird is a physical manifestation of a spirit that can be dangerous and is known to kill. But it is also known to rescue and protect people. And all of those elements are at play here." His hands flew up as he counted off one point after another on his fingers. "This person appears to control the storm and create the tornado. He's a killer, but also a protector in that he called on the storm spirits to watch over the child. There are members of the Native American community who believe the myths are grounded in reality, that the spirits are all around us, a sentient force that's part of nature, and that humans have abilities we aren't aware of, that we haven't developed. This could include the ability to tune into and be part of those natural elements, just as they believe their ancestors did." He barely took a breath. "We should speak to one of the believers, one of the shamans. Even if you don't believe, any local insights we can gain into this mystical thinking may help us understand who, or" – his expression became intense – "*what* we're dealing with."

"You're wondering," Zoe said, "if this is the case you've been hoping for. Proof of the otherworldly."

"It's out there," Zach said, expressing his frustration, "just within reach but impossible to grasp hold of. *Yet.*"

"Or maybe," Will said, bringing his voice of reason into the conversation, "we're dealing with some psycho storm freak who thinks he can get away with not one, but dozens of perfect murders."

"Themis has identified indigenous elders in Oklahoma who invoke those spirits," I advised. "And we're intending to speak with them, see if there's anything they can shed light on, particularly about the storm pendant; anything that puts us on this killer's trail."

"If you're out there on a storm path, it can get dangerous, and you need to be under the direction of professional storm chasers who know what they're doing. As I mentioned, I know the perfect team," said Zach.

I was about to suggest to Will that Zach join Zoe and me at the scene. Before I did, to my surprise, Will spoke to the professor. He wasn't showing his usual disdain for Zach's off-the-wall theories. He seemed to have let all of that wash over him without reaction. Not like him at all. "Zach," he said, "are you able to join Ilona and Zoe? We could use your knowledge of the Algonquian people as well as your storm-chaser contacts."

"Ready to rock and roll," Zach assured him.

"Will, we need more feet on the ground." I leaned forward, placing my hands on the edge of the table, shooting a demanding stare at him. "We need to know a lot more about the previous nine deaths but we're starting from scratch. No autopsies, no collection of crime scene forensics as they weren't seen as crime scenes, no linking with reports of break-ins during storms, and we are going to need all of that. Themis can search out links online, but this case also needs field agents to make inquiries to establish any personal connections. It seems to me this killer has some emotional tie to the victims, as well as to storms, and the Algonquian legends."

Zoe agreed. "And also find out why he drapes his victims with that pendant. No one else was ever likely to pick up on it, given the random nature of the deaths, but that pendant with that motif has meaning to *him*."

"It's one thing to use local office resources," Will said, "but quite another to redirect field agents to investigate a specialist team's case. I'm sorry, Ilona, I'm on board with everything else but–"

"Okay…" I cut in. I was surprised by how quickly he'd shot that down, given he'd always been as passionate as I was about acquiring whatever resources we needed.

"I'll make some calls," Marcia offered, "*but* it's a lot of ground…"

"Thanks, Marcia," I said, "but more importantly I need you to research the manufacturer and the retailers of that pendant. It's our single most important lead and I'm sending you photos for reference."

"Okay."

"As Zoe and I are heading back to Oklahoma," I said to Will, "I want to set up a command base at the field office there."

"I'll arrange it. As for the extra manpower, I might be able to pull a few strings but certainly not as many as we'd need."

"We'll take any help we can get." I couldn't help but notice Will hadn't even engaged in his usual verbal swordplay with our devil's advocate professor.

Something else is on his mind, I thought.

Chapter Eight

As we waited for the elevator that would return us to the parking station, I noticed Zoe was staring ahead as though fixed on an object, deep in thought. "You've got your something's-bothering-me look," I said.

"If there's a connection, however slight, between this orphan-care group and the killer, then surely he wouldn't mention the thunder beings; wouldn't expose such a clue, even to a child."

"No matter how careful or brilliant, everyone is capable of making a mistake in the moment."

There was a ping as the elevator doors opened, and we stepped in.

"Okay, fair point. You think it was a slip of the tongue?"

"Quite possibly," I said. "The killer wouldn't have been expecting a child to be in that house. Young Cassie was meant to be with her father that week. Something about the girl now being left alone in the house with a corpse, as storm winds smashed the place, struck a chord with him."

"In the emotion of the moment, he was prompted to reassure the girl."

"There's a good chance that could be the case. And while the 'thunder beings' term didn't mean anything to Cassie–"

"It meant something to the killer." Zoe thought about it further. "Why would he think she needed them? She's still got her mother and her father."

I pushed back a lock of hair from my forehead. "Because he didn't know it was Cassie's aunt that he'd strangled. His target wasn't Liz Markus. It was her sister, the woman whom he expected to be in her home. Alone. Carol Gainsbury."

"So, our next step is to speak with the Little Bear community group?"

"Yes. And then we need to find out everything there is to know about Carol Gainsbury and the others. What sets them apart, what's the reason that of all the people who might have been in a tornado's path, it's the single women with their own businesses who are the ones this killer targets."

***

Will was back in his office, seated in front of his PC but his eyes weren't on the screen.

Marcia walked in and sat down opposite him. "I've never seen you staring into space before."

"My mother used to say there's a first time for everything."

"You were a little distracted back there. It's not like you."

"I didn't think it was obvious."

"Perhaps only to me. You know what my husband says?"

He made a face. This seemed off-topic. "What's that?"

"That I never stop mothering. It's a force of habit from raising three energetic boys. The moral of the story is I notice when people have something on their minds.

Anything you want to share? Because, you know, another of my skills is discretion."

"Nothing, really."

"Which translates as Special Agent Ilona Farris." Marcia gave him an understanding look.

"I've had a meeting with the Acting AD, John Stafford. He thinks I allowed Ilona back to work too soon after the traumas she faced on our first two cases."

"We all think the world of Ilona, but she was determined to get back to work, and no one would say she wasn't stubborn with a capital *S*."

"Like her father."

"You knew him?"

"Yep. He was an inspiration. No surprise she wanted to follow in his footsteps."

"She insisted she was ready, and the counselor was satisfied," Marcia reminded Will. "She told me she does everything on fast-forward, and that included grieving and healing. For what it's worth, yes, we all worry a little, but she seems fine to me and to Zach and Zoe."

"We all know this new team is under scrutiny, but I can't shake the feeling John Stafford has another agenda. Frankly, I think bringing up the Ilona thing was a stretch."

"I know the type," Marcia said. "They make themselves look good by making others look bad. But he's hardly someone you'd let stand in your way."

"No, but not someone to ignore, either. I'll let you in on a little secret. Not everyone outside the commissioning panel was supportive of the UCU concept."

"But they're not going to force an about-turn, this early into the trial?"

"You can never be certain. It wouldn't be the first time money and resources have been allocated to a project that's been sidelined early. And everything's a little weird right now with this audit rampaging through the place."

Marcia pursed her lips. "If there's one thing I hate, it's internal, big-ego politics."

"No argument here."

Her phone buzzed and Marcia checked the text alert that she'd set up before joining Will. "A search response is back with the details for that pendant."

Chapter Nine

Zoe and I flew back to Oklahoma.

Later, as the sun disappeared over the city skyline, we were on the road again, picking Zach up from the airport.

"The good news is that Jock Harrow's in town and he's ready to meet with us in the morning," Zach told us enthusiastically from the back seat. "For help tracking tornadoes there's no one better."

"Tell us about him," I said, my eyes on the road.

"We were fellow students back in the day and we've kept in touch." Zach settled back in the seat, shifting his gaze from me and Zoe in the front to the lights on the highway and back again. "He's a former meteorologist turned photojournalist turned… well, a professional storm chaser is the only way to describe him." Zach's speech was rapidly gaining speed. "He's first and foremost a scientist, collecting data and images on every storm-type imaginable, and he shares that with the NOAA. He films and photographs thunderstorms, and in particular supercells and tornadoes, and sells his images to the media. He also runs tours, taking Joe and Jane Citizen for ride-alongs to experience the thrill of it all."

"Take a breath," I said. "It's what the rest of us do."

It was an old joke between us, and Zach's grin stretched from ear to ear. "Oh, yeah," he deadpanned. He shifted in the seat, fiddling with the seat belt. "I'm looking forward to this meeting with the Little Bear leader tonight.

The Native American people of this state have ancestors who lived across several regions between California and Florida, and in Canada, so they have a rich cultural history."

It was a twenty-minute drive to where Little Bear had an encampment along the river, a village-style community of homes and buildings for shared events and gatherings.

Arthur Fire Heart had one of those faces that seem to hold a permanent grin – a grin that spread wider, his eyes projecting an innate warmth as he welcomed us into his modest cottage. It was a calm night but there was a chill in the air so the heat emanating from the fireplace inside the home was comforting to us.

One of the walls in the room was devoted to children's drawings, a montage of stick figures, fields, and houses, in vibrant colors.

"Thank you for agreeing to speak with us tonight," I said, joining him in the easy chairs positioned around the fireplace. "And for looking so pleased about it as well, I might say."

His laugh was gentle. "My given Algonquian name is Ahanu," he revealed. "Which means 'he laughs'."

"Very fitting," Zoe said, basking in the Native American's presence as were Zach and I. "Makes you wonder how your parents could have been so spot-on."

"I believe our ancestors often whisper in our ears, hinting at the future, as I am sure they did to my parents on the night of my birth."

"And you anglicized your name to Arthur," Zach stated.

"I go by both, as do many of my contemporaries, because I believe I walk in two worlds. The world of my people and our ancestors, and the world of contemporary society. I am active with the young people of both and seek to be relevant in one without shutting my eyes to the other. And I can tell you, it has become a real balancing act in today's world."

"I notice," said Zach, "that your community is situated on land just outside the area of the reserve."

The old man nodded, his eyes lighting up. "Oh, yes. Oklahomans are used to intermingling regardless of race or religion; however, I didn't want to dissuade the general public from coming along to our spiritual and wellness center, or volunteering or seeking help from our community services. Positioned here, I believe it sends a message – this is common ground for all, welcoming those from all tribal groups as well as the broader community. And it has worked. People of all cultures and ancestries gather here, sharing, and working together to help others in need. It was a dream of my forefathers, and it has been my dream. My only hope is that it can be spread much further."

"Those services you mention, one of them, of course, is caring for children displaced after natural disasters, like the storms."

"It's an interim thing, if required, in tandem with the state welfare services. We are a registered charitable organization, amongst other things." He gave another of his expansive gestures. "*Many* other things. We can assist with gardening, landscaping, home maintenance, for those on our tribal land as well as those on neighboring farms – people who own properties but need assistance with the upkeep."

"It must keep you busy," Zoe commented.

"It has been an increasingly popular enterprise of ours, particularly in this age when so many have heeded the call to be concerned for our environment. Our community is one of deep spirituality, not just in its connection between people but with all of nature. It has always been our way. Our approach to land care is to be in tune with the earth, as it was in the days of our ancestors, and we bring a wealth of traditional methods to our work. Just as we care for our health with natural herbs and remedies, so too do we go about physical labor with the hands that the Great

Spirit gave us, not with the mechanical monstrosities of modern man. Just as other communities like the Amish use the horse and plow, we too rely on our hand-crafted tools and the sweat of our bodies to look after these lands without polluting the air and the rivers and the soil."

"Coming out here this afternoon," I said, "we passed a nearby hobby farm. There were workers out there on the fields, cutting grass with scythes."

Arthur Fire Heart's eyes lit up once more. "Ah, yes. We make them ourselves here at the retreat, as we do with axes and hoes and other implements. The scythe, of course, was originally one of the farming implements of medieval Europe, adopted throughout the world until mostly replaced by machines. But the folk we help love that we do not pollute their spaces with the noise and the diesel fumes of the harvesters and the chainsaws and the mowers. Not to mention that it is also far more economically viable in financially impoverished areas." He chuckled to himself.

I couldn't help but smile at the irony – the tools of another age usurping the fuel-guzzling inventions from centuries of progress. It explained farmworkers wielding hoes and similar items, and it went part way to validating the young girl's account of seeing a man carrying a stick-like object – perhaps one of those traditional implements – even though she did not have a name for it.

"I'm sure you understand I can't divulge details," I said to him, "but we are working a case in which 'thunder beings' were referenced."

Arthur Fire Heart was immediately curious. "And in which context, may I ask, was the expression used?"

"A tornado. And a child being told that the thunder beings would keep her safe."

"Ah, that is indeed the nature of the storm spirits. They protect our people and they have done so for generation after generation."

"The person who made that reference is a girl who could help us with our inquiries," I said.

I glanced again at the children's drawings that adorned the old man's walls. Illustrations of stick people working on the farmlands. In one of these, the worker held what I assumed was meant to be a scythe.

Arthur's eyes followed mine. "I see you have an appreciation of our young people's drawings."

"The girl saw a figure in her house and drew a picture of an intruder holding an item that she couldn't name," I said. "It could have been an attempt to draw something like that instrument."

"Ah. And you think that as we invoke the wisdom of those spirits in our motto, and our workers use scythes and hoes, we might know the person holding it?"

"Hopefully. Even so, any insights we gain from you into the mythology could help us."

"I have the feeling," Arthur Fire Heart said, gesturing toward Zach, "that this young man knows something of our legends."

Zach showed his surprise. "You must be psychic."

"We are all psychic. Some choose to embrace it, some ignore it, others remain unaware."

"I'm a professor of history, among other things," Zach elaborated, "with an interest in the beliefs of all cultures, including those of your people. So, I know that the thunder beings are the creators of thunder and lightning and that they are protectors of people. But I know they can also be dangerous."

"They have the power to both give and take away life," the elder explained. "They are also known to many of our peoples as the thunderers, and they are the enemy of the Great Horned Serpent of evil. It is said that when a person receives a vision from the thunder beings, they become a *heyoka*, holy men working for the Great Spirit. It is in the tradition of that belief that our motto invokes their infinite wisdom. It guides us in the work we do here for those children of the earth." His voice was soft and calm but at the same time imbued with command. His eyes met with mine. "Unfortunately, I do not know who might have said those words to the young girl you speak of during the recent tornado here, which I expect is when this encounter took place. No such story has been shared with myself or to my knowledge with any of the other helpers who volunteer their time with us."

I decided to show him the pendant. "Is this a design you have seen before?"

He took it in his hands, admiring its beauty. "No, but I must say this is a fine piece of craftsmanship" – he turned it over in his hand, and his eye caught the engraving of the creature – "and I see the craftsman has an appreciation of one of our most powerful images. The thunderbird."

"What can you tell us about that image?"

"Many of the tribes of my people tell stories of the thunderbird, known to some as *Wakinyan*, the first Thunder Being. It is said that it emits lightning from its eyes and flaps its wings to create thunder and send forth great winds. Some view it as the physical manifestation of the thunder beings and might question whether it is to be worshipped or feared. My belief is both. The thunderbird personifies the energy in the natural world. As a protector of our people, it fights off the darkness brought by the Great Horned Serpent and its many forces." He took a moment, gazing toward the window and the woods in the distance. "Just as violent weather brings life-giving rains, so too does it bring destructive winds and lightning and, of course, tornadoes. In that way, the thunderbird is showing us that to have one, we must have the other."

"As points of definition," Zach offered, "we don't know what light is unless we have darkness by which to recognize it."

Arthur nodded. "We cannot know calm without experiencing fury. This explains the dual nature of the thunderbird which, like many of my people, I believe connects the creature to the trickster, a character who abounds in so many legends from ancient times."

"The trickster?"

Arthur smiled, his eyes alight with amusement. "Trickster or clown, or the shamanistic *heyoka* of some societies, taunting the enemies of the thunder beings with practical jokes and satires." He lifted his hand and placed his palm in a vertical position, covering half of his face. "Two-faced, wearing masks."

"And what's the role of a *heyoka* for the thunderbird?"

"A sacred calling. Upholding the thunderbird's mission in protecting purity and truth from the dark forces."

"The Great Horned Serpent," Zach elaborated.

The wizened old man took a moment, nodding, as if in reverence to the spirits that were his people's protectors.

"The person we're seeking seems to know, in advance, where storms will hit," Zoe ventured. "Possibly this person is in meteorology or involved in storm chasing–"

"Knows in advance?" The elder frowned but even that was like a partial grin on his amiable face. "I think that if the FBI is looking for a man who knows the movements of the storms, then I suspect, even without you divulging details, as you put it, young lady" – he nodded in my direction – "that this man must be as dangerous, perhaps even more so than the storm itself, eh?"

I didn't answer.

The fireplace crackled, the light from the flames flickering across our host's face. "Perhaps you are looking for a *heyoka*, empowered to turn thunderstorms and tornadoes away from a certain place. Only this man, I suspect, is turning them toward it, endangering those who reside there."

I cocked my head, giving him an inquisitive stare. "But not something you believe is possible?"

It was a moment before he answered. "While there are certainly many in our community who understand the scientific view of storms, there are some who subscribe to our ancestral teachings; that humans have greater powers than they realize, that we can be attuned to nature, and do things that the modern world considers impossible."

Zach leaned forward, his intrigue growing. "Do you have any specific examples of that?"

"I have an elderly uncle" – the old man laughed – "yes, even older than myself. He's a shaman, with a far greater understanding of our ancestors than any of us here, and we still have much to learn from him. He performs rainmaking ceremonies when they are needed. Yes, a tradition ignored or disbelieved, certainly misunderstood by modern society, but it represents the forgotten relationship that all living things have with the universe. This is something you see with the creatures of the wild, who sense when storms are coming. My uncle, whom we call Longhair, talks to the tornadoes." A reflective look passed across his features. "Two years ago, there was a tornado thundering toward one of our tribal communities. Longhair and a small group of his fellow elders braved the massive winds to perform an ancient ritual, in the path of this destructive force. There is no scientific explanation for what happened next, and many call it a coincidence, but the tornado made a sudden sharp turn, sparing the people and all the homes in that community. And it is not the only known example of this amongst my people." He leaned toward us, his hands clasped in front of him. "I listen to your words, and they have a resonance; in that resonance, I hear far more than you reveal. I hear other voices, spirit voices, relaying to me the truth you are bound to conceal."

"And what are they saying?" Zach asked.

"I hear that this man you seek must be moving with the storm winds and that he is indeed a threat to others…"

I flinched, not entirely comfortable with this elder's insight in knowing far more than we were telling him.

"…one who thinks of himself as a *heyoka* on a mission for the thunderbird, or that he is himself the thunderbird, a man who brings not peace or joy, but perhaps means to reap death on those he believes are instruments of the Great Horned Serpent, convinced he delivers justice for the thunder beings. However, this man is delusional, he does not truly represent the spirit of our gods or the traditions of our people."

"Apart from those elders, are there others in the community who have sought to learn those skills?" Zoe asked.

"There are those who show interest, yes, but it is not as widespread as it was in generations past. Nor is it documented. So, no, there is no list of anyone who might have pursued this knowledge, if that is to be your next question."

Another loud crackle came from the fireplace as the flames curled and flared. I found the aroma of the woodsmoke strangely calming. "You seem to know our minds better than we do."

"We are all open books to those who know how to read the signs." Arthur Fire Heart bowed his head in reverence and then reached out, taking my hand, his eyes searching mine. "I sense you are the leader here, Agent Farris, just as I sense all three of you have a deep commitment to your mission. But I also sense you are walking into unseen danger. I will call on the thunder beings to guide and protect you." He moved his right hand and placed it over his heart. "I must also warn you that I sense this man is more than you believe. He will let nothing stand in the way of his obsession."

"It's very personal to him," I suggested.

"It goes to the very depth of his soul."

Chapter Ten

I was back in my motel room when my phone pinged. Incoming from Marcia. "Hi–"

Before I could say anything further, Marcia cut straight in. "Search results came in on the pendant but it's not good."

"What did you get?"

"Zilch."

"Nothing?"

"No pendant like this one on any online lists or catalogues. I've followed up on that with a whole heap of phone calls, to make certain, but none of the manufacturers or retailers who'd be across this sort of item could shed any light on it."

"Which means they could have been specially crafted by the killer."

"I'll stay on it, Ilona," Marcia said. "I'll run a search for artisans in the area who have the kind of skill needed for this but it's likely our man hasn't left a footprint anywhere."

"Okay."

"How did you go with the Little Bear community?"

I filled her in on the meeting with Arthur Fire Heart.

"I've also collected all the available CCTV from the storms Themis listed," Marcia said. "I've uploaded them."

"Let's hope there's a clue in there somewhere."

"One other thing. I've run the separate search you asked for, checking for connections between the original nine victims with one specific name. I think we both know you won't be surprised by what I've turned up."

I knew from Marcia's tone that at the briefing in Seattle, she had been struck by the same thought I had. "I'm listening."

"One of those nine victims," she said, "was a woman named Vema Coulston, in Oklahoma. Died three years ago; one of the earlier deaths. For many years she partnered with one of the national youth welfare assistance services. When there was a kid who was temporarily under the welfare department's care, she would foster them for the time needed; maybe a few weeks, maybe a few months. They were not hard cases, no druggies or violent kids, nothing like that, just kids who were in between homes, or whose parents were in the hospital. That sort of thing."

"Go on."

Marcia was right. I wasn't surprised by what she told me next. The search I'd asked her to undertake had found a connection between one of the victims – Vema Coulston – and one of the members of our team.

"Thanks for doing this on the quiet," I said. "Let's keep it to ourselves."

* * *

I called on Zach and the two of us went to Zoe's room. "Marcia's CCTV is in," I said.

"Already running it." Zoe was at her laptop, eyes fixed on the screen. "Not many cams in some of those country spots, and much of that older footage isn't available now. But for the more recent deaths, there's gas station video surveillance and highway speed cams."

"What do they show?"

"Five four-wheel drives with satellite dishes and reinforced steel casing, classic storm chaser-style vehicles. Four of those SUVs appear in two of the locations, despite them being in different states."

"To be expected of chasers," I said. "And the fifth van?"

"The fifth van is captured in all three of those areas and like the others, it's following the storm."

"And heading toward the victims' addresses?"

"Not enough video to be certain. And it doesn't discount a couple of the others just because they aren't shown on all of the CCTVs. But I've already run the plates that can be seen. The first three are known storm chasers. One of them is Zach's friend."

"No surprise," Zach responded. "It's what the dude does."

"And the others?" I prompted.

"The fourth van's plate can't be seen on any footage."

"And the fifth?"

"This is where it gets interesting. The fifth plate is from a minivan no longer registered, a vehicle of a different make and model to the SUV captured on the road cam. It belonged to a local building contractor."

"Where is he now?"

"Still in town, still trading. He has a different work vehicle now, and I've already verified he wasn't anywhere near any of those three recent death locations. His original van with those plates was reported stolen three years ago. It's never been found."

"That has to be our man's vehicle," I said. "Themis…?"

"On it," said Zoe. "Uploaded screenshots of the SUV to Themis's image identification software. Even from the footage, we can't be certain of the exact model. Themis will access all CCTV from the past twenty-four hours across the surrounding states for the closest visual match."

"We just need one hit," Zach said, "to pinpoint where this guy is now."

"And which direction he's headed," Zoe added.

"What have we got on the storm forecasts?" I leaned in as Zoe scanned the NOAA alerts.

"Major winds moving across from the west, predicted to hit parts of Oklahoma and Ohio tomorrow."

"And our list of single-female property owners' addresses?"

"Loaded into Themis," Zoe said. "If and when one of those severe thunderstorms is forecast in an area close to one of them, we'll know it."

* * *

It had been another long day. I was back in my motel room but found it stuffy despite the late hour and the cooler weather. I walked out onto the tiny balcony for some fresh air and to gaze out over the cityscape, my face turned to the brisk wind. My secret life was calling, but I was tired and I knew it was important to get some rest. Early in the morning, we were meeting with the storm chaser recommended by Zach.

My secret passion would have to wait.

Momentarily, my mind was cast back fourteen years, and I saw the shaft that rose above me, a vertical tunnel with minimal ridges and cracks, a shaft I'd climbed, desperate to escape from where I'd been imprisoned by my kidnappers. In the years since my teenage ordeal, donning sports gear and disguised under a hoodie, I'd often climbed the walls of the city's buildings, an adrenaline rush that filled me with the exhilaration of freedom and control.

I cast those memories aside and, in their place, I replayed the words of Arthur Fire Heart in my mind. Humans in tune with the weather spirits, who could manipulate tornadoes. *Heyokas.* "It isn't possible," I said aloud, and I could have been speaking to those very same elements. As if in response, the strong breeze stung my face, and whipped at the strands of my hair. It was as though the cold air in my breath snapped up my words, whisking them away into the darkness.

Daring me to follow.

Chapter Eleven

Carol Gainsbury woke with a start, disturbed by a grating noise coming from… where? She wasn't sure. Although she'd been staying with her elderly neighbor for over a week, she still hadn't got her bearings. She glanced at the bedside clock: 11 p.m. She'd been asleep only half an hour. Was it Cassie? Her daughter had woken with a nightmare most nights since… since… she could barely think it, let alone say it. *The tornado.*

She slid out from under the blanket, pulled on her dressing gown, and padded to the next room along the hallway. Cassie was out of bed, standing at the window on tippy toes, staring out.

"Cassie, what is it, darling?" Carol came alongside her daughter and kneeled so that she was at eye level. Outside, a strong wind blew and the sight of the treetops swaying wildly was unnerving. The movement played havoc with the shards of moonlight that broke intermittently through the scattered cloud cover.

"I heard something," Cassie said.

Carol embraced her daughter. "You've had another bad dream, honey. But it's just a dream, okay, everything's all right. Okay?"

"I saw a light."

"It's just the moonbeams, baby, and it seems like they're jumping about because of the wind and the trees."

Cassie shook her head slowly. "No, it was the man's big, burny light."

Carol froze. Her daughter's nightmares had been about the horrifying twister and about missing her aunt. She'd always woken, crying out, from her bed. She hadn't previously mentioned the strange man being in her dreams. "It's just a dream, Cassie."

The girl's eyes flicked to the window. "He's out there," she said, her lower lip trembling.

"Didn't the man say the thunder beings would look after you?" Carol's question was meant as a reminder.

Cassie nodded.

"So, he isn't a scary man, is he?"

Cassie's large, doe eyes stared back, unconvinced – the look a child gets when they regard something with a mix of awe and uncertainty, on the verge of knowing something but not fully grasping it. "But they didn't look after Aunt Lizzie," she protested.

A shiver ran through Carol's body. She took a deep breath. No, there'd been no one to look after her sister. Once again, the sharp, agonizing stab of despair tore into her. God, she missed Liz. How would she ever be able to come to terms with what had happened?

"Let's get you back to bed, honey." Carol led her daughter back to the bed, gently tucked her in under the covers, and then kneeled alongside, caressing her daughter's brow and softly singing a lullaby until Cassie drifted off.

Carol tiptoed from the room, but instead of returning to her own, she went to the wall-length glass door of the patio. She gazed at the dark field beyond the yard, at the shaking trees, the shimmer of moonlight, and she listened to the constant wail of the wind.

There is no one out there.

She thought back to the visit from the FBI and Agent Farris's request for Liz's pendant. Just procedure, the agent had said. They were following up to make certain there was no substance to Cassie's story about a man in the house, and the pendant would assist in their inquiries on another case. Farris had told her to report anything that seemed unusual or suspicious, once again, just as a precautionary measure. Really?

At first, she had believed they were just going the extra mile and showing their support. But she'd also felt a twinge of suspicion. Was there something she wasn't being told? Consumed by grief, and worried sick about the impact of the trauma on Cassie, she hadn't given it further thought.

There can't be anyone out there.

She shivered. A finger of ice trailed her spine and radiated out across her shoulders and neckline. And then she heard the grating noise that she'd heard when she woke. This time she recognized that sound. Something – or someone – brushing against the piping of the hot water system at the rear corner of the house. The wind could do that. She craned her neck, looking through the glass in that direction, and she thought she caught a rush of movement, a blur, and a brief flash of light.

She retraced her steps, this time going past her room to the small window at the opposite end of the hallway, and she peered out on the area from which came the disturbance. The house was on a large block, set back from the street, with an expanse of grassland at the back, ringed by trees. There were no figures revealed by the strobe lighting effect created by the powerful wind. No sign of any vehicles arriving or leaving the street, or stationary.

There can't be anyone out there.

She went back to her bed, but sleep had never seemed so far away, and she lay awake, tears stinging her eyes, staring into space, her thoughts running amok. She was beginning to believe that there was more to this than her daughter's imagination, more than the tornado that thundered by her farmhouse, more to the death of her sister, more than what the federal agents had revealed.

She thought back to her daughter standing by the window, silent but terrified.

She thought about the grating noise, the blur of movement, and the flash of light she'd seen. She wasn't certain what to believe anymore.

Is someone out there?

Watching?

Chapter Twelve

Day Three

Jock Harrow greeted us like long-lost relatives the moment we entered the enormous garage, robustly shaking our hands one by one and embracing Zach like a brother who'd returned to the fold after many years away. "Welcome to the madhouse," he boomed. "Now, time's short, so let's kick off by giving you guys a tour of the van. And if that sounds boring, let me assure you, this isn't like any vehicle you've ever seen or are ever going to see again."

It had been a quick trip along the I-35 S to Harrow's rambling two-acre estate and colonial-style residence. It stood alongside a working horse ranch just outside the city of Guthrie, thirty-two miles north of Oklahoma City.

The pictures I had seen of Harrow's full-size passenger van hadn't done the heavily modified vehicle justice. Seeing it live and up close was a whole other experience. Its front, sides, and rear were fitted with steel panels, giving it an appearance that was somewhere in the motor world's twilight zone between a customized off-road SUV and a high-tech, streamlined, camouflaged van.

"You're looking at our very own Tornado Tracking Vehicle, or TTV, adapted to withstand one-hundred-and-fifty mile per hour winds, heavy debris, and hailstones the size of baseballs. Those panels are 16-gauge steel, coated with impact-resistant polyurethane for added protection." He moved along the length of the van as he spoke, arms waving. "Not visible to the naked eye is a hydraulic system by which we can lower the beast's belly to the road surface. That's to ensure we don't get turned topsy-turvy if we're parked to withstand even greater gale-force winds. And she's got a 700-horsepower V8 engine. Helps to ensure our gear doesn't slow us down when we're trying to keep pace with a twister in full flight."

Sitting atop the vehicle was a radar scanner and another structure, a platform on which was bolted a T-shaped rod with connecting wires and dozens of tiny, bulbous sensor modules. Harrow's arm was raised, motioning to the van's roof. "We've our very own micro weather station," he said. "Feeds real-time, up-to-the-second data on wind speed, barometer, temperature, rain. The bottom line is that the closer we get to the action the more accurate our on-the-spot readings."

Zoe, Zach, and I followed him, clambering on board through the sliding rear door.

"People watching those TV documentaries and YouTube videos might think storm chasers are a bunch of cowboys," he said, "but as you're about to see, everything here is very scientific, very methodical, very organized."

I suppressed a grin. Everything about Jock Harrow was precisely what you might expect of a cowboy or, more to the point, a rodeo rider. He was a tall, bearded, solidly built, sandy-haired, late-thirties guy with eyes as blue as an open sky. His craggy, yet handsome features perfectly suited his denim jacket and jeans and the scuffed leather boots he wore. His voice had both a tone and a southern drawl that was somehow maddeningly laid-back but dynamic at the same time. Yeah, he was sexy. Zoe and I exchanged a subtle look.

"First up, let me introduce my partner-in-crime, Rohan Baines, but you'll call him Rowdy because... well, that's what he answers to." Harrow gestured to a man who was already in the van, seated at a media desk that was built into a recess on the right-hand side of the cabin. Positioned slightly above his desk and dual monitors there was a row of larger screens attached to the van's wall.

Rowdy was the physical opposite of Harrow – clean-shaven with a narrow face, his Native-American heritage was most prominent in his straight black hair and wide, dark, almond-shaped eyes. Equally as tall as Harrow but with a slimmer, sinewy build, he wore a checked shirt and corduroys that were more farmhand than rodeo star. Zoe again caught my eye and raised an eyebrow as if to say, not bad either.

He held up his hands in greeting and said, "I take it you guys must be crazy wanting to ride with us, because crazy is what we do."

"Don't mind Rowdy," Harrow countered. "He's still working on his conversation skills. Slow learner."

I cut to the chase. "So, what have you got going on in here?" I hoped there was going to be a lot more to these two than lame comedy routines, and I flashed a look of concern at Zach but if he noticed he didn't return the gaze. His attention was focused on this flamboyant storm chaser whom he'd known since college.

"The screens over the console here relay data in figures, graphs, maps, and images, not just from our setup on top but from the NOAA, the Tornado Prediction Center, and a whole range of weather forecasting operations. It means we can take all of that data and calculate the most likely conditions in which tornadoes form. We establish where we want to be, and when, to get the best images and collect the most useful data, which we send on to the weather boffins." Harrow allowed a moment for his visitors to take it all in. His gaze settled on me. "And I gather, from what the prof said on the phone yesterday, that you guys want to track specific tornadoes?"

"We're seeking the driver of a van, who may or may not be a storm chaser as such," I explained, "but who we've established has been heading in the vicinity of tornado-likely thunderstorms. We believe this driver can help us with our inquiries about a case we're investigating."

Harrow blew out a deep breath and then broke into a grin that seemed even wider than his face. "Now there's some genuine horsecrap if ever I heard it."

I cocked my head toward him. *Horsecrap? And this guy didn't think he was a cowboy?* "Excuse me?"

"Wasn't born yesterday." As he said that, he shot an amused expression at Zach. "Despite what Mr. Academia here might say, if the FBI wants to go into the path of a tornado, then you're not simply making inquiries. The guy you're after, or the perp as you'd call him, is the driver of that SUV. And you're figuring the only way to locate him is when he's out there on the road chasing a particular twister. Which is why you need someone like me to help you find him."

I allowed his response to wash over me. "Can we count on you?"

"You need my help, you got it."

I looked at Zoe. "Can we show Jock and Rowdy that footage?"

Zoe handed a USB to Rowdy. "Can you play this?"

"Sure." He inserted the USB into the computer and seconds later, video from the recent storms was on the screen.

"As you can see," I said, "there's one SUV with radar that's in each of those three different locations. We can't see from the video who's in the vehicle, but the occupant is a person of interest to us."

"Grainy video, and the darkness of the sky," Harrow noted, "make it hard to determine the exact make of the vehicle or its color."

"It's not multi-colored or branded like yours and many others," Zoe commented, "but it has the radar scanner atop, and it's a van."

"Could be black or a very dark gray or navy blue," I said.

"In conditions like these – heavy rain, black clouds – in the CCTV everything is dark," Rowdy offered. "Doesn't help. And there are a lot of chasers following those storms this time of year. A whole lot of them have unmarked, fairly indistinct, similarly colored four-wheel drives. Some are professionals or semi-professionals, but there's a heap of first-time amateurs, thrill seekers who think it will be a real blast to get in on the action but who give up before they can get through one season."

"It's been like that since 1996," Harrow said.

"1996?" Zoe's curiosity was piqued. "What happened then?"

"The movie."

"Movie?"

"*Twister*," Zach jumped in.

"Chasing storms became a *thing*, after that," Harrow further explained. "During peak season we get hundreds of amateurs tearing around the whole of Tornado Alley."

"Idiots," Rowdy said.

Zoe pointed to where a mass of red dots littered the on-screen map. "What are those?"

"Those are other serious chasers, guys with their beacons turned on," Rowdy informed us. "Click on the dot and the chaser's name and phone number pops up. We're a community, signaling to each other when it suits. If one of the chasers' beacons is on and he changes direction, heading a certain way all of a sudden like he knows something or his gut is telling him something, then others start to follow. Kind of like creatures in the wild following an alpha." He grinned at his analogy. "But for every dot you see, there are usually five to ten with their beacons switched off."

"They want to keep the storm for themselves?"

Rowdy laughed. "Selfish sons of bitches."

"Okay, before we go further, I've got something you need to see," Harrow said. He tilted his head toward Rowdy. "They need a real bird's eye view of what they could be heading into."

Rowdy tapped a few keys, and a new video filled the screen – aerial footage of an enormous wall of cumulus cloud, swirling at high speed, towering over the landscape and blocking the light, lit occasionally by lightning that flashed like a neon sign being switched on and off.

"What you're seeing here," Harrow informed us, "is what we look for, first and foremost, every day. Powerful, super-fast winds in the atmosphere's upper levels. This is the kind of upper-level support that builds into supercells, creating the ideal conditions for tornadoes to form." The wall of cloud churned and rotated, growing larger, and moving faster. "When we take clients out on tours, we show them this and I tell them that a tornado is a bridge between the earth and the upper layers of our atmosphere, and the more powerful the jet stream up there, the larger and more deadly the tornado." He placed particular emphasis on the words that followed. "This is what you need to see and understand. When a tornado forms and drops down, hitting the ground and rolling out across the land, it's like a bomb going off. Now, we don't take tourists into dangerous situations, and we try to get our footage and collect our data without putting ourselves in the path of a bomb built by nature. But if you want to chase down some nutter who's charging close to these things then that's what you could be facing. Except it's no longer anything like viewing the footage on YouTube. Once you're inside the hornet's nest of a severe thunderstorm, it's real and it's life-threatening."

"That's why we're talking to you," Zach said. "No one's got a better rep for getting close to these twisters while knowing how to outmaneuver them."

A female voice came from behind them. "Keep talking like that and you'll give my brother an even bigger, uglier head than he's already got."

We turned to a young woman with a wavy blonde bob, a wide, toothy smile, and a calm but cheeky demeanor, dressed like a cowgirl. She climbed into the vehicle.

Harrow introduced the newcomer. "My other partner-in-crime, my little sis, Jade."

"The real brains of the operation," said Rowdy.

She raised her hand in a curt wave. "Also the occasional co-driver, navigator, lunch-packer, PR gal, accountant, and" – she made a face at Rowdy – "the real tech guru."

I nodded and said, "Hi," then quickly diverted my attention back to Harrow. "That aerial footage, Jock. Where is that from?"

"Various sat feeds, as well as our own little eyes in the sky," he said proudly. He pointed his right forefinger skyward. "Drones, specially built and reinforced with lightweight steel casings so they can be bounced around by strong winds without breaking apart. We send them up so we can combine aerial with our ground camera shots for the media."

"But they also have another purpose," Jade revealed.

"What's that?" asked Zoe.

"If we can get them to fly into the mouth of a twister, even if a drone gets damaged, we could get live video of the insides of a tornado, while it's still in full-power mode."

I turned to Jade. "You have drone footage of previous storms?"

"Yes."

Jock Harrow didn't need to wait for my next question. "You want to take a look at all the aerial footage we've got," he guessed. "You want to see if your mystery storm chaser is in any of them."

Rowdy activated the drone footage and fast-forwarded through whole sequences, freezing it intermittently when the video caught other storm chaser vehicles.

"There's a couple there that could be the van you're looking for," Harrow said.

Rowdy froze the footage on one of the scenes. "I'd say this one's the nearest match to the videos you showed us."

"We pass SUVs like that just about every time we're out on the road," Jade told us. "We know more than a few of them, part of a community of chasers, but there's always those we haven't seen before, or don't recognize. The amateur crowd. You could chase storms for weeks or months on end and never sight this guy."

"We have certain parameters, relating to addresses in particular areas," I revealed.

Rowdy turned to us, his gaze intense. "You may be in luck. There are strong winds forecast for later today across parts of the state and in Ohio." We edged in closer as Rowdy swiveled on his chair to face the monitor again, his fingers tapping the keyboard. "Let's take a look."

The topographical map that appeared on the screen depicted the movement and expanse of a storm front across the central area of Kansas. On a sidebar column, there was a constant stream of weather data scrolling up.

"Vertical wind shear," Jade said, and then, explaining further, "a change in wind direction combined with speed, height, and lifted condensation – perfect conditions for long-lasting, rotating thunderstorms."

"The supercells most likely to produce tornadoes," Harrow added. "The Storm Prediction Center sends warnings if a tornado has been spotted or if radar shows conditions that could result in a twister." He moved alongside Rowdy, tilting his head toward the monitor. "The messages come through to Rowdy, Jade, and me on both text and email as well as flashing across the website on the main screen here."

"Which it's doing now," Rowdy commented, unfazed.

I could see that to this crew, this was just another morning on another day in the lives of professional adrenaline junkies.

"We've got a big bouncy baby being predicted," Harrow announced.

I scanned the website alert.

> *BULLETIN – EAS ACTIVATION REQUESTED*
> *TORNADO WARNING*
> *NATIONAL WEATHER SERVICE DODGE CITY KS*
> *10 AM CDT*
> *THE NATIONAL WEATHER SERVICE IN DODGE CITY HAS ISSUED #TORNADO WARNING FOR SOUTHEASTERN ELLIS COUNTY IN CENTRAL KANSAS UNTIL 830 PM CDT*

Zoe slipped her laptop from the satchel over her shoulder and fired up Themis. The same alerts were showing.

"When we're on the road, during the season," Harrow changed the subject, "our broadcast partners cross live to us for action updates. You want us to cancel those communications for this run?"

"No," I said. "Our guy will be monitoring all the regular broadcasts, so everything needs to appear normal. He has no idea the FBI even knows of his existence, let alone that we've teamed with storm chasers to hunt him down."

Harrow nodded. "Giving you the element of surprise."

I moved alongside Zoe, zeroing in on the laptop screen. "Single-female property owners in those areas?" My eyes ran down the list the moment Zoe brought it up on the monitor.

"Bingo," said Zoe. She shot me a look of alarm.

"Beth Willard, in Hays, Kansas," I read from the screen. "Five hours from here." I glanced at Harrow as

Rowdy and Jade looked on in surprise. "Can you get us there in advance of that storm hitting?"

"Maybe not for when it first hits, and twisters could form at any time. But we can damn well try to do better than five hours."

Zoe couldn't hide her excitement. "Let's do it." She glanced at Zach. "You been on one of these storm chases before?"

Before the professor could reply, Harrow laughed heartily. "Mr. Academia? He's all books and charts and YouTube, he's never set foot in the real world."

Zach protested. "That's not exactly–"

But he was cut short by Harrow. "We need to move if we're going to catch that supercell. You three need to strap into those passenger seats. Pronto." He whirled to his sister. "Jade, you stay here and man the base. We're after a particular SUV so we could use you monitoring the main computers as backup."

"You got it."

"There's an office adjoining the house with a giant screen," Harrow told us. "Jade can pull up sat and drone images and zero in with a clarity that we can't match on the monitors in here. That will help us home in on the area around us." He moved to the front of the vehicle, getting behind the steering wheel. "Rowdy?"

"All systems go," his colleague said.

Chapter Thirteen

The first hour on the road as we crossed the border into Kansas was uneventful. The skies were clear and the weather calm. I spoke with Will and Marcia about having local authorities warn Beth Willard that she could be in danger. She needed to leave her property and head to the nearest police station. Word back was that they couldn't raise her but that they would keep on it.

An hour later we passed Wichita. Every step of the way Rowdy was relaying the real-time updates from the weather services. "Thunderstorms across the Colorado/Kansas border and multiple supercell forecasts."

"Tornado alerts?" I queried.

"There was an alert for Hays, Ellis County, Kansas, fifteen minutes ago. Thirteen-minute warning."

"What happened?"

"Nothing. Fizzer."

Zach told Harrow and Rowdy about the meeting our team had with Arthur Fire Heart. "I know him," Harrow said. "His community does great work."

Zach reiterated Fire Heart's story about his uncle, the shaman, and his redirection of the tornado.

"I know the story."

"You believe they can do that?" Zach asked him.

"It's what happened. I've heard all the explanations – coincidence and so on – but that will remain one of the great mysteries. And probably of more interest to Rowdy here. He's the *thoughtful* one, went through one of those searching-for-himself phases a few years back. Didn't you, Rowdy?"

Harrow's colleague didn't rise to the bait.

"But Rowdy didn't find himself by going all new-agey on me. Like me, he figured that the true way to commune with something higher is to get out there among it, to be a part of the weather systems yourself."

Rowdy nodded. "Amen to that."

"I gather, then," I said to Rowdy, "storm chasing has, for you, a spiritual side to it."

"You could say that. But 'chasing storms' is too common a term. Not really how I see it. Following the storm path, joining its eco-system, allowing yourself to be absorbed into nature; that's how my people see it.

Communing with nature while at the same time communicating back to the human world what we learn from the storms."

Harrow laughed. "He still does some of those meditations he learned from those daughters."

I was curious. "Daughters?"

"The Daughters of Gaia, a spiritual retreat," Rowdy explained. "Good people."

A snort from Harrow. "As I said, Rowdy's the *thoughtful* one," he said.

There was barely a beat before Rowdy's comeback. "Jock likes to act all gung-ho storm warrior but deep down he's a sensitive dude. Just doesn't want his storm-channel subscribers to find out. Do you, Jock?"

There was a bellow of laughter from Harrow.

"The Daughters of Gaia. Sounds like there's more to it than the mythology of the Algonquians and the other indigenous cultures here," I speculated.

"A combination," Rowdy said. "They believe in Mother Earth as the Great Spiritual Being, and that the goddess Gaia is represented by the ancient cultures of all the peoples of the earth. Not just the First Peoples of the Americas, but the early human inhabitants across Europe and Asia. That we are all part of the one. The Daughters of Gaia absorb the beliefs and traditions of all those peoples into their teachings."

"I should have warned you not to get him started," Harrow joked.

Rowdy ignored him but there was the trace of a grin at the corner of his mouth. "Arthur Fire Heart would have told you all about the legends of the thunder beings."

"Yes. And the *heyokas*, who are given the power to speak to the storms," Zach said.

"Well, you've got to wonder," Harrow conceded. "When you get up close and personal with these twisters, the way we do, you see some damn crazy stuff. The way these babies change direction without warning, the way they demolish one building while leaving others around it intact, the way their kinetic energy can vary as much as it does from one twister to the next. It's as though each one has both a mood and a mission of its own."

"Maybe they do," Zach said.

Harrow threw his head back and laughed. "That's the crazy-ass professor I love to hear." His eyes hadn't shifted from the road ahead as we barreled along the four-lane highway. There was a moment of silence. "You want to know something, Prof?"

"What?" Zach asked.

"Part of me hopes that one day you prove one of those supernatural theories of yours, and I'm sure Rowdy thinks the same. Coz every time I see one of these twisters shooting down from the heavens, and the whole sky alight, it's totally surreal, and I have to admit there's a moment, just a moment, when I think I've crossed over into another reality."

Zoe noticed me checking my phone more and more frequently. "Still no word on Beth Willard?"

"No," I said.

"How long to Hays?" Zoe asked Rowdy.

Rowdy enlarged the GPS on his monitor. "Two hours, forty-five minutes."

"And the storm forecast?"

"They're already getting strong winds. Supercell build-up predicted for any time over the next two hours."

"Tornado?"

"No further alerts out there as yet."

Zoe leaned toward me and, lowering her voice to a whisper, said, "This guy's MO indicates he doesn't strike unless a twister sets down within a ten-mile radius of his target."

Rowdy might have been focused on his equipment, but he picked up enough of Zoe's whisper. "Strike? Strike what?"

"I think our FBI friends are chasing a very bad man," Harrow said.

I ignored their comments, turning and responding instead to Zoe. "Either way, if a twister does make landfall, he'll be there before us."

Chapter Fourteen

The sky had turned black and rain thundered against the windshield of the red SUV, challenging the windshield wipers. Beth Willard groaned, her hands gripping the steering wheel. What a hell of a day. She'd been in a rush that morning. She'd left her cell phone sitting on the kitchen bench where she'd downed a few mouthfuls of cereal, followed by a half-a-dozen sips of steaming hot coffee. And then out the door without thinking. She'd cursed herself at odd moments throughout the day, lost without that damn phone.

She'd broken up with her boyfriend of eighteen months just weeks before and it had rocked her, even though she knew it was for the best. She couldn't afford to be distracted and forgetful like this. Not now. In just forty-eight hours she was due to give a keynote speech to a group of entrepreneurial ladies at the Women's Business Collective. Beth ran an accountancy practice in the city of Hays, the economic center of Ellis County. She'd been nominated for this year's Hays Businesswoman of the Year. Hers was a boutique business in which she employed three staff, one of them a trainee.

Her boyfriend had dumped her, and she was glad. She'd been about to do the same to him. He was no Mr. Right. So why hadn't she stopped replaying the whole thing in her mind? She wasn't a teenager; she was in her mid-thirties. Older, but apparently not that much wiser in the emotional stakes.

She grimaced at the strong winds buffeting the car as she sped along the two-lane road to the partly rural outer suburb where she lived in a small house that sat on an acre and a half. She vaguely remembered from yesterday's weather forecast that there would be thunderstorms later today, but it seemed they were sweeping in sooner. The landline phones in the central business district had been down, some technical outage that was taking longer than expected to fix. She'd decided to leave the office early, beat the storms home, and spend the evening prepping for her speech. And it would feel good to be close to her cell phone. Crazy.

When the broken branch thudded against the windshield, she reacted, jamming on the brakes. As the branch was whisked away by the wind, her car swerved; spinning around, it ran into the incline by the side of the road. It stopped just a half-yard from a wide, gnarled tree trunk, and fighting off the shock, Beth breathed a sigh of relief.

After a few minutes of taking stock, nervously running her fingers through her short raven bob, she backed up, turning the vehicle and reentering the road, the rain still beating like a psycho against the windows.

I guess today isn't my day to die.

Chapter Fifteen

We were still an hour and a half away from Hays, but we had entered the storm zone. It happened suddenly, the heavens darkening as coils of thick black cloud tunneled at rapid speed across the sky.

"Incoming call from SWTV," Harrow announced to us as the rain began beating.

Rowdy raised the volume on the screen that was showing Storm Watch TV. In the foreground of a wide 3D topographical map, alive with swirling circles of color depicting the weather patterns, the broadcaster, a chubby, bushy-haired enthusiast, Grant Sawtell, addressed his viewers.

> *Maximum wind shear just now west of McPherson County, where an unusual amount of supercell activity is predicted. Conditions are ripe for some extremely dangerous weather in the region over the next eight to ten hours. And we have one of our favorite storm trackers, Jock Harrow, on the line. Jock and his crew are currently on the road in Central Kansas.*

There was a rush of static, momentarily drowning out the broadcaster's voice. "Hello, Jock. Are you there?"

"Hi, Grant. We're on the interstate, near Lindsborg in McPherson County, planning to meet that major supercell forecast for Hays, Ellis County. We've got winds of fifty miles per hour here in McPherson, building fast, rain coming and going in hard bursts, cumulus clouds moving at high speed. Rowdy's uploading some live footage to you as we speak."

"Stay on the line, Jock," Grant Sawtell said. "We're crossing to the SWTV chopper, which is not far from you. Come in, Cap'n."

"Cap'n is the showbizzy name for their aerial reporter," Rowdy explained to us. The image on the SWTV channel switched to the interior of the chopper, the perspective giving the viewer the same view that the pilot and his co-pilot had of the dark sky with its churning clouds and fiery flashes of lightning.

"Cap'n here. Hello, Grant, and hello to all our storm-watching friends out there."

"I believe you've seen some funnels?" the broadcaster said.

"You bet your sweet bippy we've seen funnels forming." Cap'n's voice had a ragged, smoky quality and it boomed through the speakers. "Weak and short-lived and nothing that's made landfall. But there's powerful vertical rotation going on at the upper levels. You can see those enormous black swirls right across the horizon, Grant, and the wind shear, moisture, and uplift data tell us we're headed for some extreme weather in several counties across the state."

"We've also got your old buddy, Jock Harrow, on the line."

Cap'n chuckled. "Love that deranged dude. How are you, Jockster?"

Harrow responded through the hands-free radiophone on his dashboard. "Who are you calling deranged? You're up there flying on the fringes of twisters that make the Wizard of Oz's tornado look like a summer breeze."

"And you're down there racing headlong into them as though they're drive-through fast-food outlets."

"Loving the banter, guys," the broadcaster broke in. "We'll check back in as the day progresses. Right now, a word from our sponsors and then we've got the Director of the NOAA giving us an update on the latest in tornado prediction technology."

I had zoned out, my focus on the laptop resting on Zoe's knee as she scrolled through the CCTV being fed through by Themis.

"Accessing cams from all over the roads leading into Hays," Zoe said. "Nothing matching the images we have of the suspected perp's SUV or the stolen number plate."

I ground my teeth, speaking under my breath, more to myself than to Zoe or Zach. "Where is he…?"

A sudden shout from Harrow cut across everything else. "Up ahead, funnel coming down, *there*–" He had one hand on the wheel, the other stabbing the space in front of him. "Hitting the ground."

An immense black column, whirling into existence out of the spiraling wind currents, emitting a roar like a jet engine as it swept across the landscape, spewed forth a stream of debris. Dust, branches, and hundreds of shapes and objects I couldn't identify.

"Wow!" Zach exclaimed.

My eyes, like Zoe's and Zach's, were wide. "Good God–"

I had seen photos and videos of tornadoes, but nothing compared to the sheer visual fury of the scene unfolding before me. It had appeared in the blink of an eye. The tornado rolled east across the field. And then, everything changed, the tornado shifted its direction like a wounded beast, thundering across the expanse of farmland directly toward us.

"Hold on tight," Harrow commanded. He spun the wheel, taking us off the road and onto the field, angling to remove us from the twister's path.

"It's fifty yards away," Rowdy shouted to be heard above the deafening sound of hard debris – branches, fences, tools, I guessed – slamming against the armored sides of the van. The winds, now at one hundred miles per hour, rocked the vehicle as Harrow pressed his foot down on the accelerator, the undersides bobbing up and down over the uneven ground.

Harrow brought the van to a stop and yelled at everyone to keep holding tight and remain still. The van lurched as the tornado thundered by on our northern side and passed.

No one spoke.

We all breathed heavily.

"It's like that thing had its sights set on us," Rowdy said.

Harrow shot Zoe, Zach, and me a quizzical look. "We might be storm chasers, but it seems that twister was an

FBI chaser. It even cloaked itself from raising any tornado alerts." His trademark hearty laughter erupted but, to my ear, this time it wasn't as devil-may-care. I sensed an underlying tone of dread. "Okay, time to get this show back on the road."

Chapter Sixteen

Beth Willard hadn't been in the house more than a few minutes, relieved to be home, and was boiling the kettle for tea, in need of refreshment. She was distracted not just by intrusive thoughts about her ex, but by the creaks and moans of the old house and the clang of metal outside. Massive gusts of wind rattled every door and window and sent loose objects flying through the air and crashing against the house and the shed at the back.

She had the television tuned to SWTV from the adjoining room, the young female presenter's voice drifting through.

> *Coal-black clouds, high winds, and a series of possible tornadoes are being reported across Hays County this afternoon. The National Weather Service is working hard to issue tornado alerts, and you can see a selection of our viewers' videos in the corner of your screen. Joining me in the studio, our resident meteorologist...*

Beth heard a man's rich baritone voice.

> *...we have confirmation of a wide range of fast-moving storms. Those reports include a 130-foot tree that came down across two properties, destroying part of a farmhouse and several sheds...*

Beth heard a voice outside, shouting. What on earth…? She went to the front window and peered out. She couldn't see anyone. Had she imagined the voice?

It was then that her eyes were drawn to the funnel on the horizon, the clouds surrounding it dark and swirling furiously. Within seconds it was much closer and a hell of a lot larger, moving at breakneck speed. She glanced at the weather-alert radio she kept on the front hallway cabinet. It squawked into life, a tinny voice advising that the Tornado Prediction Center warned a tornado was imminent and to take all necessary precautions. It's more than imminent, she thought, wondering if there was someone on the property that she'd heard calling out.

A sudden crash of thunder gave her a hell of a shock and she stepped back defensively. It felt like a sonic boom reverberating through her bones and invading her head, so much so that it was as though she'd suffered a physical assault. Her gaze settled on the window again as streaks of lightning flashed, ruptures separating one corner of the darkened sky from another, each flash leaving a momentary imprint, and for just an instant she thought she saw a figure in the distance, staring and still, resisting the torrent that swirled all around.

More deafening thunder joined forces with the wind as it howled and rammed the walls, the windows shaking uncontrollably as though possessed, one shattering, and then another. She moved closer to the window again and glimpsed a man in heavy-duty weather gear and helmet, approaching.

She opened the door.

"Ma'am," the man called out, "you're in the path of an estimated EF3 tornado—"

"Oh, Lord," she gasped, opening the door wider. "We need to get to the shelter."

The man strode forward, buffeted by the wind and he charged in, pushing her back, catching her in shock and surprise, slamming the door closed behind him.

"What—?" The word had barely escaped her lips when the man's arm rose and swung, collecting her across the cheek, snapping her head back as her knees sagged.

From the corner of her eye, Beth saw his other hand was brandishing an object but even as she did, the man cast it to the side and lunged again, pinning her against the wall, his hands encircling her neck, his fingers pressing into her throat. Beth tried to scream but no sound came, her larynx stifled by the man's fingers as he pressed deeper and harder, his face close, his eyes boring into hers with what seemed to be cold, emotionless intent. She tried to breathe but couldn't, her thoughts spiraling out of control, traumatized, and unable to comprehend why this was happening.

Chapter Seventeen

We were racing along the country road, the Willard farmhouse within sight, the monstrous funnel tearing across the field. Even though it just missed the farmhouse, the winds at the tornado's outer edges ripped up a portion of the roof and punched holes in one of the walls.

Harrow's TTV turned into the long, winding driveway of the property. Up ahead, a figure in storm weather gear and helmet ran from the farmhouse to an SUV parked at the side.

"It's him," I shouted. I whirled in my seat toward Zoe. "You go in and see if Beth is okay." I prayed the killer had been disturbed by our van pulling onto the property before he'd had time to attack the woman in the house.

"On it." Zoe leaped from the van's back door as I commanded Harrow. "We need to stop him."

The SUV rumbled across the grass, joining the driveway further back at the point where it opened onto the road.

Harrow pulled the van back out onto the two-lane road and accelerated, giving chase. The road stretched out in a straight line for a couple of miles ahead, visibility partly obscured by the veil of heavy rain.

Before Harrow had reached full speed, I watched in confusion as the SUV, already far ahead, came to a halt. The man jumped from his vehicle, brandishing what I could faintly discern as a rifle. He dropped to one knee, took aim, and I shouted, "Jock, he's armed—"

There was a deafening explosion as a bullet hit the armored front side, narrowly missing the windshield. Even though I could not hear the gunfire, with the thunder of the beating rain blocking out distant sounds, I felt the reverberations of one thump, then another. Simultaneously, the van rocked and dipped, the screech of metal on bitumen ringing in my ears.

"He's taken out the front tires." Harrow's voice was ragged as he urgently applied the brakes, wrestling the steering wheel to maneuver the van to a halt without it flipping onto its side or crashing into one of the trees that lined that section of the road.

I was out of my seat, flinging open the rear exit door.

"Ilona, what are you doing?" Zach called after her.

"It's too dangerous," Rowdy warned as the winds slammed against the sides of the van, the rain heavier.

"Stay here," I shouted back. "I need to see if there's a car in Beth's garage, I can't let this killer disappear."

Harrow had turned around in his driver's seat. "You can't go out there," he ordered. "Those winds will knock you senseless—"

My feet hit the bitumen and I launched into a run.

"Ilona!" Zach called out again.

"Damn woman," I heard Harrow growl, his voice distant now.

I had never felt anything like the pulverizing force of the wind that slammed into me, over and over. It pushed like a G-force against every one of my straining muscles. It shoved me back two steps for every three steps forward and then knocked me from my feet with a blow that could have come from the swipe of a giant's hand.

I was on my knees, struggling to get back on my feet when I felt a strong grip on my shoulder. Harrow's voice. "No," was all he said. He pulled me up, placed his arms around my shoulders, and battled the wind as he led me back to the van.

"There's no possible way of moving out there right now," he said as the two of us collapsed into the passenger seats, breathing heavily. "We just have to wait it out and call for help."

My wringing wet hair was plastered to my head. I stared hard at Harrow and then shifted my gaze to Zach. Words failed me, frustration eating at my insides. I'd known we'd be facing extreme weather, but I hadn't fully understood just how physically impenetrable it could become, or that it would throw up a barrier between me and this killer. A killer who was clearly in his element. It was as though his energy and the fury of the storm were interacting, one feeding off the other. My breathing slowed to something resembling normal. "We almost had him, Zach."

Zach stared back at me. He gave an almost imperceptible nod. "What's more, now he knows that someone is after him."

"But what made him suspicious?" Rowdy pondered. "He couldn't have known there was law enforcement in this vehicle. Jock could have driven onto the property by sheer coincidence."

"Giving chase was the giveaway," Zach declared. "He saw Zoe leap from the van, heading for the house, while the TTV followed him. If we'd been chasing the storm, we would have gone the other way. He twigged something wasn't right."

"But hasn't this guy simply drawn attention to himself by firing that weapon?" Harrow said.

"This is a highly unusual-looking van," I pointed out, "with its armored sides and gizmos on top." I glanced at Harrow. "It's seen regularly on the Storm Weather TV Channel, and our suspect would know of it."

Harrow nodded. "So, when he saw us pull up–"

"He panicked," I said. "He knew enough about your rig to know he couldn't outrun you. He wasn't taking any chances that your being on the scene might be coincidental."

"He made certain we couldn't follow," Zach said.

Another thought occurred to me. "He probably hopes the rifle shots will be written off as some gun-toting crazy storm chaser–"

"He'd have a point," Rowdy interjected in his slow drawl. "Plenty of crazy out here."

I continued, "Even if he doesn't suspect his MO has been uncovered, and this was coincidental, he'll take precautions."

"I'd say he'll ditch the SUV," Zach said.

"He'll switch to a different style of vehicle, one without radar atop, one that isn't necessarily a storm-chaser type of car." I was staring straight ahead at no one in particular, putting myself into the killer's mindset.

"Which means we've lost the advantage of identifying him on road cams," Zach said. "There are dozens of people out there on the road this time of the year, chasing storms in all kinds of vehicles."

"Hundreds," Rowdy corrected.

"Maybe he'll give it away for the time being and lay low, just in case." Zach was staring out the window at the show of lightning, as it illuminated the dark curtain of clouds in staccato flashes.

"No, this is his hunting season," I said. "Three months of storm activity during which Tornado Alley gets around a thousand twisters."

Zach nodded thoughtfully. "Yeah, I think you're right. He waits for this opportunity each year."

"And why does he do that?" I ran my fingers through my wet hair, straightening out the knots. "Because he enjoys the thrill, not just of stalking victims, but the storm chase as well, the anticipation, the precision involved in being at the location of one of his targets at the time a tornado hits the area." I paused, a shiver tracing my spine as I imagined this murderer's headspace. My eyes flicked over each of the others. "The sheer adrenaline jolt he gets when all of that comes together and he's able to move in for the kill."

Zach was tapping away at Zoe's laptop. "I'm getting Marcia to reconfigure Themis to the surrounding road cams. Let's see if we can find where that SUV goes next."

"What's Themis?" Rowdy wondered.

"A valued member of our team," Zach said without looking up, a sly grin on his lips.

"The winds have probably taken most of the cams out." Harrow moved to the driver's seat, grabbing hold of his radiophone. "But we'll get Jade to focus our sat feeds on the roads here. It's worth a try."

The radio crackled to life and Harrow said, "Hey, little sis, we're all okay but some crazy has shot out our tires."

"What the hell?" Jade said.

"I'm sending our coordinates and I need you to zero in on our sat cam on the road heading north, see if you can spot this son of a bitch's van."

"You've got a description?"

"Nothing new. Just that it's a dark-colored van with some radar on top."

Even as Harrow spoke to Jade, Rowdy was staring at me and Zach, frowning, his hand raised, his forefinger pointed skywards. "We can get some pretty neat close-ups of the ground from the sats," he said, "but I'm not confident it will help with this kind of cloud cover."

"This guy is like one of the thunder beings' *heyokas*," Zach said, glancing at me. "Drawing on the elements to cover his moves." He edged closer to the window, angling to look back at the farmhouse. "What about Zoe?"

I had already tapped Zoe's number on my phone. "It's ringing," I told Zach.

After sixty seconds the call went to voicemail.

I rang again.

"Cell tower could be out," Rowdy said.

Eyeing Rowdy and Zach, I phoned again. And then again.

On the fourth attempt, the call was answered.

"Zoe?"

I felt my face crumpling, my breath restricting, as I listened to the words on the other end of the line.

Chapter Eighteen

Half an hour later, when the wind subsided, Zach and I ran back to the farmhouse, while Harrow and Rowdy stayed with the vehicle.

Stepping through the front hallway and into the main living area, we were confronted with the sight of Beth Willard's body, crumpled on the floor beside the cracked front window – her form askew, a trail of blood running from her forehead. The victim's injuries looked identical to each of the previous murders, and precisely like a death caused by the tornado.

Zoe was sitting silently with her back against the wall on the far side of the room.

I went to her. "You okay?"

Zoe stared back at me.

Zach stood at the entry to the room, eyes fixed on the body.

"Forensics is on the way," I said, staying focused, falling back on procedure.

"We failed her," Zoe said.

I had no response.

After another minute of silence, Zoe pushed herself to her feet and walked out.

"I should have been with her when she came in to check on Beth." Zach's voice was a croak, drained of its usual, irrepressible energy.

"She's a trained agent, Zach. And it's always hard the first time you're confronted with a scene like this."

"I guess…"

"I'll go speak with her," I said.

* * *

Zoe stood in the yard, facing the dilapidated back porch, arms crossed. I walked out, joining her.

"We need to get this monster," Zoe said through clenched teeth.

"We will."

We stood in silence, gazing at the damaged farmhouse and the surrounding fields, the wind still strong in the tornado's aftermath.

My eyes still riveted to the devastated landscape of fallen trees and felled power lines, I said, "I know about Vema Coulston, Zoe." I would not have been taken aback to get a hostile response. After all, I'd covertly delved into personal aspects of my colleague's background, chasing up details that weren't part of Zoe's general Bureau profile, but at the same time, I needed to shock Zoe out of this sense of despair, refocus her on our role here.

Surprisingly, there was no anger from Zoe.

"Of course you do," she said, then turned to face me. "When Will told me he was enlisting you to be part of the team, I asked him straight up if that was because, you know, not just that he'd worked with you before but because you'd once been an item. I can be blunt like that."

"I've noticed," I said with just the trace of a smile.

"Will said no," Zoe continued. "Obviously, he would say that. But what he added was that he enlisted you because of your track record and your instincts. And the UCU was going to need strong instincts to tackle cases flagged as unsolvable. It wasn't too long before I learned exactly what he meant. So" – she cocked her head to one side – "I shouldn't be surprised, should I, that you picked up on something at our briefing and dug into it?"

"Why didn't you just tell us upfront you knew one of the victims?" I asked.

"You know why."

"Because we'd think you were pushing for this, purely on emotion?"

"Of course, you'd think that. If the situation were reversed, *I'd* think that."

I knew Zoe was right. I waited for her to open up further. When she did, her voice adopted a reflective tone.

"Vema was an incredible woman, she had a heart bigger than anyone I've ever known. She never said, 'there aren't enough hours in the day.' She said she always had the time for anyone who needed her, she'd just add those extra hours onto the usual twenty-four." She swallowed hard, resisting the urge to let her emotions take over completely. "I stayed with her for a short time while my mom was in rehab. And after I moved back home, Vema kept in touch. Every few months she'd ring or email to see how I was getting on and to fill me in on what she was up to. There was a time, when I was playing tough girl with a gang, that I never responded. Later, when I split from that scene, I wrote to her, apologized. You know what she said?" She invoked the southern drawl of the other woman. "She said, 'Girl, no need to apologize to this here mama, I heard it all before. You were just sowing wild oats and, girl, now is the age you want to be doing that, believe me, you don't want to be saddled with those oats when you're older, that's when it just gets plain ugly.' And I laughed, oh, I laughed. So yeah, seeing her name on that list, it *was* emotional."

"But there was more to it than just emotion," I said.

"Vema lived on that farm her whole life and she'd been through tornadoes before. She had a storm shelter on the grounds. I went through one of those tornadoes, down in that shelter with her. I hadn't had a nightmare about that for a long time, but when we came here—"

"You had the nightmare again?"

"Yes." Zoe took a deep breath, shrugging the memory off and refocusing. "Vema knew the drill. When there were storms, she kept her ear out for the twister alerts. Even if she couldn't make it to the shelter on time, she knew the safest places to be in the house. When I heard the news she'd died, I just couldn't believe it. But of course, I accepted it; I had to, we all had to."

"But when Themis put forward those storm deaths," I said, "and Vema's name was on that list—"

"I *knew*." Tears were brimming in the corners of Zoe's eyes. Gathering her resolve, her voice regained its more familiar confident spirit. "Normally, I wouldn't have pushed this to the forefront, not this soon anyway, but Themis has shown a cyber instinct of her own, analyzing similarities, however minor, between disparate deaths. And then when I saw Vema's name, suddenly it all made sense. If she'd been ambushed in her home, that explained her inaction, that gave credence to the similarities in all those other deaths."

"And you and Themis were right," I said.

Chapter Nineteen

Concern was etched into Will's face as he listened to the news report.

Will switched off the news as the call he'd booked with AD Stafford came through.

"Sir, I've just sent through an urgent request to deploy agents from multiple field offices."

"Bring me up to speed, Agent McCord."

"The file contains a Themis prediction and the team's analysis on a series of deaths we believe are murders camouflaged as storm fatalities. The most recent was this afternoon in Kansas. The team is on the ground there and their reports and images are included."

"Why this multiple field agents request?"

"We've identified this killer's potential targets, but the next killing could be at any one of several locations from the Texas panhandle to Nebraska. No one team can cover all of that simultaneously."

"You want agents who are on the spot seconded to your command for a manhunt?"

"We're going to need it to ensure we snare this perp wherever he turns up."

"Provided he turns up."

"Yes."

"The file's there now," Stafford said without emotion. "Let me take a look and get back to you."

"We're on a serious time restraint." There was an edge in Will's voice.

"I'll get back to you," Stafford repeated.

The call ended and Will buzzed for Marcia.

Minutes later she strode in, her manner, as always, imbued a sense of calm and quiet control. "I've just read through Ilona's update. Did you get on to the AD?"

"He's considering the request." Will leaned forward, his elbows on his desk, folding his hands under his chin.

Marcia pulled up a seat.

"He's likely to be more a hindrance than a help," Will said. "I got the distinct impression that, unlike the panel that approved the unit, Stafford has no desire to see the UCU succeed."

"I know the panel that approved the UCU has been disbanded but you could speak to some of those who were on it."

"And say what, at this point? Acting AD Stafford's tone makes me think he wants the unit to fail?"

Marcia nodded, getting the point. "Sounds childish."

"He's a Bureau veteran, entrusted with caretaking an AD role during an extensive audit. The Audit Board would see Stafford's approach as being one of procedure and pragmatism, precisely what they want to see." Will shifted, leaning back in his chair. "Can you put together a summary of Stafford's career, cases he's worked, positions he's held, that sort of thing?"

"You want to see if there's anything we should be concerned about. Or whether he's just a cynical, embittered old agent nearing retirement."

"I've met my share."

"Haven't we all."

"For now, let's just consider this as our own private piece of internal auditing."

* * *

Zoe and I stood quietly on the back porch, watching the sky as the clouds rolled away and the sun broke through, a moment to catch our breaths and collect our thoughts before heading back to Harrow's TTV. We turned at the sound of the back door creaking open. Zach approached but remained silent, sensing this need for solitude, perhaps seeking it out for himself.

There was something on my mind and these few minutes of calm had just brought it to the forefront. "When the killer learns it was Liz Markus, and not his intended victim, Carol Gainsbury–"

Zoe turned, immediately picking up on the concern. "You think he'll want to finish the job?"

I thought it through. "Carol's house has already been damaged by a tornado. There's little chance another twister will hit that area; at least, not this year nor in the foreseeable future."

"Unlikely," Zach agreed, "but it has been known to happen."

"Would he abandon his MO and just go after her, regardless?" Zoe wondered.

"Can't be discounted," Zach offered. "He'll be angry that his method failed to deliver the victim he'd targeted. But at the same time, the camouflage of a tornado is important to him, it ensures he remains invisible."

"Carol Gainsbury is staying with a neighbor whose house wasn't damaged," I said, "but her move there was no secret, no reason why it would have been."

"It wouldn't be difficult for the killer to locate her," Zoe added. "But without any proof of these crimes, we don't have the resources to place a guard on her."

I considered this. "No, but we can request the local police patrols to do a regular drive-by, keep an eye out for anything unusual, and report any storm-chaser type vehicles in the area."

"Will you warn Carol to keep an eye out?" Zach asked.

"Not yet. We may be wrong about how the killer will respond, and I don't want to create undue panic or tip our hand. We have to consider that this may not be about the individual victim. It might be purely about the type of person he's targeting – lone women on large properties in the paths of tornadoes. He may not intend to go after the one that got away."

But the reality was that I didn't know what this phantom was likely to do next.

Chapter Twenty

Marcia tapped on Will's open door as she walked in. "I've got that background on Stafford."

"That was quick."

"I don't do slow."

He laughed. "I know. Take a seat. Anything of interest?"

She pulled up a chair. "Yes and no."

"I hate that answer."

"So do I. But sometimes there isn't just one correct answer."

"Don't I know it."

"The 'no' part is there's nothing ringing alarm bells during Stafford's forty years in law enforcement. Five years with the NYPD, joined the Bureau in his mid-twenties. A veteran agent with an ordinary if unimpressive track record."

"The 'yes' part?"

"When Stafford joined the Bureau, he was assigned as a trainee to a team in NY. That team was led by a senior agent who shot dead a Hispanic man during a botched raid. On top of everything else, they raided the wrong address."

Will winced. He loathed stories like that, incidents that showed incompetence with a tragic outcome, the total antithesis of everything he knew law enforcement should be. "Go on."

"The Hispanic man was non-violent and unarmed. Prosecutors accused the senior agent of being, well, both racist and just plain trigger-happy. They pointed to several other instances involving that agent and accused his team members of complicity."

"And Stafford?"

"He was a wet-behind-the-ears rookie who'd been on the team for less than a month."

"Wrong place, wrong time," Will noted.

"Yes. Investigators interviewed Stafford's NYPD colleagues and there was an implication of discriminatory behavior, not just by race, but gender, socio-economic markers, the usual biases."

"What happened?"

"Stafford was never charged. As I said, he was new on the job, following orders, and his legal rep pointed out he had no involvement in the shooting nor was he responsible for the wrong address stuff-up. Stafford was reassigned but I guess he was tainted by his association with that incident. A stain of suspicion seems to have followed him around in those early years."

"Surely he overcame that?"

"It was over thirty years ago and one of those missteps that the Bureau has done its best to bury. But no one wanted Stafford on their team. He was punted from one team to the next. He hung in there but, as I said, his record is an ordinary one – no big wins or major busts – and he was passed over for several promotions."

"What do you think?"

"I think he's had a life-long grudge against agents who've investigated or brought down another agent, regardless of whether that other agent is guilty of a crime."

"So, just plain, old-fashioned green-eyed monster."

Marcia shook her head. "More than that, Will."

He cocked his head inquisitively.

"He's been a veteran for many years now, working out of DC. Five years ago, he put forward a document suggesting that agents involved in internal investigations should themselves be scrutinized, to ensure they hadn't 'set up' their targets by planting or misrepresenting evidence."

Will took a moment, casting his mind back. "I do recall that. The submission was tabled but ultimately the director passed on it."

"Yes, but it's a clear indicator that Stafford has a bee in his bonnet. He sees those internal investigations as something that stunted his career at its very beginning. Something a better agent would have overcome in time but—"

"Stafford isn't a better agent."

"Two weeks ago, in the wake of this internal audit, Stafford used it as an excuse to re-table that earlier submission with the planning committee. This time, he used a very timely example of the corruption charges against a member of the top brass. What's more, with the temporary reshuffle of assistant directors' responsibilities, he threw his hat in the ring to oversee the UCU, in a caretaker role as an Acting AD until a permanent replacement is appointed."

"He knew he wouldn't be considered as the permanent replacement," Will said.

"For once, Stafford got smart. By electing to stand in, he secured the role for the short time he wants it. The re-tabling of his earlier recommendation lent him some credibility for stepping in and helping out."

Will leaned forward. "Why do you think that is? To bring down the UCU?"

Marcia frowned, shaking her head again. "Not at all. I'd say he ultimately wants to take it on, replacing you as special agent in charge. Maybe he wants to satisfy that deep resentment of his, against much younger agents who've had meteoric rises."

"I hate that term."

"I know. But it's a fact for both you and Ilona. She was a star at the Criminal Cyber Response and Services Branch, that's why you wanted her on the Unsolvable Crimes Unit. But Stafford can insinuate you appointed her because of your previous relationship, and that as a result, you've put yourselves in a compromising position on the job. He's already suggested Ilona needed more recovery time from her ordeals on our first two cases."

Will mirrored both their thoughts when he said, "He casts doubt on our decision-making, gets us shifted off the unit–"

"It's not a matter of bringing either of you into disrepute, you're both too well-established for him to achieve that with innuendo. He simply seeks support for having the two of you reassigned to more suitable roles in the interim, while he steps into a much-higher little niche for himself in his final years. He wouldn't be listened to at any other time, but right now, with this audit rampaging through the place and everyone on tenterhooks, any concerns he can push legitimately will likely get the nod. All in the name of management being seen to have acted in the best interests of the audit."

"All we have is supposition, though," Will stated. "Nothing that would be taken seriously if I tried to have Stafford removed."

"Unfortunately, no. So, you both need to watch your backs. No missteps, no maverick moves by Ilona" – she raised an eyebrow, smiling – "which we both know she's capable of. And we should keep a tight rein on the professor as well because Stafford is, I expect, looking to pounce on anything that he can bend to fit his narrative."

The phone on Will's desk rang. He picked it up and listened to the voice on the other end of the line. His eyes rested on Marcia, and he mouthed the word, "Stafford."

Chapter Twenty-One

Zoe, Zach, and I trudged back along the road from Beth Willard's house to the stranded TTV.

Standing beside the driver's cabin, Jock Harrow said, "Jade managed to get a sat view of what looks like the van that fired on us. On the same road, further along, definitely heading north, but then" – he threw his arms up in exasperation – "heavy rain, and mist. She lost sight of the van and hasn't been able to relocate it anywhere along that route." He screwed up his face in frustration.

"It seems to have just vanished," Jade's voice sounded over the speaker in the cabin.

We heard vehicles and I glanced back at the house. "The forensic guys are here."

"And there's a friendly face on one of the National Emergency Crews that'll be with you in minutes," Jade told us. "They'll replace the tires and check for mechanical damage, but those bullet holes will have to wait until you're back home."

"No problem," Harrow said.

"Friendly face?" Zach queried.

Harrow winked at him. "A very good friend of Jade's, if you know what I mean."

* * *

"Zoe?"

Zoe turned in the direction of the voice, away from where the emergency crew was replacing the tires on the

TTV. A young man in a slim-cut leather jacket and a Yankees cap was standing to the side. He moved closer, night lights touching his face, and she was struck with a familiarity that she couldn't pinpoint. "Do I know you?"

"It *is* you." He broke into a bemused smile, reaching her, and he stuck out his hand. "Carson. Carson Shaw."

"Carson?" Her memory whirled into action and for just an instant the face she saw before her wasn't that of this young man, but a twelve-year-old boy, his eyes searching for adventure and his mouth warped by a mischievous grin as he sat atop a dirt bike.

"I'll race you to the treeline," he'd urged enthusiastically.

"I can't race, I'm still learning."

"No better way to learn, geek girl. Come on!"

The past dissolved and Zoe took his outstretched hand. "It must be fifteen years."

"I can't believe it's you, or that I even recognized you after all this time," he said, his eyes squinting but never leaving her face. He was lean and long-limbed, his wide-eyed expression still brimming with the enthusiasm of his twelve-year-old self. "But you still look like you, just an even better twenty-something version."

She matched his grin. "I didn't look good back then?"

He laughed. "You haven't changed. You still know how to get me all tongue-tied and twisted." His gaze took in her flak jacket and the surrounding activity. "You're with the FBI?"

"Guilty."

"Wow. I wouldn't have expected that. I would have figured you for more a techy type of job."

"I was ten. You figured what kind of work I'd do?"

He shrugged. "You were bossy and you loved your gadgets, as I recall."

"I was never bossy, and who says I'm not doing techy-type stuff with the Bureau? Speaking of gadgets" – she pointed to the camcorder slung over his shoulder — "what's this all about?"

"I'm a reporter for a local weather channel, but I freelance as well, looking to branch out. It's all over the comms about the twister that went through here. I'm told there's been a fatality."

"Yeah."

"I can never get over how brutal these things are."

Zoe changed the subject. "I never figured you for a media type, so we're even. Figured you more for mechanical stuff, like fixing bikes."

"Oh, I still fix 'em *and* ride 'em," Carson told her.

"So, you're a Kansas boy now?"

"Still based in Oklahoma but my station covers the whole of Tornado Alley. What's the FBI doing out here at a storm fatality?"

"Working a case," Zoe said.

"You can't say, of course not."

She changed the subject again. "There's some very heavy storm activity forecast for the next few weeks, so you'll be busy."

"You got that right. And I really need to keep on top of it because I'm not the only one. Reporters from other states are sniffing around these storms, including one who's been in the news herself a bit lately."

"Who's that?"

"Seattle chick. She's part of a crime-reporting podcast among other things, so I'm wondering exactly what she's out here for. Something else is going on."

"Not Brooke Goodman?"

"You know her?"

Zoe shrugged it off. "I'm Seattle-based now, Carson, so Brooke and I have crossed paths a couple of times."

Ilona and Zach, who'd been talking with the forensics crew, approached. Zoe introduced them.

"Pleased to meet you guys," Carson said, shaking their hands. "I can't believe I ran into this young lady here, talk about a blast from the past."

"I stayed in Oklahoma briefly when I was a kid, while my mom was in the hospital," Zoe explained to Zach. "I used to go to a dirt bike riding camp on Saturdays, and so did Carson."

"Small world," said Zach.

Zoe wondered why he sounded irritated. Not like him.

"You're a journalist," Ilona guessed, glancing at the camcorder.

"Yeah."

"For a moment I thought you might be one of these storm chasers that seem to be everywhere this time of year."

"I used to be during my college days," Carson said. "I studied meteorology, but then when I joined the weather channel, I had to give the chasing away. I was doing enough storm-following in my new job."

"Maybe you've come across Jock Harrow," Zach suggested.

Carson laughed. "Come across him? I chased storms with him until, as I said, I gave it away for a real job."

"Even smaller world," Zach said, angling his body and pointing to the cluster of men near the TTV.

Zoe's eyes followed Carson's gaze toward the vehicle. Carson raised his arm and called out, "The Cowboy and the Tech-head."

It took a moment but when Harrow and Rowdy recognized the young man, they raised their hands in a wave.

"I was never certain about that Rowdy Baines guy," Carson said under his breath as an aside to Zoe.

She gave a questioning tilt of her head, but Carson's mind was already on other things.

"When are you heading back to Seattle?" he asked.

"Not certain."

His eyes fixed on her. "It would be good if you and I could have a catch-up before you head back."

Zoe nodded. "That would be great."

Noting the TTV repair work was completed, Ilona said, "I hate to break this up, but we need to move."

Zoe smiled and waved to Carson as she, Ilona, and Zach strode back up the road to Harrow's vehicle.

Chapter Twenty-Two

As we watched, the emergency services workers were packing up, getting ready to move on. Harrow stepped toward them, gesturing to a man on his right. "This is the friendly face Jade spoke of," Harrow said. "Bryce Crowley of PRR."

"PRR?" Zoe queried.

"Project Response and Relief," Bryce explained. "We're a non-profit, Oklahoma-based organization but we extend our footprint throughout the Great Plains, as needed."

"Rescues and immediate after-storm assistance," Harrow elaborated. "These guys sweep in armed with chainsaws, Bobcats, and tractors, clearing fallen trees, mending fences, rounding up livestock, arranging emergency accommodation for survivors."

"Jade sometimes works with us and we're forever bumping into these jokers," Bryce said by way of further explanation. "Jock tells me you're with him on a ride-along." He flashed a wide, toothy grin. "I didn't know tornadoes were on the FBI's Most Wanted list."

"It's not the tornadoes we're after," I said, instantly warming to the man's easy manner. "We'll leave those to Jock and his gang."

We were alerted by a shout and looked around to see a man stepping out of a dark gray SUV which had just pulled up. He called out again and headed toward us.

As he approached, I couldn't help but notice the physical similarities to Bryce – lean, sinewy frame, and the same rugged features, only this man looked to be late forties, an older version of Bryce, his dark hair flecked with gray.

"My brother, Doug," Bryce announced.

Doug Crowley gave us all a wave, and then, directing his comment to Bryce, he said, "I was on the road, passing nearby and I heard the PRR were here. I hoped I'd catch you."

"Seems we catch up on the road a lot more than when we're both back home," Bryce said.

Doug acknowledged the comment with a knowing grin. Noticing my FBI-blazoned flak jacket, he said, "I didn't know the rescue guys had their own law enforcement crew with them these days."

"They're on a ride-along with Jock Harrow. He's teaching them how to handle dangerous weather," Bryce deadpanned.

His brother gave a hearty laugh.

"You staying out of trouble?" Bryce joked.

"So far. I've been up north but I'm on my way back. Got a meeting to get to. You heading back home?"

"We've been asked to head a little further north," Bryce replied. "There's a massive storm front converging just across the border into Nebraska, and we want to be on the spot for any emergencies."

"Looks like I got out of there just in time, then," Doug said.

Zoe had her phone out. "Yeah, the updates are coming through from the NOAA." As an aside to me, voice lowered, and motioning me and Zach away from the others, she said, "Themis alerts that one of the targets lives there, in Alma."

I turned to Bryce. "My team needs to get across the border, to Alma," I said. "We're actually on the trail of a suspect, and he's been alerted to Jock's rig giving chase to him."

"Wow. Okay…"

"I don't suppose…" I stopped. Pleading was not my style, but the hell with it, I thought, we really need his help. "Would you–"

Bryce Crowley cut me off. "You're wanting a different ride to go north looking for this guy?"

"Yes. We have an address; it's just a matter of being dropped off nearby, so we can advance covertly, on foot."

"We can help with that. We're heading that way anyhow and we'll just about squeeze the three of you in. It's just under two hours to the border, so we need to move."

Doug Crowley was already moving off. "I'll leave all you important people to it," he said.

I thought I detected just the slightest hint of contempt in his voice, and I noticed Bryce frowning, giving a slight shake of his head. Some kind of sibling rivalry going on? I wasn't paying any attention to Doug as he walked back to his SUV but from the corner of my eye, I caught him pause briefly before getting into his vehicle, staring back in our direction.

"Rowdy and I will follow but we'll keep our distance, stay out of sight, and be there for when you need to come back," Harrow announced to me, and then, throwing a glance around, he said, "Time to get this show on the road."

Chapter Twenty-Three

It had been less than a week but Carol Gainsbury was restless and impatient to get back to work. She had good staff, but her business wouldn't run itself. And as much as she appreciated the kindness of the neighbor who'd taken her and Cassie in, she didn't want to overstay their welcome. She needed to be in a place of her own again and she thought it would be better for Cassie to be back in school. Her daughter needed the distraction as much as she did. They couldn't hang around this house, in a state of shock and grief, forever.

Her phone rang and the call display showed it was her ex-husband, Jason. Again. If he hadn't been ill the previous weekend, then Cassie would have been staying with him instead of at home being minded by Liz while Carol was out.

But she couldn't blame Jason.

He was still the last person she felt like speaking with right now, but she took the call anyway.

"Is Cassie still having the nightmares?" he asked.

"I'm afraid so."

"Have you thought about my suggestion she spend a week or so with me?"

"It's too soon, Jase. She needs time and right now I think it's best if she's back in school."

"Is that what the counselor thinks?"

"We're seeing her again in a few days."

"Does Cassie still see some phantom figure in these nightmares?"

"Yes."

An edge crept into his voice. "I don't like the sound of these nightmares, Carol."

"Do you think I do?"

"Surely a change of scene could be good for her?"

He'd never shown this much concern for Cassie – or her – during their short-lived marriage, or even now he seemed happier living over the border. Always self-indulgent and carefree, but never with the edge to his voice she was hearing now.

If you hadn't been sick. She bit her lip. Stay civil.

"I think it's best I keep her close for now. We'll see what the counselor says."

"What about the place you're staying?"

"What about it?"

"You can't stay on there and it's likely to be ages before the house is repaired."

"I'll sort something out."

There was a long silence. "I'll call you after Cassie's seen the counselor," she said.

He ended the call and Carol reflected that he hadn't even asked her how *she* was faring after the death of Liz. He'd barely touched on it the first time he'd called after the news broke. Their break-up had appeared amicable to all who knew them but there was a cold, self-absorbed side to Jason Gainsbury that few were aware of.

He doesn't seem to give a damn how I am.

That thought no longer made her sad or angry, but it did send an odd shiver down her spine.

Chapter Twenty-Four

Marcia looked on as Will answered the call from Stafford.

"The UCU will have backup from every field office across the Midwest and the Plains, if and as needed," Stafford said. "And, of course, each one of those agents has contacts with local police that can also be called upon."

"Thank you."

"What's the plan?"

"The first step, in the event of tornado alerts, is to contact potential victims and have them go to the nearest police precinct for safeguarding."

"This killer, of course, won't know that."

"No. And the next step is to be ready to act when a tornado hits and the killer makes his move."

"You'll need to catch him in the act to make any charges stick," Stafford warned, "and if the intended victims are no longer there–"

"We don't know which location he's likely to turn up at next," Will said, "and we think he now suspects we know about him."

"Why is that?"

"An incident that occurred less than an hour ago in Hays, Kansas. My team sighted the unsub and attempted pursuit. There's a report coming through."

"So, you've lost the element of surprise."

"Possibly. Either way, we can't risk the lives of any of those women. If we can't nab him in the act then we'll have to place him at the scene of the previous crimes to make the case, but first, we've got to get him off the street."

Will wasn't expecting Stafford's response. "I suggest that you recall Agent Ilona Farris at this time. You'll have dozens of field agents on board and any one of them can fill her place on this assignment."

"Agent Farris is with the team that's already on the road in Central Kansas. And she has a depth of knowledge and background on this case."

"That may be," Stafford shot back, "but I now have further independent advice that after two traumatic incidents, each within a month of the other, Agent Farris should have taken a longer leave of absence and more counseling. On your first case, she suffered a harrowing encounter with the man you called the Piper. On your next investigation, she was trapped in equally terrifying circumstances by another psychopathic killer. She's barely taken a breath and now she's charging into the path of tornadoes. I have legitimate concerns, for her, and the agents relying on her."

"Agent Farris was cleared for duty, and I need her in the field. Is this a direct order, sir?"

"It's your unit," Stafford said, a professional distance in his tone. "It's a recommendation that is part of the internal audit and I'd suggest you take it seriously."

Will bit down on his lower lip, rolling his eyes at Marcia. "I'll discuss the matter with Agent Farris."

"Keep me posted." Stafford's tone was ice-cold as he ended the call.

Marcia shifted in her chair. "I gather he has well and truly started playing his games."

Will gave a slow nod but said nothing further. During their time working in a different unit two years ago, he did not remember Ilona playing outside the rules, particularly the safety rules, in the way she had recently. Headstrong and opinionated, yes. Relentless in her pursuit of answers on a case, yes. A star on the rise. But a risk-taker to the point of putting herself in harm's way? No. Should he have been more concerned? Even though Stafford had another agenda, had he nonetheless touched on a nerve? Will mulled it over, uncertain.

* * *

Will made an immediate call to Ilona to tell her they could expect backup from relevant field agencies and police precincts. He didn't mention the other matter. He needed time to think about how best to handle it.

"There's intense storm action forecast for southern Nebraska," she said, "and one of the targets lives near the border, in Alma. The lady's name is Megan Tarrant. We're on our way but the killer has a head-start."

"I'll get onto the local field office to escort her from her home," Will responded.

"Will, this killer will be suspicious if he sees Jock's TTV again, so we've hitched a ride with an emergency rescue and relief crew. If we can get a roadblock set up at the border, we could stay there to intercept him before he crosses. Or, if he's already made it across, then the border checkpoint could nab him if he heads back this way."

"Leave it with me," Will said. There was absolutely nothing in Ilona's manner or her command of the situation on the ground to suggest there was a problem with her. He'd make a call to Zoe for her on-the-spot insights, but he was certain that wouldn't change anything.

I'll be damned if I'm going to let some trumped-up little bureaucratic agent railroad my team or this investigation.

Chapter Twenty-Five

Will was back on the phone to John Stafford, asking that the Acting AD make the roadblock request directly, at senior level, to the Nebraska Police Commander. A short while later, after getting Stafford's confirmation that the blocks were underway, Will called the local state commander. "I believe you're ready to roll with the border roadblocks?"

"Copy that, Agent McCord," the man replied. "I understand your suspect is likely to be crossing into Nebraska, or on his way back."

"Correct."

"The highway has troopers setting up as we speak. And your locally assigned field office agents have started arriving at the site."

"Good," Will said. "ASAC Farris will arrive there within the hour and she will be the on-site coordinator. Just to clarify, all SUVs and vans are to be stopped and searched for weapons as well as for scythes, hoes, in fact, all farming tools, traditional or otherwise."

"Copy that," said the commander.

* * *

The FBI chopper swooped across the US-183, transmitting its video of the border area to Will in Seattle.

In the PRR rescue rig now stationed near the checkpoint, I received the same feed.

My phone rang and the field agent in Alma came on the line. "No sign of Megan Tarrant at the house here. There's heavy wind but despite the alert, no twister eventuated. But one of our guys did catch sight of a van that could be the one you're after." The static on the line flared and then died down again; the man's voice was distorted, as though he were speaking underwater.

"Got that," I said, "but it's hard to hear you."

"These winds are playing havoc with our comms," the field agent replied. "Let me move to another spot." The level of static subsided.

"Go on," I said.

"We dispatched one of our vehicles to follow the van but it's wild out there with heavy downpours. It hampered our progress, and we lost eyes on the van."

"Understood," I said. "We need to find Mrs. Tarrant."

"Hold on." The man in Alma was suddenly distracted. "One of my guys is waving me over."

I waited as the static surged, ringing in my ears, and then it fell away again and I listened to an unintelligible babble of voices in the background. I exchanged an anxious glance with Zoe and the fear in Zoe's eyes said it all. Had we lost another woman to this monster?

The static ramped up over the field agent's voice as he came back on the line. "We've found Mrs. Tarrant. Alive." I breathed a sigh of relief as the Alma agent continued, "Her storm shelter door was faulty, so she'd gone across to her neighbor's farm. All safe and sound."

"Thank you, Agent," I said. "Maintain high alert on the lookout for that van."

"Yes, ma'am."

I turned to Zoe. "The woman is okay, but the killer's van has done a disappearing act. Again."

Zoe's eyes were glued to the data scrolling across her cell phone display. "The storm cell is dying out as it heads further north, no further extreme weather predicted across that state for the next week. But there are heavy storms forecast back around the Kansas/Oklahoma border from tomorrow." Her eyes narrowed as she lifted them from the phone. "Maybe he made it to Alma just before the field agents set up their ambush there. It would explain how one of them sighted the van in the distance. The killer would have found Tarrant's house empty, or maybe something spooked him and he never stopped at the house at all. Either way, his next best opportunity is back in Oklahoma."

"Another potential victim?" I queried.

"Roberta Wills, in Watonga."

Chapter Twenty-Six

Day Four

It had been a long night. Heavy storms had erupted across the state line but passed without forming twisters and without widespread damage. The border check had not identified a suspect. I worried that the killer had already made it back across before the roadblock was in place. In which case he was most likely heading to the south.

As dawn broke, a long line of vehicles was forming as police officers and agents performed what they told drivers was a routine inspection. They looked at driver's licenses and recorded license plates and VINs. I wondered how many of those drivers would be complaining that severe weather was an inappropriate time for such an operation. Little did they know. The information gathered was transmitted to the UCU where it was processed by Themis for any connection to the other data held on the case.

No alerts came back. My anxiety rose as I checked my watch. Time was moving at a snail's pace. Where the hell was the killer? Had he even traveled this far north after all?

I'd been certain — we all had — that he would be heading to where the next build-up of extreme storm activity was forecast. The whole northern sector of Oklahoma was on alert.

What if the killer had a different plan in mind?

Where else might he be?

Zach, Zoe, and I had spent the night bunked in the back of the emergency rescue team's truck, but sleep had been intermittent.

The aroma of coffee in the early morning had never smelt so good. I savored the taste as I pulled up a detailed map of the surrounding regions on my laptop and I split the screen, simultaneously running the weather forecasts.

What am I missing?

My phone rang. "Another hour," Will said, "and we'll be well past the point of the suspect being able to pass there and still make it to Oklahoma for the predicted supercell activity."

"You'll be packing up the roadblock?"

"No choice."

Another thought occurred to me. "What if something delayed him? Mechanical failure? Maybe he's still on his way?"

"Good point. I'll have Marcia check with the roadside assistance organizations and any calls they've received."

"Okay." I ended the call, frustrated.

I returned to scanning the maps and the weather forecasts. There was breaking news. The severe storm cell build-up in Oklahoma was happening sooner than forecast. One tornado alert had already been raised.

"Are you seeing this?" Zoe said, watching the same streams of data on her device.

"Yes. I'm sending Will an update now. We'll need local field guys dispatched to Roberta Wills's home straight away. Even if our perp isn't there yet—"

Zoe nodded. "We still need to take every precaution."

I blew a puff of air, dislodging a loose strand of hair that had dropped over my right eye, just as Bryce Crowley stuck his head into the van. "Some folks are stranded on a roof near Holdrege," he said. "The river has flooded."

"You need to head out," I said.

"Yeah."

"Thanks for the ride here."

"Sorry you haven't got the result you're looking for."

I shrugged. "We'll get out of your way."

"You're heading back to Oklahoma with Jock?"

I nodded. "Maybe we'll run into you back there."

Bryce shot me a captivating grin. "I'd rather run into you than one of the EF3s they're predicting." And with that he was back outside again, issuing orders to his crew.

* * *

It was a half-day drive to Watonga, in Oklahoma's northwest. Rowdy sat up front alongside Harrow who drove, allowing some privacy to me and the others in the back of the TTV.

Zach didn't waste any time expounding on the theories and thoughts that had been streaming through his mind. "Think of predatory animals that patiently lie in wait to ambush unsuspecting prey, pouncing when the moment is right," he said. "Like tigers. This killer is like that. He watches and waits for the right weather in the right place at the right time and he's been doing this for years."

"Playing a long game," Zoe said.

"The hunt is as much a part of the thrill for him as the actual kill," Zach continued. "The hunt for the right location at the right time. The hunt for a severe thunderstorm that includes one or more tornadoes."

"But he's specifically targeted businesswomen who own their properties," Zoe said. "There are at least another fifty of those women out there who fit that profile, in areas that haven't been hit by tornadoes, and maybe never will be. What's his plan for them?"

I fixed her with a stare. "You're thinking his MO will change?"

"Evolve. Yes."

"Won't happen," Zach countered. "Not in the foreseeable future, anyhow. The tornadoes are significant. They mean something to him. And as long as it's surrounded by a severe thunderstorm with powerful winds, he's got the cover he needs to camouflage a killing. But what if there's more to it than just watching and waiting for those conditions? Take the Nebraska storm. It's as though it was purposely redirected away before we arrived."

I watched him and waited, sensing where the professor's thoughts would lead. It was, after all, familiar territory.

"What if he can somehow shift the weather patterns he needs away from one place and towards another? The thunder beings grant their *heyokas* the power to control storms, and that is exactly what appears to have happened."

"Except that's impossible," I said.

"But is it?" he said. "There's a truth behind every legend, every myth, every religious ideology, Ilona."

Despite the speed with which they were delivered, Zach's words were clear and brimming with his unique blend of passion and wonder.

"Every belief and every story handed down through the generations has sprung from something experienced or observed, but so many of these have been hidden or distorted over time, or discarded by so-called progress." He breathed a sigh of frustration, but his eyes didn't dim, and his speech didn't slow. "Losing that ancient connection with the spiritual is not a form of progress. Far from it. So, in a sense, discovering the truth of those legends, proving the reality within the myth, is a bridge to reconnecting with everything it means to be human." He raised both hands with his palms upturned. "It can help us understand what the essence of evil is." This was Zach the criminologist merged with Zach the supernaturalist. "The answers are never closer than when we're looking through the perspective of people like the Native Americans – people who are strongly connected to the ancients." He cocked his head toward me. "And you were on the money when you said that this killer has some personal connection to the legends."

"And you have a theory on that," Zoe guessed.

"A *heyoka* will undertake missions for the thunder beings, as Arthur Fire Heart explained. In another life, old Fire Heart would have made a criminologist because I think he was spot-on with his speculation that this killer sees himself in that light." Glancing at me, he said, "Do you have Cassie's drawing?"

I pulled it from my satchel and handed it to him.

He stared at the drawing for a moment and then held it aloft. "I know the girl who drew this was very young, that this is a simplified distortion of what she saw – but it could be likened to some sort of storm god." He couldn't stand and pace in the back of the TTV, so instead, he shifted and turned constantly in his seat, barely drawing breath, the drawing in one hand, his other motioning wildly. "We've seen from the pendants that this killer identifies with the storm-controlling thunderbird, and the lightning bolt it depicts. The girl's drawing shows a man holding what could be considered a lightning bolt. And we know the women this man targets are in the path of a tornado."

"He's doing the twister's work for it," I said.

"Yes. As though he's a living, breathing part of the tornadoes, a special kind of *heyoka*, just as Arthur Fire Heart speculated." Zach paused briefly before waving the piece of paper again. "Delivering death. Seeking out what he believes are servants of the Great Horned Serpent. Controlling and using twisters to mask his actions."

I played along. "A trickster," I added.

Zach nodded.

Zoe adopted the role of devil's advocate. "Okay. But why?"

"The answer lies with the victims. What do they have in common?"

"Apart from being single women on farms who run businesses… nothing."

"What else do we know about them?"

I visualized the names and photos from the police records. "Black, white, Hispanic, Asian, none from cultures that identify with the thunderbird. None were Native American."

"The killer views the lightning bolt as representative of himself but also something that women from other cultures can recognize."

"You think this is a Native American acting out a vendetta against women of other cultures?" Zoe asked.

"Not necessarily. The imagery isn't about his victims, it's about him, about his delusion." Zach took a breath, choosing the right words to convey his theory. "The thunderbird and the lightning bolts are the images with which he identifies."

"Adopting a persona," I said.

"Exactly." Zach fiddled with his glasses. "What worries me now is that while this killer sees his victims as being infected with the evil of the serpent, if he knows the FBI is on his trail then he will view us as the same – agents of the serpent, trying to stop the good work he thinks he's doing."

"And you want us to believe he has some extraordinary power to control the tornadoes," Zoe said, eyebrows raised, her mouth twisted into a shape that was neither a grin nor a frown.

"Many societies have held a belief in man's ability to manipulate the elements." He countered with an animated but serious expression – a look that reminded me of an orchestra conductor's performance. Zach illustrated his first point with a theatrical raise of his right forefinger. "India's historical records tell of enlightened groups of people, called *rishis*, who chanted mantras known as Vedic rituals, summoning rain." His middle finger indicated the second. "In medieval Europe, the Finnish people were believed to harness the weather with special abilities, a belief that persisted for centuries. Yes, it sounds ridiculous to the educated, and yet at the same time, as Arthur Fire Heart pointed out, we have no problem accepting that animals, reptiles, and birds can predict weather patterns. And their senses are so attuned to the earth that they evacuate an area before a natural disaster hits" – he tapped his temple – "as though they're telepathically receiving messages. And if one species is tuned to those rhythms, why not people who are highly empathetic to the elements? Geo-sentients, who could reverse that kind of telepathic messaging?"

"Reverse? You mean, as in sending a message that *creates* weather patterns?" Zoe said.

"Studies have been made into geo-sentience. They've been unable to unearth any evidence of it and yet–"

"Sorry, Prof, but I don't accept for a minute that this psychopath can control the weather." My tone was dismissive. "I do think, as Arthur intimated, that the killer probably believes he can."

"Ilona, he zeroes in with uncanny accuracy when tornadoes strike near intended victims. Something is going on with this guy."

"When we catch this freak, maybe you can have him studied like some kind of lab rat. But first, let's concentrate on trapping him like the rat he is," I said.

Zach shrugged off the dismissal as though it was par for the course. "Either way, if he knows we're on his trail, he'll be hellbent on doing whatever it takes to stop us."

Zoe and I nodded in agreement, but neither of us had anything to add to that. "The one thing we can ascertain so far about the victims," I said, "is that they were women who ran their own businesses. Did those women, perhaps, belong to the same business club or committees, or had they attended the same seminars or conferences?"

"I'll get Marcia working with Themis to check on that," Zoe said.

What we all needed right now, I decided, was some quiet time and rest. It was a long ride and after a while, I snoozed.

* * *

I woke to the sound of my phone ringing, and the field agent on the scene at Roberta Wills's home in Watonga brought me up to date. "Miss Wills is out of state at a conference," he said, "so the house is deserted. We've had it under surveillance but there have been no vehicles approach."

"No tornadoes?"

"No. The heavy storm and tornado activity is further south."

"Thanks for the update. There is no further need for you to maintain your surveillance there."

"Understood, ma'am."

I related the conversation to the other two. "This killer," I added, "does his homework. He'll know Roberta Wills wasn't at the house and with no tornado action, he had no reason to travel there."

"We should have known Roberta Wills wouldn't be there," Zoe said. "I'll make certain Themis is programmed to search for any current travel arrangements, reservations, or other plans that any of the suspected targets might have made."

Another call came through. "Special Agent Farris?"

"Speaking."

"Agent Farris, I'm the local state commander. Frank Hewson."

"Yes, Commander?"

"I understand you're on your way back to Oklahoma City."

"We're half an hour away."

"Urgent matter. I need to see you and your team in my office as soon as you can be here."

I felt my pulse race. "What's happened, Commander?"

My heartbeat pounded in my ears at his reply. "Something that will need to be discussed in person, and in private."

* * *

At the Oklahoma City Police Headquarters, we were escorted by a constable through to the office of the commander. A stocky, military type, he rose from behind his desk and came around to shake hands with the three of us. "There's someone else here you need to meet." Hewson gestured to the other man in the office. Broad-shouldered and sharp-featured, with longish dark hair, dark eyes, and smoldering, mixed-race good looks. There was some Native American blood pumping through that honed physique, I thought. My curiosity was at fever pitch. What was going on?

Stepping forward, the man nodded his head to each of us. "I'm the one who fired those gunshots at you in Hays," he said.

Chapter Twenty-Seven

"Detective Dan Walker," Commander Hewson said, introducing the police officer.

Walker offered his hand. "I'm not as formal as the boss, so Dan is fine."

"We've been aware for some time," Hewson told us, "that there's a gang of looters targeting storm-damaged homes or homes deserted ahead of tornado alerts. We believe this has been going on for several years, and twelve months ago, in consultation with my counterparts in the surrounding states, we came to realize there's a network of these gangs operating across the region." He took a breath. "Four months ago, Dan went undercover, joining up with the local gang." He looked to the detective to continue.

"The gang functions in pretty much the same way storm chasers do," Walker explained. "A van with radar on top, and onboard computers monitoring the weather forecasts. We roam the storm-hit areas, follow twisters if we come across them, and move in when we sight a damaged house that's a likely score. I've managed to win the gang's trust, so now I'm also acting as one of the forward scouts. We'll pull up nearby, I'll go in on foot to make certain the place is empty and safe from any falling debris. If it is, I alert the other guys, they back up the van and we move in."

"You were there to scout Beth Willard's farmhouse in Hays," I guessed.

He nodded. "When I sighted Jock Harrow's vehicle, I recognized his rig from his media reports. I was in the house, and I'd just seen Beth Willard's body. I high-tailed it back to our van and we took off. What I didn't expect was that the TTV would follow. I wasn't sure why Harrow was on our tail, wasn't sure if it had anything to do with the body in the house, but I couldn't have him catch us, couldn't have the gang caught while I'm still working undercover to determine the big brains behind this network. I phoned in the incident and reported the body in the house as soon as I was able to get a private moment away from the others."

"So, you shot out our tires to make certain you couldn't be followed," Zoe said.

"Doing that not only allowed us to escape, but it won me brownie points with the other guys. They got a kick out of seeing me shoot at our pursuer. In reality, it was best I fired the shots because I'm the only one good enough to make certain I hit the tires and that no one was hurt."

"You almost hit the windshield," I pointed out.

Walker winced. "I aimed low. I guess, with those winds some of the bullets got swept up. But I know that rig's heavily reinforced, and I was never going to take any shots that could cause injury."

"What did you do after you'd stopped us from following?" I asked. "The last we saw, you were heading north."

"Pulled off onto some back roads. Eventually rejoined the interstate and headed back here."

Which is most likely what the killer did, I thought.

"We'd been asked to respond to any FBI requests and were told you were on the road with Harrow," Commander Hewson said. "When I saw Sergeant Walker's report come through, I called you straight away. You needed to be aware that the gunfire wasn't from the perp you're hunting."

"The commander's briefed me on your investigation," Walker added.

A silence fell as we absorbed the implications. We had not encountered the killer in Hays after all. There'd been no sightings of the killer in Alma or Watonga.

I bit down on my lip.

Where is he?

"Have you come across corpses on any other burglaries?" I asked.

"No," said Walker.

"You must sometimes encounter people in the homes you enter?" Zach said.

"When the storms are most severe, people are either in a storm shelter or they've left the area. Those are the houses the gang is scouting for, houses abandoned but left untouched, or largely untouched, by the winds. We then fill the van up with electrical goods, valuables, some furniture, and we're gone. When I rush in to check out a house and there are people inside, I simply exit just as quickly, and we head off to scout the other properties."

Zach shifted his weight. "Incredible."

"This gang of looters you're running with," I said, "could one of the other guys be sneaking off to those houses, after your raids, and attacking the occupant?"

Walker shook his head. "No. We're bundled up together in the van, and there simply isn't an opportunity for that."

"And it's always the same group of guys?" Zoe asked.

Walker reflected on this. "Mostly."

My eyes locked on his. "Mostly?"

"There are five guys in total in this region," Walker explained. "From time to time, there might be four of the five on a job. One of the guys might be otherwise occupied but will always let us know if they're unable to show. But there's always at least four of us, including the driver."

I probed deeper. "Is there one of the five who regularly doesn't show?"

Walker took a moment to cast his mind back. "When I think about it, yeah, the only guy who sometimes stays away is Billy Joe. Billy Joe Garrick."

"What can you tell us about him?"

"Thirtyish. He's been doing this sort of thing since he left school, small-time criminal stuff. Hell, probably while he was still in school. He has an attitude, but all these guys do in some way or other."

"Was he with the gang in Hays?"

"No."

"Has he connections with the Native American community, or an interest in their culture or in storm chasing?"

"Not that I'm aware of. He watches those extreme weather channels. Loves that sort of macho stuff, but that's about all."

"We need an address," I said. "We need to get eyes on him, as well as check out his movements on the dates the killings occurred."

"I'll get you that address."

"What happens with the stolen goods?" I asked.

"Our head guy, Davie, delivers them to some warehouse, as do the heads of the other looting gangs."

"A central depository," Zoe said.

"And the mastermind behind these robberies collects it from there," I supposed. "Do you know where this warehouse is?"

"That's what I'm trying to find out. It takes a while to win the full trust of these guys. But I've done that. Now I'm waiting for the opportunity, which I think is imminent."

"What opportunity?"

"Sooner or later, they'll ask me to be the second man when they make a delivery to the warehouse. It'll be a lot safer and surer than putting a tail on them and having it go belly up."

"And once you know the address from being on the spot–"

"We lie in wait. When the mastermind, as you call him, goes to pick up the stuff, we move in."

"I expect you've sneaked photos of these gang members," I said.

"Yeah."

"Do you have one of Billy Joe?"

Walker navigated to the image on his phone and held it up for us to view. "Anyone you know?"

I shook my head and the vacant stares from Zach and Zoe were answer enough from the two of them. "Can you send me that?"

"Sure."

I tapped on my phone and held it up, for Walker's benefit, so he could see my list of all the addresses of the killer's victims. "Did the gang attempt to rob any of these places on those dates?"

Walker cast his eyes over the list. "Only three of those are from the period I've been with the gang," he pointed out. "And no, none of those are places we hit. But as for the other, earlier addresses, I couldn't say."

"Once you nab your man at that warehouse, we'll need to interview the looters. There's a chance one of them has seen, heard, or knows something that could lead us to the man we're after."

"You've got our backup, anything you need," the police chief said.

Walker nodded his agreement.

"Actually, there is something else you can do," I said, my eyes on Walker.

His gaze hadn't shifted from mine. "What have you got in mind?"

Chapter Twenty-Eight

On the way out of the police chief's office, I made an observation to Zoe and Zach. "We called on a heap of resources at short notice for that roadblock."

Zoe frowned. "It probably won't sit well, given it turns out we were chasing an undercover cop on a covert mission."

I grimaced, aware that this development could impede our investigation. As we passed the front desk, I saw a familiar figure leaning over the counter in conversation with the officer there.

Sighting us, Brooke Goodman turned and broke into a wide grin. "Speak of the devil, or should I say, devils," she quipped, tossing her mane of dark, shoulder-length hair.

Brooke was a passionate, ambitious journalist, who a couple of months earlier had suffered the loss of a family member to a psychopathic killer. Subsequent events had seen her career propelled forward by her involvement with Aiden Sharpe's crime watch podcast, *One Voice*. After our experiences together on the Piper and Whistler cases, Brooke and I had formed an uneasy bond.

It was no surprise that Brooke had dealt with her recent tragedy by digging deep into her work as an investigative reporter. But I was surprised to see her here, in Oklahoma City.

"Don't tell me you're down here chasing storms?" Zach said.

Brooke made a face as if to say, 'good idea'. "Close. Chasing a story that I predict is close to breaking. Storm looter gangs."

I was curious. "What led you to that?"

"An old friend of yours and mine." Brooke teased, enjoying the chance to be mysterious. "Detective Radner."

In my previous role with the CCRSB, I assisted the Seattle Police Department when they launched a crackdown on the rising wave of urban climbers and parkour runners. An irony that had never been lost on me, given my own secret obsession. A driving force in that operation, Detective Paul Radner had a personal as well as a professional stake in the outcome. His daughter, Sarah, had fallen to her death while in the company of those daredevils. Radner believed that one of the climbers, the leader, was responsible for the tragedy.

"Why would Detective Radner be involved with anything going on down here?" Zoe asked.

"He has video bloggers shooting the rooftops in several cities, including this one, casting a net for urban climbers he thinks were involved in his daughter's death."

I was silent. Radner hadn't revealed that to me. Was he pursuing this on a personal level, and not as an official police investigation? If so, he would be keeping his actions close to his chest. I knew he'd been warned by his superiors that he needed to focus on his job, and not on personal matters. His daughter's death had been ruled an accident but, even if that were the case, Radner believed the other climbers with her were guilty of reckless endangerment.

"Here's the thing," Brooke continued. "The detective was sent a video of a night climber in Oklahoma City who had the same build and clothing as the Seattle climber he'd previously wanted to speak with, the one who stopped a suicide jumper and was captured on camera several times. The one they suspect could be a woman." She took a breath, allowing a beat. If she expected a response from me, she didn't wait for it. "Radner also confided that the local cops down here suspected there was a gang of looters targeting storm-damaged properties. I called your office. I wanted to pick your brains and ask if you could reveal if you'd heard anything about that, and I was told you were currently on assignment in Oklahoma. I couldn't believe it."

Warning bells sounded in my head, my mouth suddenly dry. Had the savvy reporter put two and two together?

I can't remain silent. That will alert Brooke that she's on the right track if, in fact, that's what she's already thinking.

Deflect, I told myself. Instinct chimed in. Give Brooke something that would lead her thoughts off in another direction. "We're also here because of the looters."

Brooke's confusion was evident. "That's hardly an FBI matter."

"Brooke, if I say any more, then I have to stress that it's strictly off the record."

"As per our arrangement?"

"Yes." I had previously demanded Brooke stop watching and following me. Brooke had wanted to be on the spot for breaking news whenever my team solved a case. In return for Brooke backing off, I promised that when I could release case details, the reporter would be the first to be alerted, the same kind of deal I imagined Brooke now had with Radner.

"Agreed, so shoot."

I breathed deeply. I'd successfully diverted the reporter's attention. It seemed Brooke hadn't imagined a connection between me being in Oklahoma at the same time the Seattle urban climber had been filmed here. Now to completely redirect the focus, I needed to invent an angle that would intrigue Brooke sufficiently without revealing the true nature of our investigation. "There's a suspicious element to some of the recent storm deaths, which may or may not involve the looters. We're running a preliminary study."

Brooke gave an almost imperceptible nod, taking it in.

Quickly moving to redirect further, I asked, "I get that you're here to follow up on this story about looters, but what has that got to do with Detective Radner recruiting video bloggers?"

"A couple of weeks back," Brooke said, "Radner arrested two climbers. He grilled them and found out that they knew a guy they said was with Radner's daughter the day she fell. According to these two, this guy – a ringleader amongst the climbers called Mark Gorton – left town soon after Sarah Radner's death. He figured there'd be heat from the cops looking for climbers, and – get this – this guy Gorton was also a petty thief. When he was climbing and roaming rooftops, he kept his eye out for unattended apartments or houses with easy access and burgled them."

Zach chimed in. "But he left Seattle?"

"That was what these climbers told Radner. Spilled their guts hoping Radner would let them off with a warning and a promise not to climb buildings. These guys had heard through their underground network that Gorton was somewhere in the Plains and that he was not only climbing and urban exploring down here but also in a gang burgling homes, taking advantage of storms."

"Go on," I urged.

"Radner wanted to track this ringleader down and he was surprised to learn that police down here had an investigation underway into a network of looters. And that they had an undercover cop infiltrating one of the gangs."

"The commanders want information that will lead to the boss of these gangs," I said. "I know about that. And Radner divulged all of this to you? Another one of your deals?"

Brooke shrugged. "I hardly think of them as deals, Ilona. More an understanding that's mutually beneficial."

"And why was this deal beneficial for Detective Radner?"

"I had learned about his obsession from my contacts, and I started probing into the climber scene."

"You were the one that led Radner to those two climbers," I said. "And now Radner's got himself involved with this local police op?"

"He'll be able to interview Gorton once arrests are made."

I knew what that would mean to the detective.

"And I expect, if he can prove it, he'll want to charge him with manslaughter," Zoe said. "I guess it would be a kind of closure for him."

I remained silent. *Would it?* I wasn't certain anything would ever divert Radner from his crusade to clamp down on urban climbers who put themselves and others at risk.

"Zoe!"

We turned to face the far side of the lobby. Carson Shaw had emerged from an office, walking alongside a uniformed officer.

"Not sure who's stalking who," Carson joked, reaching us.

Zoe shot back, "Storm chasers, ambulance chasers, I'm starting to wonder where you fit in."

He laughed.

Zoe introduced him to Brooke.

"Ah, the opposition," he said. "I wondered what a high-profile out-of-town reporter was doing here, but I'm guessing now it's about the multi-state storm looters."

Brooke flashed her wide, magnetic smile, casually flicking back a strand of hair. "Not the opposition," she said. "I'm Washington, you're Great Plains, so we don't need to compete. If anything, we should collaborate, or at least share info."

"I'm good with that," said Carson.

"And I'm not so high-profile, either." Brooke chuckled.

"You might not think so but breaking that Whistler story on your podcast made an impact," he said.

Gesturing to Zoe as well as to me and Zach, Brooke said, "And this is the team that worked that case."

Glancing at Zoe, Carson showed his surprise. "That was you?"

"*Us*," Zoe corrected.

Brooke pressed a card into Carson's hand. "I've got to rush, but here are my contact details. Call me and we'll trade notes, we'll see what we can dig up if we combine our resources."

"Sounds good," Carson said, "but what's the rush? You got a lead—?"

With an enigmatic wave, Brooke was gone.

"You know about the looters?" Zach said to Carson.

"Yeah, there's been a series of reports the command here has linked. I sussed there was an investigation underway and I'm trying to pry out whatever details I can."

The young police officer Carson had been walking with moments before, came over. "Okay," he said to him, "here's what I'm cleared to tell you about the looting that's been reported…"

Standing to the side, voice lowered, I remarked to Zoe, "Those two seemed to hit it off." It had been hard not to notice the spark between Carson and Brooke.

"Both reporters," Zoe said. "Maybe they'd make a good match."

"You and Carson seem to be getting on as though you'd never been out of contact."

Zoe shrugged. "That's because it's like stepping back in time, and he was a good friend. We had some laughs at that dirt-bike camp."

"Have you ridden since then?"

"Once or twice, but I never really had the time to pursue it."

"Maybe it's time to have another shot."

"We've got bigger fish to fry right now," Zoe responded with a hint of sarcasm as she rolled her eyes, "and you're not one to be lecturing others about pursuing leisurely interests." Changing the subject, in a rare expression of frustration, Zoe said, "As for Brooke Goodman, I'm starting to wonder if that girl is stalking us."

"Stalking?"

"She's a great girl and I know she's suffered a dreadful loss, but she turns up like a bad penny at every one of our investigations. Even here."

"I've spoken to her about keeping a professional distance from our investigations."

"Maybe she also needs to hear that from Detective Radner," Zoe said.

Carson turned back to us as the officer moved away. He raised his eyebrows as realization dawned. "I gather you're also here about this looting."

"Yes." Better that's what he thinks, I thought, rather than the real reason.

"I understand there's a national police initiative to investigate further."

"Given the weather angle," Zoe said, "I guess it's the perfect story for you to cover while branching out at the same time."

"Ideal," he said. His eyes met hers. "You got time for that catch-up?"

"Now?"

"Yeah."

"I really wish I did, but no—"

Throwing a glance at me, Carson asked, "You likely to catch any bad guys in the next hour?"

"Maybe not in the next hour."

Carson returned his gaze to Zoe and held up his right forefinger, signaling the number. "One hour. That's enough for maybe two drinks, and a catch-up on about a quarter of the time since we rode those bikes."

"I really haven't—"

"Forty-five minutes. Final offer."

"I'm sure we can spare you for a while," I said.

Zoe smiled, and I could see the tension ease in her shoulders. "One hour, tops."

"Not a minute more." He gestured to the exit. "I know the perfect place, not far from here."

∗ ∗ ∗

"What was all that with Brooke before?" Zach asked me, referring to the cover story I'd fed the reporter.

"Keeping her close while at the same time keeping her at a distance. A delicate balancing act. We know she can come in useful."

"I'm inclined to agree with Zoe. It's starting to feel like we're being stalked." He tipped his head in the direction of Zoe and Carson as they departed. "And speaking of reporters stalking us, do we really need Zoe catching up with this guy?"

I observed Zach. He looked disappointed. Was that a tinge of jealousy I was detecting? "Maybe he'll come in useful as well," I said.

If Brooke was nosing around the urban climber scene and exchanging notes with Detective Radner, then it was to my advantage that I keep her close and prevent her from stumbling upon my urban climbing secret.

My thoughts whirled back to the undercover operation we'd almost blown. *Focus.* And to the harsh truth that if looters were out there targeting damaged homes, then it muddied the waters in determining which of the vans belonged to the looters, and which was the killer's.

Chapter Twenty-Nine

"I survived because I was in our basement," Carson said. "My mother should have been there as well."

"What happened?" Zoe asked. She and Carson had been filling each other in on the years since they'd last met. Cradling beers, they'd slid into a booth in a bistro dominated by dark oak, a horseshoe-shaped bar, and walls lined with photos of country music stars from another era. The pivotal point in Carson's life, the death of his mother, an event that informed his later career choice, struck a nerve with her. And it had occurred just six months after the time she'd lived in Oklahoma, with Vema.

"My mother told me to get down to the basement." There was a quiver in his voice, but he swallowed and cleared his throat, quickly regaining his composure. "She said she'd be with me in a minute. But her body was found a quarter of a mile away, so she must've been outside."

"Do you know why?"

"Yeah. She said she saw a man, one of the field workers, and she wanted to go and shout out to him to come inside for shelter."

"So, she'd gone outside—"

"Yeah," he said breathlessly, reliving the moment, "and the twister got her. Our home was damaged. Mostly the exterior, the awnings were found hundreds of yards away..." His voice trailed off.

"And you were in the basement," she said, stating rather than asking.

He nodded but didn't speak. The sorrow in his eyes was visceral, as though it had just happened.

Zoe felt a pang of regret that he was revisiting that despair. She rested her chin against the knuckles of her left hand, watching him, subconsciously lowering her guard to draw his words, his feelings, closer to her. She rarely did this; she'd certainly never done it with any of the guys in the old Harlem gang, the other students at Quantico, or with her current team, not even with Marcia. There had been too much hurt in the past, too many times she'd had to rely on her own strength, not someone else's. But there *had* been Vema, back when she'd spent time in this part of the country. Maybe that was the reason she felt this affinity with Carson, because they'd been friends during that brief but happy time, and because she knew that shortly after, he'd suffered.

But right now, there was something else, something troubling, something prodding her. "Do you know who the worker was, the man your mother went outside to call out to?"

He shook his head. "I never saw him. He would have been one of the field workers on our neighbor's property."

"What would he have been doing on your mother's land?"

Carson shrugged. "I don't know. I've never thought about that. The neighboring farm's border was very close to our farmhouse, so—"

"Would this worker have been one of the volunteers from the Little Bear community?" Zoe asked, her mind racing.

"Maybe. I know that they help a lot of the local farmers."

"The Little Bear helpers use traditional tools. Did you ever see workers out there with traditional tools, like scythes and hoes?"

"Sure. They used them for clearing the land. Why do you ask?"

"Curious nature. Just wondered what happened to that worker she saw. Was a man's body found as well?"

"No, there were no other bodies found." There was a beat as he considered this.

"I gather he must have found shelter somewhere."

"But that would mean he took off and left my mother out there after she'd gone to help him."

"I'm sorry, I shouldn't have brought it up," Zoe said. "I'm not being very good catch-up company."

He shook his head. "No, no, not at all. I'm glad you mentioned this." He reached for his drink and sipped. All of a sudden, the look on his face was haggard. "What if one of these looting gangs was operating way back then? What if it was a looter my mother saw?"

Zoe shot him a reassuring look. "Unlikely. It was, after all, fifteen years ago. Long before any reports of widespread looting during the tornado season."

"I guess you're right," Carson said.

Of course, the looters could have been operating longer than first thought, but it led Zoe to now wonder whether the storm killer had been out there much longer than they'd suspected. She pushed the idea aside for now, changing the subject to happier thoughts.

* * *

Outside the bistro, they exchanged kisses on the cheek before going their separate ways. Zoe watched as Carson waved and walked away along the street. She took her phone from her purse and connected with Themis, telling the AI the address of the farm where Carson had lived as a boy. "Check real estate records for the neighboring property," she directed. "I need the name of current and previous owners, and if there are any business or IRS records from fifteen years ago, of farm workers employed by the owner." Carson hadn't remembered the name of the neighbor and wasn't sure if the property still had the same owner. She wanted to see if she could locate that neighbor and talk with them. She would also need another meeting with Arthur Fire Heart to ask if he could shed any light on a volunteer from that time who might have worked on that property.

Her curiosity was piqued, and she wanted to find the man that Carson's mother saw that day.

Chapter Thirty

"I've withdrawn the request," Stafford said, "for state and federal resources to assist the UCU on this so-called case." He shook his head in anger. "I cannot believe we mounted a roadblock for what turned out to be a wild goose chase.

And it could have derailed an undercover police operation."

Will couldn't shake the impression that it was all pretense. He remained tightlipped. There wasn't much he could do but cop the spray.

"This gives rise to my concerns that this unit has suddenly gone way off-course." Stafford stared icily at him.

He's better at icy stares, Will thought.

"I know a unit leader is under pressure to keep delivering. You're ambitious, I get that, you rose through the ranks at a rapid pace, but what this project doesn't need is a leader whose ego has got the better of him. A special agent in charge who is personally influenced by a team member with a reckless approach."

"I don't let ego get in the way, John, and no one could have known we'd cross paths with an undercover police operative." Will's voice was firm. "It's thrown a spanner in the works, but it doesn't change the fact there's a killer out there."

"It changes everything," Stafford shot back. "It means the unknown persons seen at the site of the other deaths were looters. All the other 'evidence' – and I use the term lightly – is circumstantial. The injuries are consistent with storm-inflicted wounds. The medallions could have been bought from a traveling artisan. They don't add up to a storm killer. If you're going to continue looking into this, Agent McCord, then you would want incontrovertible proof of the crimes, and you'd want it pronto."

"The concept of the UCU," Will countered, "is to take on cases likely to remain unsolved. Taking unconventional approaches alongside the conventional. Pushing boundaries like this will lead to some missteps, yes, but with all due respect, you're overlooking the basic premise this team's been built upon."

"That may be, but the UCU is in a trial phase," Stafford responded, calmer now but just as cold, his jawline set like an immovable vice. "Let me be clear: presenting to the

Internal Audit Board that the UCU is charging into tornadoes with a reckless bunch of storm-chasers, in pursuit of a killer who does not exist, almost destroying a long-term police undercover op in the process, and with one of the agents having faced personally traumatic incidents in just the past two months, is hardly a visual that instills confidence."

"I can't agree," Will protested. "There is still the evidentiary connection of the pendant that each of the women was wearing when they died."

"Have you sourced the origin of those pendants yet?"

"We're working on it."

"But there could be hundreds or more women across the States wearing that design."

Will shrugged, his frustration rising.

"There is no way," Stafford said, "I can continue to direct our field offices to make themselves available to your unit for this case." He released a pent-up sigh. "I approved that support against my better judgment, taking into account the UCU's start-up track record. The detail on this case was sketchy to begin with, and I have to question now whether you ignored your own better judgment launching into this, pushed by Agent Farris–"

"That is not the case," Will cut in sharply.

"I hope not." Stafford went quiet, leaning back in his chair as though giving himself the space to adjust to his newfound power and authority.

Will had had enough of this. "Will that be all?"

"There's something else. I need to let you know about another case I'm pursuing under the umbrella of the UCU."

Will sat straight in his chair. "And what is that?"

"During Agent Farris's time with the CCRSB, her team investigated the Seattle arm of a national business network, and ultimately all of that network's interconnected businesses. They arrested the owner and CEO, Brad

Carstairs, on tax evasion and money laundering and he's currently serving twenty-five years."

"I know of the case," Will said. "I worked on the investigation in its earlier stages before my move to DC."

"Ah, yes, for your promotion." Stafford's tone barely concealed his contempt.

Will said nothing.

"The Carstairs crime family had their fingers in the pies of many more criminal activities on top of the one the CCRSB nabbed him for," Stafford said. "I'm flying to DC to oversee a further interrogation of Carstairs. My inquiries have shown that there are several other inmates in the same prison who were involved in Carstairs's crimes, although they are serving time for other, unrelated activities."

"I'm not sure I understand what that has to do with this new interrogation of Carstairs, or the UCU," Will said.

"I'll have Carstairs transported from the prison to our DC HQ for the interrogation. But I'll also make certain that word spreads among the prison inmates, not only that he's being taken to a special interrogation center, but the unit interviewing him is the one responsible for cracking the high-profile Piper and Whistler cases. I expect those inmates will panic, believing that Carstairs is throwing them under the bus in return for a deal to reduce his sentence."

Will nodded, seeing the strategy. "Those inmates will freak out that they'll get extra time based on Carstairs turning state's evidence," he added.

"Yes, and as a result, we'll get them to turn witnesses themselves, which will bring a raft of extra charges we can lay on Carstairs, and others whom we don't know about at this stage."

"This doesn't fit the UCU's remit," Will pointed out, "which is to tackle cases pinpointed by Themis."

"Regardless, it will add to the roster of the UCU's successes, and help the unit get the nod once its trial period is over."

"Definitely worth pursuing. When do we head to DC?"

Stafford shook his head. "You need to stay here, put an end to this so-called storm killer investigation and get yourself and Agent Zoe Marshall focused on another case. I'm bringing in one of the Bureau's top terrorist interrogators who will play some serious mind games with Carstairs, giving the once-mighty crime boss a taste of his own medicine." It was said without any hint of dark humor, Stafford's expression remaining as granite-like and icy as always. "Transporting him from the federal prison to the special interrogation rooms will already have served to destabilize him further."

"Good psychology," Will conceded, feigning approval while making certain there was nothing in his demeanor to reveal his true thoughts. He'd wondered what Stafford's next moves would be and he certainly hadn't anticipated this. Will had a lawman's antennae for sensing when someone was not the kind of person they pretended to be. What was John Stafford really up to?

Chapter Thirty-One

Zoe joined me back at the motel, and I texted Zach, who was in his room, asking him to join us. While we waited, I asked Zoe, "How'd it go with Carson?"

"Good catch-up."

"Nothing more?"

Zoe shot me a curious look. "No. What do you mean?"

"I couldn't help but notice you were instantly comfortable in Carson's company."

"Good memories."

"You can tell me to take a running jump if I'm getting too personal, but do you do much dating?"

"None."

"No?"

"I suppose you could say I'm a serial flirter."

"And what's stopping you from moving to the next level?"

"A little thing called Themis."

"I get that. And it's been one major achievement."

"Oh, yeah."

"But there comes a time…"

"Yeah. There *will* come a time. But not yet."

"And why's that?"

"There's still a lot to focus on. Like getting this project fully cemented into the FBI's psyche."

That wasn't something I would disagree with. "Fair enough. But just saying, you really seemed to light up when Carson was around."

"Friend zone," Zoe said.

"Strictly?"

"Strictly."

I knew when to back off. I flashed a wide grin. "Got it."

"But there is something that came up in conversation."

"Oh?"

Zach arrived, giving a wave as he walked in, and pulled up a chair while Zoe filled us in on what she'd learned from Carson about his mother's death, and about the fieldworker his mother had seen.

"You're thinking something doesn't add up," I guessed.

"I've got Themis chasing up details. I want to establish who Carson's neighbor was back then."

Zach changed the subject. "Not knowing it was Dan Walker and the looters in the van at Beth Willard's place, we assumed it was the killer and that he'd gone north to Alma. But the real killer never headed that way, nor to

Watonga; it seems he already knew that tornadoes weren't going to eventuate in either of those places."

"He outguessed the forecasts," I said.

"Or he had something to do with causing a change," Zach jumped in, excited, again raising his theory. "We've heard from Arthur Fire Heart about shamans who controlled the weather and redirected tornadoes, shamanic incidents that science hasn't been able to explain as anything other than coincidences. What if science can't explain it because it's real? What if this killer *does* have the skills that those shamans have?"

"That's crazy..."

"Or a perfectly natural, untapped human ability."

"Let's put ourselves in this guy's headspace," I said, resetting the focus. "He likely traveled back this way from Hays, though we can't be certain he's based here in Oklahoma. Could it be that in between his journeys from one killing to the next, he sometimes stays on the road, in motels or trailer parks, not always returning to a home base? It would mean he's not madly zigzagging all over the place, which could maximize his chances of success." I flashed a look at Zoe. "Could that be his MO?"

"I'll have Themis backtrack to previous seasons, see if there's a pattern."

"He wouldn't just sit around in motels scanning weather reports," Zach protested. He looked a little miffed that I'd redirected the discussion away from his theory. Even so, he shifted effortlessly into investigative mode. "This is not a mind given to idle time. He has to keep busy, doing something that has meaning for him. Think about it. If he believes he's doing the bidding of the thunder beings, could he be going somewhere to commune with those spirits immediately after a kill, perhaps as a form of validation, or a moment to be re-energized by the thunderbird?"

"Re-energizing," I repeated, drawn to the idea. "What about a Native American community, something along the lines of Little Bear but with a purely spiritual focus?"

"A shamanic church or retreat." Zoe whirled around to the keyboard. "Initiating a search." It took Themis less than a minute to respond.

"Native American spiritual churches, retreats, and communities in this region," Themis's mellow and distinctive voice responded through the laptop speakers. "The Daughters of Gaia, in Sand Springs; The Earth, Air and Sky Retreat to the west in Wheeler, Texas; and north, the Spirit and Shaman Community in Phillipsburg, Kansas. Unfortunately, there are no digital records of people visiting or staying in the accommodation or studying at these organizations."

"We're going to have to rely on old-fashioned phone calls," I said, "and hope they keep manual records." I recalled that one of those retreats, The Daughters of Gaia, had come up in conversation with Harrow and Rowdy. "We're also looking for a trail that the killer left behind at diners, motels, and gas stations each time he visited one of those areas before or after a killing."

"He may not have used his real name," Zach said. "Even though he doesn't expect anyone will ever identify these deaths as murders, he'll likely play it safe so that there's no paper or digital trail."

"Let's hope he's overlooked something." I tried to sound more hopeful than I felt. "We check the hotels and motels for credit card payments, and if he used cash transactions, as I'd expect, did he sign in with his real name and license details? We're looking for a name that consistently shows up in a given place at the same time one of the murders occurred in the area."

"When the killer pinpoints a supercell near his target, he's got limited time to act," Zoe added, "so he needs to know exactly how to find his target's address and the best way to access the property as quickly as possible."

"It helps if he's been there before," I said, picking up on Zoe's line of thought.

"Exactly."

"He could have a job that makes that possible without attracting attention," Zach offered. "A tradesman or a door-to-door salesman."

"Makes sense," I said. "We'll compile bank statements from all the victims going back a few years. Zoe, let's have Themis pull out any phone records and payments to a common contractor or services provider."

The ping on Zoe's phone alerted her that there was an update from Themis. "Zoe, update on your request for the owner of the property neighboring that of Carson's mother fifteen years ago. Collette Rayburn had owned the property, which operated as a poultry farm."

"Rayburn?" I queried out loud, the name ringing instant bells.

"Is she still the owner?" Zoe asked.

"Collette Rayburn died three years ago from storm-inflicted injuries. She was the first of the deaths flagged as being victims of an undetected killer."

Zoe exchanged a sharp glance with me. "If this killer was around fifteen years ago and Carson's mother was one of his victims," she began, her mind spinning.

"Then Collette Rayburn wasn't the first."

"Themis," Zoe said. "Are there any records revealing who might have worked on the Rayburn farm back then?"

"No records found."

We would no longer be able to query the since-deceased Collette Rayburn about the worker, but we could query Arthur Fire Heart about volunteer workers from that period. Zoe gritted her teeth, and I saw the sorrow in her eyes flare into anger. "We need to find this man that Carson's mother saw."

Chapter Thirty-Two

I held up my phone, showing Arthur Fire Heart the picture of Billy Joe Garrick. "Does this man look familiar to you?"

Arthur studied the picture, responding almost immediately. "Oh, yes. I remember that young man. I haven't seen him for a while now, maybe a year or two. But he spent a little time with us, he and some friends."

"Friends?"

"Yes. I recall a small group."

"How many?'

Arthur took a moment, frowning. "I can't be certain, but I'd say three."

"All male?"

"Yes."

"Was one of these men Native American?"

He pursed his lips, digging deeper into his memory. "So many have come and gone, spending just a little time with us, since those three. But yes, I seem to remember that one of those young men had the blood of our people."

"When young people volunteer to work alongside your members, do you give them training with the traditional tools?"

Arthur's genial smile widened. "Of course. There is always one of our experienced persons acting as a mentor."

Zoe leaned forward, taking on the other aspect of our inquiries. "Fifteen years ago, a woman named Melinda Shaw died when she was caught in a tornado. She'd gone outside her farmhouse to call to a farmhand from her neighbor's property, and we'd like to find this man."

"How may I help with this?"

"The worker was most likely one of your community volunteers."

Disappointment clouded Arthur Fire Heart's eyes. "Fifteen years ago?"

"Yes. I know it's a long time…"

"Our community here was much smaller then. We had volunteers helping out, but at that time we did not have workers out on other properties. It was another four or five years before we began to reach out in that way."

"There's no chance a volunteer might have offered their services to a farm?"

The old man shrugged. "I could not say for sure it never happened. But it was certainly not our practice at that time, and if someone did help out this person you speak of, it's not something I would necessarily have known about or remember. Not after all this time."

"I understand."

"The person we're looking for is very knowledgeable when it comes to when and where tornadoes are likely to form," Zach said to Arthur, "so much so that I can't help but wonder if he's a shaman, or at the very least has trained in shamanic ways and has used them for nefarious means."

A cast of sorrow passed the old man's eyes. "It would disappoint me if that was the case. But, of course, it is possible. All things, the good and the bad, are possible."

I handed him the sheet of paper on which I'd scrawled the names of spiritual retreats in the region. "We're checking on people who've visited these centers."

"And you'd like to know what I know of these retreats?"

"If you have any insights, then yes."

He gazed briefly over the names and then raised his head. "This is the one you might find of most interest. Certainly the closest. The Daughters of Gaia, in Sand Springs, not far from Tulsa City."

"They hold shamanic studies?" Zach asked.

"Yes. And they are very good. And very careful about whom they invite into such studies."

"Once again, I have to thank you for giving us the benefit of your local knowledge," I told him.

He bowed his head, a sign of deference, and then, raising it once more and grinning, he said, "Should I consider myself a special agent in your Federal Bureau?"

I couldn't help but return the grin. "Perhaps not a special agent."

"But most definitely our best consultant," Zach said, and then, with a nod and a wink, he added, "Well, second best."

The sound of a lone drum drifted through the open window, with the intermittent rattle of a shaker joining it, and then the beating of further drums. "Ah, I am late to the pow-wow," Arthur said.

"Pow-wow?" Zoe queried.

He laughed. "Sounds so very old-time movie-ish, doesn't it? In fact, it is our community's song and dance ceremony, held each week, and our people here, and any who wish to visit, can participate. If you can spare a few minutes, perhaps you'd enjoy viewing the opening?"

"Lead the way," I said.

He led us through a hallway and a rear exit of the large cottage, onto an expanse of field, oval-shaped, edged on the closest side with the buildings of the community, with meadow stretching away on the other sides, and beyond that, a slight rise into the woods. "Our shamanic elders enjoy a strong connection with the elements, and they express this interconnectedness in music and dance. Something in which we have a rich culture. Our ceremony is also part of our mission to teach our younger generation the traditional ways of our people so that it is not lost with their immersion in modern society. We often stage these pow-wows with festivals, carnivals, and sports events. The elders relate the stories of our ancestors and pass on their wisdom and their knowledge of how the spiritual realm interacts constantly with the physical world."

It was a warm day, sunny, the sparsely clouded sky a cobalt blue. A large group of the locals stood in a wide semi-circle, and within this, there was a troupe of men and women; some playing drums, rattles, and bells; some singing; some dancing around a small fire – the men garbed in traditional breechcloths, leggings, and buckskin jackets decorated with beads; the women in long, wrap-around dresses and shawls.

Arthur gestured to the drummers. "The hand drums are crafted with animal skin, soaked and stretched taut across a wooden hoop. This is then laced onto the hoop and tied at the other side of the hoop in a distinctive design. The big drums are made so that they can be played by more than one person at a time, and singers pitch their voices to complement the various tones of the drums."

His voice was filled with such pride that I could feel the same sensation rising within me. The performance was well underway, the rhythm was hypnotic, and I was drawn into the magic. It was akin to the exhilaration I experienced when I was climbing, attuned to the space that surrounded me high above the earth, in sync with the birds, in awe at the infinity of the natural world.

There was a sudden cry of alarm from one of the dancers, a middle-aged woman, and she fell to her knees, shaking. The other performers abandoned their performances and went to her.

Arthur Fire Heart moved toward her at a brisk pace. "What is it?" he asked her as he reached the group, kneeling before the woman.

She was clutching her chest as though something had struck her. "I feel it… so strong…" She gasped for breath.

"Feel what?"

She winced, not wanting to say the words out loud. "The evil one."

As the others consoled her, Arthur said, "Is it like something physical…?"

"Yes… close by."

"Deep breaths. We shall work together to drive the Serpent away." Arthur gestured to the others, and they joined their voices in one deep, resounding, uplifting chant.

Standing back from the group, Zach, Zoe, and I watched in amazement.

The woman began to calm down, and then she pointed off to the woods, her voice a croak. "Watching…"

All eyes looked in the direction she indicated and on the crest of the rise that skirted the forest, there was a rustle of leaves and scrub, a fleeting glimpse of movement, of a dark shape. A forest animal? Or someone watching, someone who didn't want to be seen?

I raced across the open ground to the spot where I'd seen the disturbance. I wasn't sure if I believed the woman, and this might be nothing more than a deer, but I was compelled to be certain that something else wasn't going on.

But what?

I reached the edge of the woods with Zoe and Zach right behind me. I pushed through a dense undergrowth of buckbrush and juniper, with gnarled patches of blackjack oaks towering overhead, blocking the sunlight. After a couple of minutes of tramping forward, I stopped and listened. No rustle of hurried movement ahead. No cracks of twigs and branches.

"Anything?" Zoe whispered, coming close.

I raised my hand as a signal for silence and continued to listen. Faint whistling of the leaves in the soft breeze. The shrill of a bird. But nothing more. "If there was someone, they're gone."

We returned to where the group had now dissipated, the ceremony deferred for a short while.

Arthur Fire Heart stood quietly, his head slightly raised, his eyes on the horizon, his gaze shifting to us as we approached. "Those of us trained to heightened sensitivities have now detected the traces left behind by that presence. Someone observing. Someone... or perhaps I should say some *thing*... malevolent."

"There didn't appear to be anyone out there," I told him.

"A physical emissary of the Serpent can be gifted with the silence and the invisibility of the spirits."

"Is there a reason this malevolence would be watching?" Zach asked.

Concern crossed Arthur's face. "Evil always watches but it is not always as overt. I fear that on this occasion it is your visit here that has drawn out this dark heart." I exchanged glances with Zoe and Zach as Arthur gestured for us to follow him back to the house. "If that is the case, then I believe that our sensing of the presence is a godsend. It serves as a warning that the one you seek may also be seeking you. He thinks he is erasing evil, when in fact it is *he* who is being controlled by the Great Horned Serpent."

Chapter Thirty-Three

After saying our goodbyes to Arthur, we headed out to our hired car, this time a white Audi. Although it weighed on my mind, I pushed away thoughts of the dancing woman's collapse and her and Arthur's warnings of a watcher in the woods. A malevolent force. Surely not, and yet I had myself, inexplicably, as I'd run into those woods, felt the same strong sense that there had been someone spying. Someone who had run when they'd realized their presence had been detected. Perhaps I'd simply been caught up in

Arthur Fire Heart's charismatic ways and words. There was no way that the storm killer could know that the FBI was aware the tornado deaths were murders.

If someone had been in that scrub, watching the team, then who? And why?

We stood by the vehicle for a moment as I brought the focus back to Billy Joe Garrick, one of the main reasons we'd been talking to Arthur. I held up my phone with Garrick's photo displayed. "He looks to be early to mid-thirties, so Garrick would have been around eighteen to twenty, fifteen years ago – when these murders might have started. He's had access to traditional farming tools, has spent time here learning about the American Indian legends, and could have been here volunteering back then."

"And he's also one of the looters," Zoe added.

"He could have been the forward scout for the gang before Dan Walker got involved," Zach said.

"And still could be on those occasions when Walker isn't." I slid the phone into my jacket pocket. "He could have murdered those women and then raced back out to the van, telling the others the place wasn't suitable."

"And they head off, unaware one of their members has just committed a murder," said Zoe.

"Walker will be on the spot," I pointed out, "if any of the upcoming robberies target the address of a potential murder victim. He'll alert us if that happens, and if Garrick's the man, we'll also have the chance to catch him in the act." It was what I had asked of Walker during our first meeting, and I'd given him our list of potential targets.

We were heading back to our motel in the Audi, Zoe driving this time, me in the back passenger seat, making a call to Rowdy Baines. "Rowdy, you told us you once spent some time at The Daughters of Gaia retreat."

"I think it was Jock who brought it up, but yeah, I did. If I had the time, I'd probably revisit the place. Great for meditation and it's run by a brilliant, beautiful soul, Agnes Night Moon."

"And they have classes on the ways and wisdom of the ancients?"

"The best. Very immersive. As you're probably aware, in Greek mythology, Gaia is the Goddess of the Earth, the ancestral mother of all living things, and is paid homage to by New Age groups from many different cultures and countries. Has this got something to do with the man you're after?"

"The person we want to speak with might have sought out spiritual groups."

"You think he's spent time at Gaia?"

"We'd like to find out."

"It makes sense," Rowdy said. "And The Daughters of Gaia is probably the best place to start with that line of inquiry, it's easily accessible from the surrounding states and it's also the most welcoming, thanks in no small part to Agnes. Of course," he added, making light of his comments, "this is just between you and me. Don't say anything to Jock." He laughed. "Just another piece of what he calls mumbo-jumbo to poke fun at."

"Mum's the word." I already had an incoming call as that one ended. I glanced at the caller ID and frowned. "John Stafford," I told the others as I answered.

"I know we haven't yet had the opportunity to meet in person, but I wanted to have a word with you, Agent Farris, about your current investigation and the setback you've encountered."

I straightened in the seat, tightening my grip on the phone. "Setback, sir?"

"It seems clear from the incident with the undercover detective, Dan Walker," Stafford said, "that the houses you believe a killer ran from, were, in fact, houses from which a looter was running."

"Except, sir, none of the houses we identified had been robbed."

"Do you know that for certain?" Stafford's tone was antagonistic. "Jewelry and other valuables could have been taken. Those houses were severely damaged, the interiors in disarray. Did relatives or anyone else do a full inventory under those circumstances? Would they even have known precisely what valuables their relative had?"

My reply was tentative. "No, we can't be certain."

What the hell is this all about?

"Have there been any significant developments there today, Agent Farris?"

"We're following up on several lines of inquiry–"

Stafford didn't wait for me to finish. "I agreed to considerable resources in other field offices being made available," his tone accusatory, "but in light of the Hays incident involving Detective Walker, there is no longer any real evidence to support this theory of a storm killer. I'll discuss this further with the internal audit people, and I've spoken with Will McCord, but in the meantime, I strongly suggest you rethink your view on this so-called case, take extended leave, and consider further appointments with the counselor."

"Sir, I–"

"I have an urgent call coming in, so I'll leave it at that for the moment." He ended the call abruptly and I was left, phone in hand, staring at the screen.

"What was that all about?" Zach asked.

I looked at him but was guarded in what I said. "I wish I knew." I immediately called Will.

"I just had the most bizarre phone call from the Acting AD," I blurted out the moment he came on the line.

"He's a strange man."

"Strange? He strongly suggested I drop this case, take extended leave, and get counseling. Spoke to me like I was some kind of PTSD madwoman."

"He may have a point." Will's attempt to lighten the situation fell flat. There was a moment of silence on the line that seemed to last longer, accentuated by the lack of any laughter from me.

"I'm all for improvements that help stamp out corruption or incompetence, but Stafford seems to be targeting me for no good reason."

"He's using the broader machinations of the internal audit to push some personal agenda," Will said. "Marcia and I are looking into it."

"What does that mean?"

"It means Marcia's trying to find out what she can about his history with the Bureau. And what it is that he's trying to achieve with these… recommendations of his."

"I don't like the sound of this, Will. We don't need this crap going on while we're mounting a crucial investigation. Hell, we don't need this sort of BS at *any* time, period."

"Stay focused, Ilona. I'll keep you posted on Stafford."

I'd barely ended the call when all of a sudden, I was thrust forward, pressing against my seat belt, as Zoe applied the brakes and brought the vehicle to a halt by the side of the road.

"What is it?" I said as Zoe pulled her phone from the dashboard's storage shelf.

"Urgent weather update from Themis," Zoe said. The AI's voice came over the speakerphone. "Multiple tornado activity is predicted across Kiowa, Washita, and Caddo counties with severe supercell build-up faster than forecast. Alerts have been issued for New Cordell and Anadarko."

"Anadarko," I repeated. "One of the women on the list is an Anadarko resident."

Zoe called up the list and scanned for the Anadarko address. "Millie Hargraves."

Zach tapped a number into his phone. "I'll call Jock. We need him to get us out there now."

I started tapping another number into my phone. "I'll have the local cops get out to the Hargraves' place. Hopefully, they haven't been called off by Stafford."

"That's what that call was about?" Zach said.

I nodded.

Zoe's voice was ragged as she turned in her seat to face us. "Either way, this killer's always a step ahead and he could already be there."

Chapter Thirty-Four

"You want me to break the speed limit," Harrow shouted to me in the back of the TTV as we raced toward Anadarko. Jade was beside him in the passenger seat, and Rowdy was back at their HQ, manning their sat equipment.

"Yes."

"If we get pulled over–"

"We've been designated as an emergency vehicle."

The sky was darkening rapidly as though a mad artist was furiously brushing it with black paint. Shards of lightning split the air and the trees were whipped by the wind into a manic dance.

"Ilona," Harrow barked. "Up ahead, on the left."

I shifted forward and craned my neck, looking out the front passenger side window. A van with a radar dish on top was standing stationary on the grassy embankment beside the highway. The dark coloring and the model of the vehicle were a possible match.

Why was the van stopped here in the middle of nowhere? Was it worth pulling over, losing time, this close to our destination?

"Let's take a look," I said.

Zoe spun to face me. "Can we afford–"

"No, but we'll only take a minute. Something odd…"

Harrow pulled in front of the other van, screeching to a halt, and Zoe, Zach, and I piled out of the back.

"No one at the wheel," Zach announced as we ran back to the vehicle, his eyes focused on the front windshield.

We tried to open the doors but they were locked. Peering in through the front windshield, I could just make out that the back of the van was partitioned off. There were no signs or sounds of life.

I cast my gaze over the surrounding fields, taking in the cattle grazing on a far-off knoll, the hills in the distance misted with low-lying clouds and sheets of rain. No shelter nearby. I guessed it was at least a mile or two across those fields to the Hargraves' property. Too far to walk and certainly no time to cross that amount of ground with a twister bearing down. This couldn't be the killer's van, but where was the driver?

"Something about that van seems oddly familiar," said Jade, who had jumped from the TTV and joined us.

"Wouldn't that be the case with most of these storm-chaser vehicles?" Zach said.

She nodded. "Yeah… but…"

"No idea why?" I prodded.

Jade's brow furrowed as she thought hard. She shook her head. "Sorry, no."

There was no time to speculate further, the minute was up.

"Let's go," I ordered, and seconds later we'd clambered back on board the TTV and we were hurtling along the road.

"Here she comes," Harrow cried out as the TTV turned into the long, straight driveway leading to the Hargraves' farmhouse. On the horizon, I saw the funnel swirling into existence, its wide base spinning and driving it in a direct route to the house.

Meteorological graphs moved over the satellite pictures on Jade's screen. "That baby is up to 140 mph," she said, "I'm guessing we could be looking at an EF3, and if it hits any part of that house…" Her words trailed, her inference obvious, as we held on, rocking up and down as the TTV bounced along the stony driveway, buffeted by the winds.

"There's no van at the house and we've not seen one leaving," Harrow called out.

"Millie Hargraves should be in her shelter, then," Zoe said.

Harrow brought his rig to a standstill and we watched as the tornado's direction shifted, veering south of the house, but as it passed, the edges of the funnel cut through a part of the building, shattering its south wall and crushing a portion of the roof. "Dear God," breathed Zoe.

"Or Thunder Gods," Zach quipped but it was without his usual exuberance, his eyes fixed in awe on the sheer force of this fast-moving column of destruction.

The twister passed and the winds subsided, and I felt an odd sensation as an eerie, dark calm descended over the landscape.

Harrow drove forward, pulling up a short distance from the ruined building. Moving carefully, to avoid exposure to the loose and falling timbers and windows, I approached the front door. It was splintered but otherwise intact. Rain gushed in random bursts, the intermittent lightning accompanied by the low growl of distant thunder.

I called out for Millie Hargraves.

Zoe located the storm shelter, on the west side of the house, and she called out to me and Zach. She lifted the shelter door, arming herself with her pistol as a precaution. I came up alongside her, with Zach, Harrow, and Jade holding back, looking on.

Zoe and I peered down into the shelter. It was a small space. "Empty," I announced. Stepping away, I then led the way through the front entrance of the house, motioning for Zoe to back me up, and for the others to keep their distance. Although there was no sign of the killer, nor any indication he'd been here, vigilance was essential. I moved with speed and stealth, every muscle primed for the unexpected.

"God, no." I stopped, staring down at Millie's body lying on the floor amidst broken glass and misshapen pieces of furniture. Her inert form was beside a dividing kitchen/dining counter and a flash of lightning through a shattered window illuminated the scene. Fragmented slivers of half-light flickered. I knelt beside the body, checking for a pulse. "She's gone. But… warm. Still very warm."

Zoe was frozen to the spot, staring. "He was here before the twister hit, but–" she sucked in a lungful of air "–he can't have gone far."

Zach was in the doorway, listening, only a part of the crime scene visible to him. There was a bang as part of the house shifted and something somewhere crashed. "The house is too unstable," he warned.

Zoe and I stepped back outside. I scanned the empty miles of surrounding fields. The winds that were left behind in the wake of the tornado were still strong and we had to brace ourselves to maintain our footing. "He must have been on foot after all."

"That van?" Zoe started.

Rushing to the TTV while gesturing, I said, "That has to be his and we can beat him back to it."

As we rumbled back down the driveway and onto the road, I glanced out on the fields, alert for a lone figure traversing the landscape.

"Jade," said Harrow, "can we get a bird's eye view with our drone?"

"Already on it," Jade said, "and I'm trying to raise Rowdy to send the images through."

Four minutes later we rounded the bend to the spot where the mystery van had been stationed.

It was gone.

"Now what?" Harrow said.

"We need to find him," I said. "Jade, any chance we can spot the van?"

Jade shrugged. "Right now, no pics are coming through, and I can't raise Rowdy. Comms are down. Massive storm interference."

Zoe expunged a breath of sheer exasperation. "No way he could have crossed that distance in so short a time."

"Zoe," I said, "we've still got Themis accessing CCTV live feeds?"

"Checking that" – Zoe's fingers flew across her keyboard – "but most of the systems are out."

"He must have been at the house earlier than you thought," Jade suggested.

I shook my head. "No. Millie Hargraves hadn't been dead more than fifteen, twenty minutes. I don't need a coroner's report to tell me that."

Harrow momentarily averted his eyes from the road, glancing at me, intrigued. "Then how? And why park his van way out here?"

It was Zach who replied. "So that it's never near the death scene, never observed. And maybe the distance between the van and the farmhouse is no problem–"

"Don't say it," I cut across him, my voice weary. I was in no mood for his theories, but Zach was back to his unstoppable, unflappable self.

"No problem for someone with the powers of a *heyoka*."

PART TWO

Chapter Thirty-Five

Day Five

I woke to a call from Local Area Commander Frank Hewson, ten minutes before my wake-up alarm. "There's been a development."

I cleared my throat, found my voice. "What's happened?"

"Detective Walker got a call at dawn. He's been instructed, with one of the other guys, to drive to the warehouse and pick up goods for transport. But that's not all. He's been told the boss he's never seen will be there and wants to meet him."

"And when he does, you'll raid the warehouse."

"We're tracking his movements via his phone. We're able to hear everything he hears, and we'll be ready to pounce. You and your team are welcome to listen in."

"We're on our way."

* * *

Joining Hewson in his command center, I watched the live stream from the officers' helmet cams as they surrounded the warehouse with their semi-automatic rifles raised. They ordered the occupants to come out with their hands in the air. Walker and two other men appeared – Walker playing along, maintaining his undercover role.

Hewson indicated a row of monitors that ran along the far wall. "Now that we have the head man and the location of this warehouse," he told me, "I've got simultaneous arrests being made of the other gang members."

I glanced at those monitors, and one in particular, that showing Mark Gorton, the Seattle climber who'd come here over two years earlier and joined this band of thieves. He was the man Detective Radner had long been searching for. I watched as he was handcuffed and led away from his apartment by two police officers.

"By the way," Hewson said, "about your office's request to have the local precinct's daily patrols include, for a few days, the street where Carol Gainsbury is staying. I've seen a report, which they're sending to you. It's a quiet area and there's been no suspicious activity of any kind detected."

"Good to know," I said.

* * *

Given access to Gorton's place, Zoe, Zach, and I walked into a tiny, dusty, one-bedroom apartment, the furniture sparse and threadbare. Ashtrays overloaded with cigarette butts littered the armrests of the lounge and there was a pile of unwashed dishes in the kitchen sink. "Bachelor pad," Zoe quipped. "This remind you of your place, Prof?"

Zach winced. "I'm hurt."

She grinned. "You might finally find your evidence of other life forms in here."

"Spread out, search everything," I said. "Let's see if there's anything here that points to a connection, either knowingly or unknowingly, to the killer." I headed to the door at the opposite end of the room. "I'll take the bedroom."

Alongside a rumpled, unmade bed was a tatty single chest of drawers, with strips of paneling hanging loose. There was a small window that was partly open, a breeze ruffling the thin lace curtain that hung over it. I rifled through the drawers. A few clothes in two of them, and in the third, a bunch of foolscap-size papers with rough penciled layouts, something that didn't fit with what we knew of Gorton, or with any of the other items we found in the apartment.

Chapter Thirty-Six

With Zoe and Zach alongside me, I watched the interrogation from behind a wall of one-way glass. Walker was glaring at Mark Gorton while Detective Sergeant Paul Radner, seated alongside the undercover cop, began his questioning. As per his arrangement with the Oklahoma PD, Radner had been given access to interview Gorton. The moment he'd received the alert that Gorton had been arrested, Radner had got on a flight from Seattle.

"I'm Senior Detective Paul Radner, Seattle PD, but of course you know who I am, don't you?"

Gorton was all lean and angular shapes, his wavy, collar-length brown hair giving the impression it was permanently tousled. He stared back, trying and failing to suppress his disbelief. He cleared his throat. "Should I?"

"You were urban climbing with my daughter, Sarah, when she fell."

"I don't know what–"

Radner slammed two photos down on the table. "Recognize these guys? Your fellow climbers. They told me they were in conversation with you before you left Seattle. You told them you were with her."

"You can't prove–"

Radner cut him short again. "Think very carefully before you answer the next question, Mark. And remember it's an offense to lie to a police officer." He paused for effect, his eyes boring into Gorton's. "Did you push my daughter over the side of that building?"

Gorton's lazy expression changed, his eyes widening. "No way," he blurted out. "She was a good climber, she was doing fine. There was a freak gust of wind, no one…" He stopped abruptly, realizing too late the mistake he'd made, lured into admitting his presence at the time of Sarah's death.

"You encouraged Sarah and others to undertake dangerous, illegal urban climbs. At the very least, in addition to your involvement in these robberies here, you will be charged with reckless endangerment. At the worst, either manslaughter or second-degree murder."

Gorton's voice was ragged, his breath coming in short, sharp bursts. "I didn't cause her death," he protested.

"Tell me in detail everything that happened that day." Radner barely contained his fury, his voice so hard and so cold that even I didn't recognize it. "Start from the very beginning. Cooperate with me and with the sheriff's office about the robberies, then with the FBI – who also want a word with you – and the courts will take all of that into consideration. Is that clear, Mark, do you understand how serious these charges are? Do you understand how your cooperation could go a long way to lessening the sentence a judge imposes?"

Gorton swallowed hard, giving a slight, almost imperceptible nod of his head.

* * *

I was looking at bundles of pages, maps grouped into geographical regions, each with dozens of rough, hand-drawn layouts of properties, showing the locations of houses and storm shelters. I pushed them across the interview table towards Gorton. "What's this?"

Gorton's drawl was punctuated by underlying hostility. "All the places we've robbed, and some we didn't. We made notes of where we'd been, what loot we took, and drew layouts of the places."

"Why?"

"All those homes will be deserted for a while, and a whole lot of them have underground shelters that are roomy and well-stocked. If any of us was ever in danger of being caught out, or in some kind of trouble with the law" – he shrugged, as though there would be nothing unusual in that – "and we needed a place to hide out, then there's nowhere better. No one's checking out those shelters on abandoned properties. The boss man has another side to his business – some kind of service for crims who need a place to lay low for a couple of days, maybe longer, while they're making other arrangements. That's why he gets us to collect the information."

"This other side to your boss's business. Do you know if it's active?"

Gorton was silent, brooding, his eyes flicking anxiously around the room.

"Let me remind you, Mark, that your full cooperation here today will be viewed very favorably by the courts."

"Yeah. I know of a few guys who used the boss's service." He sneered, displaying his contempt that his 'boss' had failed to keep the gang safe from arrest. "Some entreprender he turned out to be."

"Entrepreneur," I corrected. "How well do you know the other guys in this gang?"

Gorton had already been interviewed by Commander Hewson after Radner had left the room. He was tired but his speech was still punctuated by turns of childish arrogance. "Who wants to know?"

"None of us have time for your crappy attitude, Mark. How well do you know the other guys?"

"Not well."

"You spend any time socializing with them?"

"The burglary runs usually lasted at least a day or two. After that, we'd grab a few beers at a bar, blow off steam."

"What is Billy Joe Garrick like?'

"How do you mean?"

"Anything about him that struck you as a little off?"

Gorton shrugged. "He's a loner if that's what you mean by 'off'."

"What was he doing when he wasn't on the raids with you? We know he often didn't turn up."

"No idea. But he often said he needed to get out on the open road on his own, and I know he used to get around a few of the states."

"How do you figure that?"

"Whenever we were on a run over the border, whether it was Texas or Nebraska, he always seemed familiar with the area."

My back straightened in the chair. "Did he know more than he should about the properties you were casing?"

"You mean, like, had he been there before?"

"Yes."

Gorton shifted in his chair, shrugging. "Don't know. Maybe."

"We've brought in all the other gang members except for Garrick. He no longer lives at the address he'd given your boss."

"Like I said, he's a loner. And a bit of a drifter, always moving around."

"You know where he's living now?"

"As far as I know he's been living in the back of his van."

"Van?" My nerves tightened. "A storm chaser vehicle?"

"Hell, no." Gorton sneered. I figured that was as close as this guy ever got to laughter. "It's a seedy little nineties Ford minivan. A rust bucket if you ask me."

"You don't know where he parks it?"

"Anywhere the mood takes him, I'd say. Billy Joe's one strange dude. I don't even think the van is his and I don't think the boss was going to keep him on. Too unreliable."

"Wouldn't he be a liability if he knows all about these robberies and the boss sacks him?" I asked.

"Guess that's why the boss kept him around."

"You think he stole this van he's living in?"

Gorton shrugged again. "He never seemed bothered driving it around town so no, I don't think it's stolen."

* * *

Bill Rowland was a short, wiry, balding man with a boxer's nose and a nasal voice. "I'm not the top dog," he protested.

I was back behind the one-way glass, with Zach and Zoe. Watching.

"Just the middleman, you say." Walker was sitting across the table from him in the interview room.

"That's right. The big boss contacts me by phone, a different burner every time. Gives me instructions. I just carry them out in Oklahoma, Kansas, and Texas, and believe me that's enough, keeping track of the gangs in those states, and doing it remotely so that I was never seen. You can check my phone, you'll see all the calls from unknown numbers, right before he arranges for me to shift goods from the warehouse."

"And where do you move those goods to?"

"A truck stop on the interstate. I pull in, another truck with guys I've never seen before pulls in, they transfer the goods over and then they're gone."

"What do you know of this big boss's operations in other states?"

"Nothing. You think he's going to let anything on to a middleman like me? But I picked up, from things he said, that he's got guys running similar setups in Nebraska and Ohio, and I don't think that's all."

"You've no idea who this man is?"

Rowland went to raise his arm in ignorance, forgetting it was chained to the table, and he winced as his arm snapped back. "None."

"And the maps that the agents found in Mark Gorton's apartment," Walker pressed. "Gorton told us they were drawn up to show storm shelters that could be used if ever needed. For use in a whole other criminal operation."

"I wasn't involved in any of that. As I said, I already had my hands full. The boss told me what he wanted me to know, and what he wanted me to do, and nothing else. He's a ghost, and one thing I can tell you, once he knows this part of his business has blown up, he'll vanish. It'll be like he never existed in the first place."

* * *

Zach rubbed his chin and scratched at his cheek. "Organized groups of looters, as well as storm shelters used as temporary havens for criminals. This whole thing is even bigger than the police first thought. Still in its early stages but actively being expanded. I think Rowland was telling the truth about each state being run by a small-time crim. Each one reporting to a big network boss."

"Do you think this big boss Rowland speaks of has anything to do with the killings?" Zoe asked.

Zach was quick to answer. "No, he wouldn't want anything going on that could attract unwanted attention to his business."

"But sometimes," I said, "even the most cautious mind can get reckless." I flashed on my more daring urban climbs and wondered whether I was talking about myself.

"There are no vehicles registered to Billy Joe Garrick," Zoe said, her focus drawn away to her phone's screen as Themis lodged its search result.

"Okay, so we check for all of the Ford minivans manufactured through the nineties which have a current Oklahoma license plate." I was pacing. "There has to be a record somewhere for this vehicle Garrick is using."

Minutes later, Zoe said, "There's more than a few, all housed on farming properties outside the city." She scrolled down the list and then, all of a sudden, her neck stiffened in surprise.

"What is it?"

"A name I didn't expect to see," Zoe said.

Chapter Thirty-Seven

Carol Gainsbury was out on the country road. Always busy, she had never previously walked the area surrounding the neighborhood homes, and the walk afforded a whole different perspective than what she saw when driving. She reached the junction with an intersecting road which ran along the far western aspect of her neighbor's land and then, further back, curved around the adjoining forest.

She felt in that moment as though she could go on walking forever; something was liberating about it, a sense that if she stopped and stood still, the real world would come crashing back. Rushing in with all the grief that had been tearing her apart.

The small-acreage properties here backed onto a forest of big bluestem tallgrass that licked the trunks of small, gnarled blackjack oaks. The morning sun dappled the landscape. If she closed her eyes, holding in her mind the serenity of this road and that islet of woodland, she could almost believe the horror of the tornado and her sister's death were not real. But the moment passed too quickly, and she knew she had to get back; she didn't want to be apart from her daughter for too long, even if Cassie was in the care of their elderly neighbor, Fiona Elderslie.

Her phone pinged with a text from her ex.

*I still think it would benefit Cassie if she came to stay
with me for a while. Perhaps you could bring her? A
road trip here and back might be good for you.*

She had no intention of responding. Not right now,
anyway. Typical Jason. He wanted to comfort his daughter
but couldn't be bothered to come to visit. And then trying
to couch the idea of a trip being something that would be
good for her.

What an ass. What is going on in the head of that shallow man?

He was only across the border in Amarillo, a three-and-
a-half-hour drive from El Reno on the I-40. He was an
insurance claims investigator, sure, they were busy, but
even so, he could have taken some time off for a family
emergency.

* * *

Returning to Fiona Elderslie's house, Carol found that
Jason had made a video call to her iPad and was speaking
with Cassie. She stood in the doorway to the living room
and listened in.

"Are you coming to be here with us?" Cassie asked.

"I'll be coming very soon," Jason Gainsbury said,
blowing a kiss to the camera. "In the meantime, lots and
lots of Daddy's kisses, just for you."

"When is soon?"

"Daddy has some work stuff to finish and then I'll be
there, or…" He hesitated.

"Or what, Daddy?"

"Maybe you'd like it if your mom brought you here to
stay with me for a while. Would you like that, hon?"

The girl didn't respond, she just shrugged, unsure.

*She's only five years old, Jason. She's been through a harrowing
experience; she doesn't need to be unsettled or confused any further.*

Carol let out a frustrated breath, but she didn't enter
the room to interfere. She didn't want to take away any of
the limited time that her daughter was getting from her
father, even if it was just on a video link. And she didn't

trust herself to speak with him. She needed to stay calm and in control of her emotions, for Cassie's sake.

When the call had ended, Carol went and sat beside her daughter on the floor. "That was good, darling, you got to talk to Daddy."

"Are you taking me to stay with him?"

"Would you like me to, honey?"

"Only if you stay with us." The little girl threw her arms around her mother.

"Maybe we could do that soon." There was that word again, Jason's word. *Soon.* Carol bit her lip, sorry she'd used it.

"Not too soon," Cassie protested. "I like it here with Mrs. Elderslie."

Sun streamed in through the double glass doors that led to the veranda. Mrs. Elderslie, an energetic eighty-year-old, was tending her garden bed in the backyard.

Carol hugged her daughter closer and stroked her hair. She felt the presence of Liz, watching them with her comforting, sisterly smile. It wasn't hard for Carol to imagine Liz's distinctive, throaty voice. "You and Cassie should be fine, sistie." But then Carol's imagination took a dark turn, fracturing her sense of calm with images of Liz, terrified, confronted by the storm, the roar of the tornado ringing in her ears, and Cassie's dreams of a man in the darkness, shrouded in dust and debris. The ghost of Carol's sister's voice took on an alarming tone. "Keep Cassie close and keep your wits about you, sis. Be very, *very* careful." Thoughts crashed through, of the FBI's visit, their request for the pendant, and her fears in the night that there had been someone snooping on the property.

She shuddered. Was her subconscious, through her vision of Liz, trying to tell her something?

Chapter Thirty-Eight

"To what do I owe the pleasure?" Bryce Crowley from Project Response and Relief said as he opened the door to me and Zoe, ushering us in, his grin replaced with a questioning look as he saw Detective Dan Walker bringing up the rear. He smoothed down his dark hair as he led us into the living room.

Jade came through from an adjoining area. "Here's trouble," she said jokingly.

I introduced Bryce and Jade to the detective.

"We're looking for the driver of a nineties Ford minivan," I explained, "so we're calling on everyone in the region that has one of those vehicles registered, and your name came up."

"Ah, the Ford mini. One of my brood." Bryce pulled up some wicker lounge chairs and gestured for us to take a seat.

"You've got quite a few cars registered to you," Walker commented.

"Seven, maybe eight." He flashed a grin. "I'm losing count, must be getting old. It's a boyhood hobby, buying and fixing up old vehicles, and I've got the space for them in the barn out the back. What I don't have these days is the time to indulge myself, so they're sitting pretty idle and have been for a while. My older brother's the same."

"Doug?"

"Yeah, the guy you met when we were out on the road."

"Where is this Ford minivan of yours?" I asked.

"That one's not here. I loaned it to my nephew, must be a year or more ago. He was down on his luck, needed something to get around in and get to job interviews, that kind of thing. It's not worth much so I was happy to let him use it for a while."

"You don't seem old enough to have a grown-up nephew."

"I'll take that as a compliment. He's my brother Doug's boy, and Doug's fifteen years older than me."

"Why didn't he loan one of his own cars to his son?"

"Doug isn't around much."

"So, your nephew's a Crowley, not a Garrick named Billy Joe."

"That's right." Bryce showed his confusion. "Who's Billy Joe Garrick?"

I handed him a photo. "He's wanted in conjunction with a series of robberies. Do you know him?"

Bryce glanced at the photo, tugging at his collar as he did. "My nephew rents an old farmhouse with a couple of other guys. I don't know them. Saw them once in the back of the van when I happened upon my nephew in town – this was ages ago – and that face is vaguely familiar." A shrug. "He could have been one of them."

I didn't respond immediately. My eyes had been drawn to his neckline. Bryce had been in a rescue worker's outfit when I'd first met him but this time his upper chest was visible beneath the unbuttoned top of his casual, checkered shirt. He was wearing a pendant and light was glinting off its silver surface, just below his Adam's apple.

I squinted, looking closer.

There was an engraving with a lightning bolt zigzagging from a cloud. Not the same as the one worn by the killer's victims, but similar in style. I pointed to the pendant. "Where did you get this?"

"The pendant?" He shrugged. "Who remembers? Probably some local fair, years ago, back when I first started in emergency work."

"The image suits."

"Yeah. Storms."

"I haven't seen that styling before."

He laughed. "Neither had I."

"What's on the flip side?"

He turned it over, revealing a plain surface. "Nothing. Why?"

I didn't respond. I wanted to press him further as to whom he'd bought it from but didn't want to seem unnaturally curious or raise suspicion. From the corner of my eye, I saw the confused expression on Walker's face. He would be wondering what the hell I was doing asking about Bryce's pendant when we were here on official business.

I thought of another approach. "I'd love a pendant like that. It'd make a great souvenir. Where do you think I'd find that fairground hawker?"

"Good Lord. After all this time? Your guess is as good as mine."

"That one time I met your nephew," Jade interjected, "I seem to remember he wore a pendant. It looked like something similar."

Bryce considered this. "I'd forgotten about that but yeah, you're right."

"You ever visit one of those fairgrounds with your nephew?" I sensed Walker leaning forward, becoming agitated, and I flashed him a look, my eyebrow raised, praying he would get the message that I knew what I was doing and remain silent.

"Not with my nephew," Bryce said, remembering, "but I sure did with his dad."

"Maybe your brother bought one as well, and passed it on," Jade suggested. She was speaking to Bryce, but her eyes were fixed on me. She'd ascertained that I had another reason for the questions.

Bryce shrugged. "Most likely."

I took a deep breath, shifted in the wicker chair, bringing the focus back to our search for Garrick. "Do you have an address for this place your nephew rents?"

"Sure." He rattled it off and I watched as Zoe tapped it into her phone's address book.

"Are you heading there now?"

"Yes."

"Then I'll follow," he said. "I hope neither of his housemates is this Garrick. But if one of them is, and there's any trouble, I've got a good rapport with my nephew, and I might be able to help keep things calm."

"You think that's necessary?"

"I hope not, Ilona. My nephew's a good guy but he's not the sharpest tool. My brother confided once he was concerned about the company his boy was keeping."

"Perhaps his father should come out to the house as well."

"I'll call him but even though I sometimes run into him out on the road, he's often not that easy to get a hold of."

As we headed out to our cars, Bryce made the call, and I could see that on this occasion he was in luck and his brother answered. Or had Bryce spun me a line about his brother being difficult to contact?

"Doug, I need you to meet me at Nathan's place. I'm headed over there now with law enforcement officers. They need to question Nathan. You should be there. *You really should.*" There was a tension in Bryce's voice that I hadn't heard before.

"Any chance there are weapons on the premises out there?" Walker asked Bryce.

"My nephew has a permit for a hunter's rifle."

"Then I'm guessing the other guys do, as well," Walker said.

* * *

The farmhouse was on a small block, the result of the owners having sold off large tracts of the land, retaining the house and a couple of acres as a rental.

In the hired Audi, we followed Bryce and Jade, who were in a recent model Hilux, and pulled up on the long grass of the paddock beside the house.

Jade waited alongside the Hilux as Bryce led Zoe, Walker, and me to the front door.

The door opened and a skinny, stringy-haired young man grinned from ear to ear and high-fived his Uncle Bryce. "Hey, Rescue Man, what's up?"

"I've got some law enforcement friends with me. They've got some routine inquiries about the minivan, and they'd like to speak with you and your house buddies." Bryce's tone was as folksy and non-threatening as anything I had ever heard. "Able to spare a few minutes?"

The grin evaporated and the young man looked unsure. "I guess."

"This is Nathan," Bryce said to us, introducing his nephew as we walked through the entry alcove and into the living room.

A voice called out from just outside the front door. "Hello?"

We turned to see Doug Crowley stride in, and I remembered the craggy features and dark hair spiked with touches of gray. "Hey, Nathan."

Nathan stared at his father but didn't respond, a facial twitch his only acknowledgment of his arrival, nothing like the spirited response he'd given his Uncle Bryce.

Nathan's house buddies were sprawled across a sofa and playing a video game. A glance convinced me that neither of them was the man I was looking for.

"So, where's the van?" Bryce asked his nephew.

Looking sheepish, Nathan said, "I loaned it to a friend."

"I loaned the van to you, Nathan," Bryce said, irritated, the folksiness gone and his voice taking on a tone of disapproval. "For *you* to drive, not for you to loan out to buddies."

"I know, I know."

"Some things never change," Doug Crowley said but his comment didn't solicit either a reply or even a look from Bryce or Nathan.

I held up the photo of Billy Joe Garrick. "Nathan, is this the guy you loaned it to?"

Nathan reared back when he saw the photo. "Yeah. Billy Joe. Why have you got a photo of him?"

I ignored the question. "What's your relationship to Billy Joe?"

Nathan looked to his buddies, as though their confused expressions could be of help. "He lived with us for a while and still crashes on the sofa from time to time. He's a bit of a weirdo, likes to get away and be on his own a lot, that's why he doesn't stay here permanently."

Bryce didn't hide his annoyance. "Then why the hell did you loan him my vehicle?"

"Yeah?" Doug echoed.

"He wanted a van he could live out of, and sometimes he parks it out the back here."

One of the other young men spoke up. "He's a friend but we wanted him out of here; it was crowded, and we'd had it with his moods. I've got a car I share with Nathan, so we figured we'd loan the Ford mini to Billie Joe."

"He said he'd return it soon, once he had one of his own."

"Oh, yeah, sure," Doug said.

I was wishing now that Bryce hadn't been able to contact him. It was obvious he didn't want to be here, and his presence wasn't helping.

"What's this all about, anyway?" one of the other guys asked as he casually keyed something into his phone.

Walker strode forward, snatching the phone away and glancing at the text on the screen. "You're warning him," Walker said as they heard the gunning of an engine outside. Running to the window, I saw the minivan hurtle from around the back and onto the road.

Walker was already racing to the door. Glancing back as he did, he called to me, "Arrest these jerks for misleading police. I'll go after Garrick."

Chapter Thirty-Nine

"I've been doing some more digging, behind the scenes," Marcia said, striding back into Will's office. "Stafford has a big house in an elite suburb, regularly goes on international vacations, never short of funds. All attributed to his wife's inheritance from a family business that was closed down long ago. Except that the inheritance was minimal. I expect it enabled a fake paper trail so there would never seem anything suspicious about Stafford's finances. But if the money didn't come from there, where did it come from? Even though he resents the agency's young Turks" – she grinned at her reference to Will and Ilona – "he's had a cushy ride, never in the front line, always behind the scenes, and he and his wife will retire a hell of a lot wealthier than any other agent."

"Go on." In all his years at the Bureau, Will had never felt a sense of unease like this one. The sense of being attacked from within.

"I programmed Themis to run an extensive search, pulling in anything and everything, business or personal, on Stafford. Once a month, dating back years, Stafford has a golf game with old friends at a prestige club in DC. Occasionally, there is a photo of the group in the club's internal newsletter. Eight years ago, one of Stafford's friends had a son who went pro on the golf circuit and one of those photos was run in external media, *Golf Pro* magazine. Themis found that photo and has identified that the person next to Stafford is none other than the crime boss, Brad Carstairs."

"Stafford has known Carstairs personally for years, without anyone having any idea," Will said.

"What's more, Themis also highlighted that prior to Ilona's team's success in charging Carstairs, there had been CCRSB investigations, years before, none of them going anywhere, and in at least one instance that was because of evidence that went missing."

Will stiffened. "Stafford would have been in a position to tamper with evidence. The perfect underdog to remove or shred evidence."

Marcia nodded. "No one's watching Mr. Nobody."

"So, do you think his unimpressive work history was deliberate?"

Marcia raised her eyebrows and frowned. "Perhaps not deliberate, I'd say that's just who he really is. But at the same time, it's a perfect cover. In return for being one of Carstairs's helpers and being rewarded handsomely for it."

Will breathed in. "So, what's he up to with the UCU?"

Marcia adjusted her glasses, a subtle move that she made when deep in thought. "I'm not sure about that, Will. But Carstairs has plenty of dirt on Stafford, he could easily expose him—"

"Which means Stafford has little choice but to do his bidding."

"Blackmailed."

Will mused over the possibilities. "It suits Carstairs to have Stafford in a position of some authority, even if only for a short time."

"And it suits the Internal Audit Board. Stafford's exactly the vanilla flavor they need right now to fill that gap and dance to their tune. Except he's secretly dancing to Carstairs's."

"In which case," said Will, "why the hell is Stafford initiating this uber-interrogation of Carstairs?"

Marcia leaned forward. "There's a list of underworld identities, whom we believe Carstairs had connections with through the years. This morning, Stafford asked me to provide him with that list. I didn't read anything into it at the time but perhaps he intends to use that information for this interrogation of Carstairs." She raised an eyebrow again, confused. "The question is, to what purpose?"

A buzz alerted Will to an incoming email. He glanced at his screen. "Stafford. Requesting an immediate meeting. Maybe I'm about to find out."

Chapter Forty

"I've just come from my sit-down with the internal audit people," Stafford said, waving Will to the guest chair. "They're moving at breakneck speed, and they're determined to show that there's been a major house clean, with audit teams dispatched to every field office and resident agency."

"The director made that clear," Will acknowledged.

"No stone left unturned, and they've roped in high-level consultants for financial auditing, fact-checking, and of course, counselors for psychological assessments."

"You mentioned that."

"There is no question," Stafford said, "that Themis is a brilliant piece of software, *but...*" He accentuated the word, pausing briefly for effect. "It's still a work in progress 'as its self-learning algorithms develop' – to use Zoe Marshall's words – and there are, as with all such endeavors, flaws to be ironed out. Some of the AI predictions are strong, well worth pursuing, but others appear to be, at best, fanciful, according to an independent study by several of those consultants. As I made clear previously, McCord, a hard stick is being applied to all projects, including those utilizing AI. Now, there are some pressing matters to be addressed."

Will suppressed his irritation. "Such as?"

"The Board agrees with my recommendation that Agent Farris take stress leave and undergo a series of additional counseling sessions. Once cleared to return she will be reassigned, possibly back to her previous unit. You understand this is nothing personal, a restructure that's in everyone's best interests, and I will speak again to Agent Farris about it."

"Sir, as I said before, Agent Farris was assessed by our internal counselor and cleared for duty. In fact, that assessment agreed with Agent Farris's judgment that she was better off keeping busy."

"There's a difference between keeping busy and charging into harm's way in a storm-chaser vehicle that's come under gunfire and has narrowly avoided a tornado. For Christ's sake, McCord, this is not a Bond movie. I'm well aware that Farris is a passionate agent, but she's gone too far, endangered herself and others, and I have to question your role in enabling what I can only consider reckless behavior."

"My role?"

"I don't say it's intentional, but she's been allowed too much free rein."

Will ignored the personal slur. "Management approved Farris as second-in-command. It wasn't purely my call."

Stafford leaned across his desk. "Let me tell you something, McCord. A wise old agent once said to me that a race car driver can't win the race without taking two or three pit stops along the track. Those pit stops ensure the performance of the vehicle. And high-performing federal agents need to take the physical and emotional equivalent of those pit stops to go on achieving at their maximum level. Given the multiple stress factors she faced in a short period, it is now judged that Agent Farris didn't have the necessary R&R. That, in turn, would explain lapses in judgment not just with this storm-chasing business but across those previous cases.

"I want you to take a cold, hard look at her actions," Stafford continued, "putting aside her track record for just a moment."

He had the unnerving ability to stare at someone while talking to them but avoid any direct eye contact at the same time.

"On the UCU's first case, and without backup, Agent Farris approached an isolated location that she believed housed the unsub, and she was subjected to a near-fatal encounter. She took only a brief, less-than-counseled break before launching back into fieldwork where, separated from the team, she was trapped in a hostile environment at the mercy of another psychopath. Once again, minimal stress leave taken, and just weeks later she's in a vehicle headed into a tornado."

"Those incidents have been explained–"

Stafford cut him short, his tone sharp. "This isn't about individual explanations. It's about questions raised by this continuing, clearly erratic behavior. Her actions in the field have been far more gung-ho than they were when she was in the CCRSB. Why? What's different?"

Will's nerves tightened.

"I note that Agent Farris pushed to keep Professor Silverstein on as a consultant."

"His input has been invaluable."

"Really?" Stafford wasn't convinced. "I see he's a professor of multiple disciplines, criminology among them, but he also has a reputation for being outlandish, to put it mildly. Published a book with outrageous ideas about the supernatural, and gives talks on the subject to nerdy fringe groups."

"He has his quirks."

"The FBI needs to maintain a high bar regarding those we consult with," Stafford said, "and given the changes being wrought as part of this audit, there are concerns that this man hardly fits the bill. Understandably, you would speak to him on the Piper case, given his knowledge of the European medieval era. But I see no reason for him to be an ongoing consultant with clearance relating to Themis."

"His expertise has been put to good use."

"He's not the only expert in those fields, McCord, and he's a bit of a nutter. And then there's his influence on the team—"

"The professor's input is kept strictly to what he can verify about historical periods and mythologies, and his insights as a criminologist. He can be a good devil's advocate but beyond that, he doesn't influence the team with his interests in strange phenomena."

"And Agent Farris?"

"She's his toughest critic." Will's gaze was unflinching, and he clenched his fists, willing himself to remain calm.

"Nevertheless, I'm revoking the professor's clearance and I'm directing you to consult with others with similar expertise if and when needed."

Will shifted in the chair, frustration gnawing at him, but he didn't offer anything further. As Marcia had suspected, Stafford had an agenda and he was pushing forward with it, dressing it up as a restructuring that addressed the Internal Audit Board's overall strategy.

"I can see that Marcia Kendall's foreign language skills helped your first two cases," Stafford said, "but the Board is promoting a back-to-basics approach."

"Meaning?"

"She's assisting the UCU on a part-time basis in between translation projects. There's now a view that she's better employed full-time in translation work."

"Marcia is also programming Themis."

"Which is Zoe Marshall's area of expertise." He shrugged, his expression showing contempt.

"Yes, but Zoe is spending more time in the field—"

"The directive," Stafford didn't wait for him to finish, "is that Agent Kendall will be redeployed to a special translation project currently underway, and another agent, an experienced field operative who also has cyber skills, will join the team. Think about it, McCord. It's a natural progression for the unit coming on top of its impressive start, and more importantly, part of a plan to ensure the unit stays on that track. And if the interrogation of Carstairs under the UCU banner helps solve other cases, you can be assured of the team's place in the Bureau's future."

Will had no trust whatsoever in Stafford but returning to his office, he wondered if there was a fragment of truth in his words.

He'd briefly wondered himself about Ilona's hunches, leading her to track down the Piper, and the man known as El Silbón, the Whistler. Coincidence, recklessness, as Stafford believed, or was there more to it, something she hadn't revealed? That thought had troubled Will on more than one occasion.

Even if there was a ribbon of truth to Stafford's words, that ribbon was being raised as an enormous banner, legitimizing the restructure of the team, not in Stafford's image, but for the vengeance of the man pulling his strings.

Will gazed out over the city skyline, mulling over the conversation with Stafford and its implications.

He checked his phone. A missed call from Ilona. No message. But on his desktop PC, he sighted an interim report that she'd just emailed. He pulled up the report. Another tornado death, this time in Anadarko. And another report, outlining the Oklahoma police raid and arrest of the storm looting gang and the man believed to be running the operation. He read quickly, scrolling through Ilona's account of both the police interviews with members of the gang and her own. There was an attachment, and he opened the document to see photos taken on Ilona's cell. A series of scribbled layouts of tornado-damaged farmhouses and the storm shelters positioned alongside them.

He looked up as Marcia strode into his office, her disapproving expression tipping him off as to what was to follow. "I've just had a call from the Languages Team and a meeting with Stafford."

"I know."

"I told them I didn't want the reassignment."

"And they told you it was non-negotiable. They needed you."

Marcia nodded, speechless.

"There's not much we can do about it right now…" He spread his hands in a gesture that signaled both frustration and sympathy. "When does the translation department expect you to report?"

"I'm to take a few days' leave and report next week." She angled her head, watching him. "But what I do in my spare time is my business, so…" She flashed a grin. "What can I do to help?"

Will's mind flashed on Stafford's words from one of their previous meetings. *'I'm bringing in one of the Bureau's top terrorist interrogators. Carstairs will be getting a taste of his own medicine… transported to the special interrogation rooms at HQ…'*

Will diverted his attention to his computer, tapping the keyboard and bringing up the document that Ilona had attached to her email report. He glanced at the screen, his mind racing, and then he turned back to Marcia, keeping his voice low. "Did you identify any others closely associated with Stafford who might also have benefited financially?"

"I've identified several agents who have worked with Stafford at some point over the years and remained in personal contact. Men who remained under the radar, so to speak, like Stafford, but none of that necessarily means anything."

"Do any of those agents work out of field offices in the Great Plains?"

Marcia consulted the notes in her folder and her expression showed her surprise. "Yes. Texas."

"Nicely positioned in Tornado Alley," Will stated. "And Stafford asked you for that list of criminal contacts believed to have been in business with Carstairs. Contacts he might be able to call on."

"What are you implying?"

"I need to pay Stafford another visit. Use some of his misdirection techniques on himself."

"How?"

"Ilona's report is in on the latest tornado death. And there are developments in the storm looting investigation."

"Stafford won't be interested."

Will raised his right forefinger. "He will if he thinks there's something about the case he can use to his benefit."

"About the killer?"

"No."

"Then what?"

"I think I know what Stafford is up to."

"And by the look on your face, you have a plan of your own to stop it."

He shook his head. "The opposite. I've got a plan to ensure it goes ahead."

Chapter Forty-One

I was back in my hotel room, toweling myself dry after stepping from the shower when my phone rang.

On the other end of the line, Stafford spoke quietly and calmly, as though there was nothing personal or dramatic about his words, delivering the outcome of his meetings with the audit board in a matter-of-fact manner. "As a result, I'm directing you, Agent Farris, to take extended leave immediately, give yourself some well-deserved R&R, and you're to undergo some additional stress counseling with a board-appointed psychologist. After which, reassignment to another team will enable a fresh start."

"Sir, I respectfully disagree–"

"And I respect your opinion, Agent, but I'm overruling both you and Agent McCord on this. And I hope, further down the line, you'll thank me for intervening. It's only in the best interests of your long-term health, the UCU, and of course, your career."

"Sir, we're in the middle of an investigation–"

"An investigation that is going nowhere," he shot back. "The latest information I have to hand is that a local named Garrick was detained and questioned about his movements by the OPD. You've cleared him of being in the vicinity of all the recent murders."

"Yes."

"Agents McCord and Marshall will wrap up any loose ends and close that investigation down in the next day or so. Your orders will be sent through but for now, Agent Farris, are we clear?"

"Couldn't be clearer."

Straight after the call ended, I phoned Will. "What the hell–"

"Take a breath."

"You knew about this?"

"It unfolded late this afternoon. I'm sitting here with Marcia and she and I were as blindsided as everyone else."

"You should've called me–"

"You were behind closed doors, in those interviews, and Marcia and I have been digging into Stafford's background."

"I've had missed calls from Marcia," I said, checking my phone log.

"She's in the same boat as you, Ilona. Reassigned. And Stafford's sidelining the professor as well."

"Will, we can't stop now."

"I know that."

"There's been more than eleven deaths that we know of. How many more if we don't put an end to this?"

"I'll do what I can to have Stafford and the Board's decision overturned," Will assured me, "but in the meantime–"

I cut in. "I'm not stepping aside."

"Ilona, you know how these things work. There's no choice until I can get something sorted."

"This killer–"

"I'm heading down there myself – I intended to join the team tomorrow regardless – and I can carry on from where you've left off."

"You can't do this alone."

"Zoe's still on board and doesn't she keep reminding us that Themis is the equivalent of a hundred investigators?"

"A thousand." I wanted to grin, but my jaw was set solid, my teeth biting down on my lip.

"For tonight, just try and get some rest."

"What are you going to do about Stafford?"

"Right now, I need sleep. Tomorrow, I'll give it further thought."

There was a pause and I wondered if he was holding something back. He'd once told me that even when he wanted to hold back, he'd never been able to do that where I was concerned. Bouncing his thoughts off me had always come as natural to him as breathing.

"I've got the ghost of an idea," he revealed. "We'll speak tomorrow."

I had no sooner ended the call than a text came through from Zoe.

We need to meet. My room. Urgent.

I pulled on a blouse and jeans and headed along the first floor, reaching Zoe's room at the same time as Zach.

Zoe didn't avert her gaze from her laptop as we entered the room. "Themis has pulled roadside cam footage near the homes of some of the victims."

"And here I was, hoping for pizza," Zach deadpanned.

Zoe ignored him. "Three of the recent victims, one in this state and two in Texas, had properties on a road not far off the main highway. In each case, there's a road cam that spans the junction where the off-road connects with the highway."

"And there's footage for the times of the murders?" I asked.

"Yes. And the only access to those properties is from turning off at those junctions."

"So, we've got the killer's vehicle on camera?"

"No."

"No? If those junctions are the only points of approach—"

Zoe cut back in. "Then the killer has to have turned there. But there's no sign of him. Not in the lead-up to the killing or the thirty-six hours prior, and we can keep looking further back but—"

"We'd be wasting our time," said Zach.

"Then how is he getting to those properties, and at precisely the moment he needs to be there?" I said.

"Everything points to this killer exerting some form of control over when a tornado hits," Zach added. "And somehow, he appears at his victim's home just ahead of a twister, without seemingly making a physical approach."

Zoe threw him an incredulous look. "You think he's spiriting himself there as though he's part of the storm?"

"It fits with some of the stories that have been passed down by the Algonquian people."

"No," I said. "There has to be a reasonable explanation. Something else is going on." This hardly felt like the right moment, but I couldn't avoid telling them about the call I'd received from Stafford. "On top of all that, I'm afraid I've got some bad news."

Zach was uncharacteristically still while I told them about the reorganizing of the team. It was as though he believed that if he remained motionless then none of what I was saying could become true. "W-T-F, Ilona," he said.

"Are they mad?" Zoe added.

I shrugged in frustration. "Tell me about it."

"I know there's a massive internal review rocking the Bureau," Zach said, "and I can understand the unit wanting to show *me* the door but, Ilona... you and Marcia? There has got to be something more to this."

"Internal politics."

Zach was no longer still, but pacing, arms gesticulating. "The worst things afflicting organizations are the egos and the internal politicking. Makes my blood boil."

Zoe spoke, her tone solemn. "Seems we've got a narrow window, maybe twenty-four to forty-eight hours to kickstart this investigation before Will has to close it down."

Chapter Forty-Two

Sitting in my motel room, anticipating my return to Seattle and my enforced leave, I felt confined and restricted. Trapped. A shiver ran the length of my spine and then leaped, engulfing me, and it was not unlike the sense of hopelessness I'd felt fourteen years earlier when I'd been kidnapped and held in that dark space at the bottom of a deep shaft.

I didn't, of course, feel the terror of that ordeal, but I did feel the loss of control and fear for the lives that would be lost at the hands of this killer, this phantom that Stafford and others no longer believed existed.

I couldn't just leave it to Will and Zoe. And Zoe, I knew, would never give up on this, driven as she was by the death of Vema Coulston. She was young and feisty, and a wild card; I worried that she would pursue the case on her own if it came to that. If Will was forced to close the case, there was no way I could leave Zoe to carry that burden.

For weeks on end, I had steeled myself against the emotional and psychological fallout from the previous investigations. I'd resisted counseling as that meant mentally revisiting those ordeals. I'd ignored the suggestion that I take extended leave. Was this new man, Stafford, right in having me step aside, pending reassignment? Had I pushed myself too far? If I was to remain as objective as I always had been, then I had to at least consider Stafford's words, no matter how much I disagreed with them.

I thought back over the past two months, factoring in Stafford's supposed perceptions. Did he have a point? Did I need to retreat for a period of rest, reflection, and recovery?

Damn that.

I needed to plunge headlong into my work. Into *this* case. A killer shadowing storms throughout Tornado Alley. Unknown. Undetected. Precisely the kind of impossible case that Themis and the UCU were created to tackle. The kind of investigation, like the previous two, that could take us in unexpected directions with emotionally destructive fallout. You had to be able to compartmentalize, to shield yourself psychologically, something I'd trained myself to do since those moments of terror in my mid-teens.

Self-counseling.

I'd developed what a Bureau psychologist had once told me was a cold indifference that enabled me to stare into the dark and to keep pressing forward.

We all have our ways of maintaining our sanity.

I tried to resist the urge to break free, to climb, but the more I pushed the thought away, the stronger and more persistent it charged back.

Climb.

I caught an Uber to the outer rim of the city and then I wandered the streets, exploring until I found a narrow, twisting, barely used alley at the back of a cluster of old-style buildings. Brick architecture with ledges, ridges, windowsills and piping, perfect for my needs.

No street cams here. In the recessed doorway of a closed factory, I unzipped my duffel bag and swiftly changed into my hoodie, track pants, and sports sneakers. Stashing the bag, I stepped back into the alleyway and then ran and leaped onto a bin, using it as a springboard. I pivoted, grabbed hold of the piping and slithered my way up, deftly maneuvering my body with the help of every protrusion of brickwork – my adrenaline spiking, energy coursing through me as though inner fireworks had been launched; every nerve, every muscle primed to propel me toward freedom.

As always when I climbed, I had flashes of my attempt to climb out of that deep tunnel in which my teenage self had been imprisoned. I'd taken control. I'd escaped.

Residing deep within my psyche there was a fear that if I didn't climb, my spirit would become stagnant, that I would lose control and slowly succumb to all the tiny, daily fears that we carry in life.

Irrational thoughts and my common sense knew that.

This fear was *itself* just one of those tiny, daily fears, and that was the irony. Regardless, my soul still craved the exhilaration of roaming the quiet world above, where my spirit would always be free to soar. Never to feel the loss of control and the hopelessness that descended on me all those years ago at the base of a shaft on a deserted nuclear power site.

A crow observed me as I clambered up over the side and onto the roof. It watched me with a heightened curiosity and then, as though in acceptance of my right to be up here in its domain, it cawed and lifted off, resuming its journey.

Positioning myself on the roof's edge, I tilted my head and gazed at a night sky alive with a smattering of stars. A gentle breeze touched my cheeks.

I watched as a flock of birds that I couldn't identify – silhouettes under the starlight – wheeled across the sky and then made a sudden, sharp turn in startling symmetry, always a wonder and a mystery to anyone observing. And in that instant, I knew exactly what I needed to do to change the direction of the investigation and to stay on this killer's trail before I had to leave Oklahoma.

I returned to the motel and, noticing Zoe's light was still on, I knocked gently on the door. No answer. I peered through the small front window and although the view was partly obscured by the lace drapes, I got a distinct impression the room was empty.

It was nearing midnight. Where had Zoe gone at this hour?

Chapter Forty-Three

At this time of night, the office spaces at the FBI's Oklahoma City field office had the atmosphere of having been abandoned. The empty desks with the piles of paper, the rim-stained coffee mugs, and the hum from the computers created the impression that people had suddenly and inexplicably vanished, leaving behind a mystery that begged answers. Zoe was in the comm room, using one of the PCs there to remotely access Themis. She was immersed in the screen when she answered the call from Ilona.

"I noticed you weren't in your room."

Zoe laughed. "No surprise you're not getting any sleep. And there's no way I was going to, not after that bomb you dropped."

"Where are you?"

"Local field office. I had to get out of that room, and I was tired of accessing Themis on my laptop. I wanted to use the network power here. I can't believe what's happening, Ilona. Without the state field offices giving us the manpower, and with the team dismantled…"

"You and Zach are still on it, and Will is joining you." There was a pause before Ilona added, "And I haven't left yet."

"It will be more than we can handle. Supercell activity across Oklahoma and northern Texas over the next week will be at unprecedented levels. There are more than a dozen potential targets–"

"I've been thinking about those pendants," Ilona said, and her words forced Zoe to focus. "When he was younger, Bryce and his brother picked up pendants from a traveling fair. Marcia had an expert study the pendants for comparison, and even though he's working from emailed photos, the expert believes they're from the same craftsman. So, the question blazing in my head is, if the mother of your reporter friend, Carson was an early victim, did he place his trademark thunderbird pendant around her neck? If he did, then he's had a ready supply, back then and through the years. He is either the craftsman himself or he commissioned that particular design from an independent artist. Either way, he's the only person who has those pendants. Marcia established they don't exist in retail outlets and national jewelers don't recognize them."

"Fifteen years," Zoe repeated, her voice drained, as though she hadn't taken in anything Ilona had said. "Fifteen years of preying on victims. We know who his targets could be, but tornado alerts are only raised within the hour, and often only within minutes." Her anxiety level rose sharply as she spoke. "No way we can be there in advance at all of them and without the extra manpower; we're back to the needle in a haystack scenario. How in hell do we find him?"

"I'm working on an idea. But I also want to know for certain how long this killer's been active. I've got Marcia checking the records of Carson's mother's death to find out if she was wearing that thunderbird pendant when her body was found."

"And if she was," Zoe said, "and if she *did* encounter this storm killer, and if Bryce's brother, Doug, as a young man, bought something similar from the same artisan, then that craftsman has been selling his wares at carnivals for the past fifteen years…" Her voice trailed as the scenario took shape in her mind."

"And the killer is still getting them from the same source," Ilona said.

* * *

Zoe returned to her motel room and was pacing, hoping by now that Ilona was getting some rest. Her mind was doing cartwheels. She wondered whether Melinda Shaw had jewelry from that same vendor that Doug Crowley and others had visited back then. She figured there was a way she could find out from Carson about any jewelry his mother wore, without alerting him to what she was up to. She sent him a text, hoping he'd see it first thing in the morning.

> *Hi, Carson. Thought it might be good to get together once more time before I head back to Seattle, and maybe when we do you could bring some old photos of you and me and your mom from back during those dirt-biking days, for a trip down memory lane.*

A moment later she was startled by her phone ringing. It was Carson. "Hi. I'm still up," he said.

"So, you're a night owl on top of everything else."

"Look who's talking." He laughed. "Great idea, to get together one more time. I've got heaps of photos in an old family album somewhere. In fact, I've just found one on my computer of you, me and my mother. You're going to love this; I'll send it to your phone. And there's another one, of the two of us with that lady you lived with when you were staying here."

"Great."

"By the way, how is she going, that lady you lived with?"

"Vema Coulston. She died when a tornado damaged part of her farmhouse, same as what happened to your mom."

"I'm so sorry. When was this?"

"A couple of years ago. After she died, her daughter inherited the farmhouse, and had it repaired. There's a shed out back of that house heaped high with Vema's old things. I know the daughter means to have it cleaned out one day, but she's never got around to it."

"You're not going to tell me–"

"Yep. That old bike of mine – well, it was Vema's because she paid for it… it's still there, as far as I know."

"Would the daughter let you borrow it?" Carson asked.

"Oh, yeah." Zoe swallowed hard, the memories and the emotion getting to her. "I'll never forget how Vema got a bike for herself. Went riding with me on three or four occasions, on weekday afternoons. That's the kind of woman she was. Always on board with my interests. Always supportive." There was a lilt in her voice and a teary shimmer in her eyes, but she shrugged them off and smiled fondly as though Vema was sitting there with them and she was smiling back at her.

"We should also go for a ride for old times' sake before you go back," he said.

Zoe's eyes lit up. "Definitely."

Her phone pinged and she opened up the first of the attachments on the text message.

"You got the text?"

"Yes."

The photo was of her and Carson sitting astride their dirt bikes with Melinda Shaw in between them, wide smiles, hamming it up for the camera. Her heart swelled at the memory of the joy, tinged by the stark reality that such a tragic fate awaited Carson's mother.

And then her eyes widened in surprise. She zoomed in on to the area of Melinda Shaw's neckline and the pendant that hung there. The craftsmanship and styling were similar to the pendant worn by Bryce Crowley and the pendants placed by the killer on his victims.

Zoe took a closer look at the image engraved on the pendant. The silhouette of an American Indian rider atop a galloping horse.

"Your mom was such a lovely person. I wish I'd met her more than just a few times. I know she and your dad split up when you were much younger, but you never mention him."

"After my mom and dad divorced, he took off and I didn't see him until just once, years later. I went through one of those phases where you're curious about a missing parent. I tracked him down, took a while, as he was largely off the grid, living in a trailer, doing odd jobs at carnivals. He wasn't interested and he closed the door in my face."

"Sorry to hear that."

"I'm not. It answered my questions. He's a cold-hearted nobody. A reverse role model for everything I don't want to be, and it was obvious he was a heavy drinker. Anyway, I've long since moved on from that. And hey, can I ask a favor?"

"Sure."

"If you guys find those looters, and if they know anything about the man that was on my mom's property that day…"

Zoe could hear the choke in his voice. "You want to be the one to write the story."

"It would mean a lot to me. It would mean everything."

"You'll have some stiff competition."

"Brooke Goodman?"

"She follows these cases like a hound dog."

"I don't need to scoop her," Carson clarified, "I just need access so I can write an in-depth, personal piece for the local press."

"Well, I've got something to say about that."

"You have?"

"You *are* going to scoop her. If there is a story to report, then you're going to write it before anyone else."

"You'll help?"

"You bet. The memory of your mom deserves it."

After she ended the call, Zoe sat for a while, phone in hand, staring at the pendant that hung around Melinda Shaw's neck. And then she plugged into Themis to run a raft of searches on pendants and fairs.

Chapter Forty-Four

Day Six

Zach boasted of having gained a good night's sleep and Zoe felt a pang of uncharacteristic jealousy, having barely managed a few hours. Right now, she'd kill for more shuteye. Ilona and Zach had joined her in her room for a quick, light breakfast and to go over her findings via Themis from the evening before.

"There's an arts and crafts publication that's been publishing in the Midwest and the Great Plains for decades," Zoe said. "It carries a listing and a locality for all the folk-art fairs that are staged throughout the year."

Zach shook his head, incredulous. "There's a listing going back fifteen years?"

"The magazine's digital edition is archived, and Themis could access the directories going way back."

Ilona was suddenly wide awake. "What have you found?"

"There is a jewelry artisan who's had a stall at most of these fairs, traveling across at least three states. I couldn't find any contact details for him, but his stall is called Shaman's Cave, and he's at a fair that's in Bartlesville all this week."

"If he's the creator of the pendants–" Ilona began.

"He's not the killer, Ilona. Themis has cross-matched the data, and the dates of the fairs don't correspond with any of the killings."

"Bartlesville is about a two-and-a-half-hour drive," Zach said.

Zoe held up her phone, showing the other two the photo of Carson's mother. "Look at the necklace Melinda Shaw is wearing. Same design style."

Ilona glanced at her watch. "We can be in Bartlesville mid-morning. The shaman should be able to tell us if he fashioned this killer's thunderbird pendants. And if those pendants belonging to Bryce Crowley and Melinda Shaw are from his hand as well."

"I guess you're not heading back to Seattle this morning, then."

"Figured Stafford would want me to have a day of rest before heading home," Ilona teased. "I'm booked on a flight tomorrow morning to keep him happy."

"But you're not giving up," Zoe stated.

"Not in my DNA."

"You said last night you were working on an idea. If questioning the shaman doesn't point us in the right direction, something tells me you've got a plan B."

"If we haven't got the backup resources and we can't find the needle in the haystack," Ilona said, "then we have to draw the killer out and lead him to where *we* want him to be."

"Agreed."

"Can Themis pull in the latest and most detailed storm forecasts for Oklahoma and northern Texas and southern Kansas?"

"You want to concentrate on the easiest areas to access from here?"

"Yes. Let's get those forecasts and overlay them with our suspected list of targets. And then, I think there's a way we can direct the killer's movements to where we want him to be."

* * *

The NOAA Storm Prediction Center watched for the most likely areas that tornadoes would develop, issuing forecasts forty-eight hours in advance. Drawing on satellite imagery and computer modeling, they fine-tuned that information with Severe Thunderstorm and Tornado Watches within a few hours, and Tornado Warnings closer to the event.

Zoe and I singled out the closest areas with the most severe forecasts.

There were three obvious choices: supercell storms forecast for Vernon in Northern Texas, Wichita in Kansas, and Woodward in Oklahoma. Each was approximately two-and-a-half hours' drive from Oklahoma City. Each one of those towns had a few women living alone on rural properties. Just two of those – one in Wichita, and one in Woodward – ran a small business, one of them being an internet-based retail site that the woman operated from her home computer.

"He'll choose one of those," I said, "except that on this occasion, we're going to choose for him."

"By removing one of the potential targets," Zoe guessed.

"We make travel arrangements for one of them that can easily be checked and found on the net, and we move that lady to a motel. I can't be seen to be involved but you and Will can organize it, using UCU funds."

Zoe nodded. "That leaves just one woman that he knows will be on the property and who will be within easy reach."

I indicated one of the names on the list. "Courtney White has a small property between Woodward and Fort Supply. We shift her to a safe house and Will waits on the property in hiding. And there's someone that Will and I know who can partner with him."

"But to catch the killer in the act, we need someone on the premises masquerading as Courtney White."

"You're looking at her," I said.

* * *

"Not a chance." Will's brow furrowed as he stared at me in the video link. "I'm not putting you in danger, in the crosshairs of a deranged killer."

"It's a standard Bureau maneuver," I reminded him. "An agent acting as a decoy."

"Even so, until and if I can get you reinstated to the team–"

"Will, this is our one big and immediate chance to catch this monster. There isn't time to jump through the hoops to get someone from the local field office, especially with all the bureaucratic restraints Stafford is enforcing, and Zoe doesn't have the experience."

Zoe disagreed. "I can do it."

I ignored her offer. "Will, we can't pass this up. If I've anticipated the killer's moves correctly, if he goes for this target, then we've got him. Marcia can arrange for each of those women to be moved and for the fake travel arrangements to be put in place."

"Stafford will never–"

"Make a captain's call to use me one last time before I head back to Seattle," I said. "Don't tell Stafford until after the fact. In the meantime, the team will be visiting an artisan we believe could have created those pendants, as well as one of the spiritual communities that the killer could have visited while on the road. While I'm still here, I don't see any reason why I can't tag along."

* * *

As the call ended, Will asked himself again whether he was cutting her too much slack; whether, as Stafford had intimated, she had been acting erratically and was far more gung-ho than she'd been at the CCRSB.

He shook his doubts off, still certain that Ilona's strengths and skills far outweighed any of those concerns. The last words he'd said to Ilona before the call ended had been, "I will be there, in the house, to ensure you're safe, to make certain there are no unforeseen circumstances."

Don't tell Stafford until after the fact.

If his suspicions about Stafford were correct, he hoped it wouldn't come to that.

He was going to be walking a tightrope as he'd have to juggle the storm-killer intercept with something else. With Marcia's help and her programming of Themis, crunching specific data, he had another, very different intercept planned, and he would need backup. Assistance he couldn't risk requesting from the FBI's Oklahoma field office.

He needed to go and see Stafford before the Acting AD left for DC. First, though, he placed a call to someone else who was currently in Oklahoma.

Senior Detective Paul Radner of the Seattle PD.

Chapter Forty-Five

Will entered Stafford's office and placed a printout on his boss's desk. "This is the latest report on a tornado-related death. It could hold the evidence I'm looking for."

Stafford did not attempt to conceal his irritation. "What evidence?"

"Take a look."

Stafford cast his eyes over the printout. Before he could refute what he was seeing, Will delivered the line he'd rehearsed a dozen times in his mind. "The looters threw a curveball in our investigation, but it forced the team to adopt a different focus. We believe the killer could have a connection with the looters. In the meantime, another case has opened up. We've discovered the looters have also been identifying deserted, storm-damaged homes, with secure shelters that can be used as temporary hideouts for criminals."

Stafford was staring hard at the printout. "Temporary havens for fugitives?"

"Think about it," Will continued, maintaining an even, considered tone. "No one is looking for a fugitive in the storm shelter of an abandoned, damaged home in rural areas throughout Oklahoma, Texas, and Nebraska." He took a breath, allowing a moment for the idea to cement itself in Stafford's mind. "Easily accessed, unseen havens for people who are evading the law. Temporary accommodation while arrangements are made for transport, false IDs, and longer-term placement."

"So, the UCU's discovery of these maps," Stafford said, "has exposed this whole other enterprise."

Will gave a satisfied nod. "Something the unit can take credit for."

"Are there fugitives in any of those shelters right now?"

"Unknown. I suggest we direct our field officers down there to search the most obvious spots. And if it leads us to the instigator of this fugitive network, then it will be another breakthrough for the UCU."

Stafford was unnaturally still as he stared at the report and the attached layouts. Will could imagine the wheels turning in his superior's mind.

He's taking the bait.

Stafford shifted his focus slowly from the printouts in his hand to Will. "Good call." He placed them on his desk, then folded his arms and raised his chin, his eyes on Will. "You concentrate on either proving this killer theory of yours in the next twenty-four hours or closing down that investigation. In the meantime, leave these maps with me. I'll follow up on these with the field office people in those states."

* * *

"You're on a late-night flight to Oklahoma," Marcia confirmed.

"Yes. And Stafford is on a redeye to DC tomorrow for the Carstairs interviews, arriving at the same time that Carstairs is on his way to HQ in the back of a police van."

Marcia cast a quizzical eye over Will. "Do you think Stafford is using Carstairs's criminal contacts to refute anything Carstairs says about him? His way of freeing himself from Carstairs's suspected blackmail?"

"No. Too contrived and, ultimately, too unreliable. Regardless of what assurances he might be able to get from underworld figures, Stafford could never be certain they would follow through and help him out."

"So, what's this all about?"

Will slipped a sheaf of papers from a folder and pushed them across his desk. "These are the papers Ilona sent through. Drawings depicting farmhouses and storm shelters."

Marcia pulled up a seat and took a closer look at the hand-drawn maps.

"I believe I know what Stafford's planning," Will said. "And I've given him a little bit of help without his knowing it. By early tomorrow we'll know if I'm right. In the meantime, I need you to program Themis to access specific roadcams outside the Capitol."

Chapter Forty-Six

The old man looked at the enlarged print of Carson's mother in the photo. "Oh, yes, this is mine." He gazed longingly at the picture and then handed it back to Zoe. "I have dozens of designs. This is one of my earlier works, and I crafted many pendants from it, but I have long since moved on to other images." The warm, ethereal tone of his voice had as timeworn a quality as his wrinkled skin and long, gunmetal-gray ponytail. He gestured to the stands that stood around his enclosure, a wide range of his pendants and medallions and other trinkets hanging from them.

I took the thunderbird pendant from my bag and handed it to him. "And this one?"

His eyes opened wider in surprise as he took the pendant in his hand, turning it over as though reacquainting himself with an old friend. "It is a long time since I have seen this one. On rare occasions, I receive an order from a customer to produce a special design, often for a group of friends or a family, or a social club. Such an order is usually for half a dozen or so. But I will not forget this one, eh? An unusual, striking design idea, sent to me as a rough drawing of what was wanted. And such a large order for a simple fairground hawker like me." He chuckled to himself.

"How many?"

"One hundred. It took me a year to complete the order, as I also need to keep up my work for the fairs." He shrugged. "That timing didn't seem to bother my customer, provided I could give him some in advance."

One hundred, I thought. It meant that the killer had enough to last him a long time.

"I supplied a half-dozen, to begin with, to keep the customer happy," the old man continued, "and the rest later." He handed the pendant back, his eyes settling on me. "Perhaps you already know this? Perhaps you are that mystery buyer?"

"No," I said.

"If you never met your customer," Zoe asked, "how was the purchase made?"

"I was contacted by phone. The drawings and payment were sent via the post."

"You delivered the items by the same method?"

"In a satchel. Yes."

"Do you still have the address?" I asked.

His shoulders rose and fell. "It was a post-office box number but no, I'm afraid I have no records." He gave an apologetic look. "I am no businessman, just an old-school craftsman, a creature of these ramshackle fairs."

"Did you ever wonder why this customer wanted a hundred of these?"

"Oh, perhaps at the time, but I never had the chance to enquire, did I? I thought perhaps for a retail endeavor, though I have never seen any of these, anywhere. May I ask your interest?"

"The buyer may be able to assist us with a case we're pursuing," I said. "We appreciate your help and I do have just one further question. When did you receive this order?"

The old man considered this for a moment. "I would say a little over three years ago, four at the most."

"Not what we expected to hear," Zoe said later as she, Zach, and I walked across the fairground and back to the Audi. The shouts of excited children drifted across from the carnival that was operating on the far side of the markets.

"It points to the killer not having used the pendants earlier but making them a part of his ritual from the time of the Collette Rayburn murder."

Zoe sucked in a deep breath. "Which means that around three years ago, once he had these pendants, he escalated the frequency of the killings. But why?"

There must be something else to this, I thought. My mind was in freefall, echoing the same question. What had prompted it? What happened – what changed – three years ago?

* * *

Our next stop, on the way back to Oklahoma City, was to the spiritual retreat known as The Daughters of Gaia, in Sands Springs.

Many of the emergency fire and rescue crews had stayed nearby in motels at differing times, some of whom might have been visitors to the retreat. A compilation of lists of those motel guests showed that Bryce Crowley was among the emergency workers who had stayed nearby within the past twelve months. It also included a few traveling salespersons, just one of whom was Bryce's brother, Doug.

Zach, Zoe, and I sat in a spacious room with Agnes Night Moon, the woman who ran the retreat. "I wanted to ask you," I said to her, "whether you could recall a frequent visitor, someone who always visited before or after heavy storms?"

"Not specifically, although there is sometimes a familiar face or two from the emergency crews during those periods," she replied, nodding gently. She was a tall, elegant First-Nations woman whose deep, dark eyes seemed to convey pearls of age-old wisdom.

I showed her photos of Bryce and Doug.

"I couldn't say for certain I recognize either of these two men." She was apologetic that she couldn't be more helpful. I could tell she was an intuitive woman but even so, she surprised me when she said she could sense that we were pursuing a dangerous person who carried the stain of evil in their soul.

"Yes," I said.

Zach leaned forward, grasping the moment. He shot a glance at me and Zoe. "I've been doing some more research into geo-sentience," he said, before focusing his gaze on Agnes. "There's a body of thought that extreme weather conditions and natural disasters release waves of psychic energy on a frequency that highly sensitive people – empaths – are tuned to. Do you know of people who have experienced this?"

Agnes gave a gentle smile. "It is extremely rare, young man. These people, geo-sentients, are impacted on a physical, emotional, and spiritual level, like a warning system of impending disaster. You think the person you seek has such abilities?"

"I do," said Zach.

Agnes's gaze took in all three of us. "Whatever it is you are facing, you must take great care." She walked with us to the door of the main homestead as we left, and her voice was solemn. "I ask the Great Spirit to stand beside you, and to keep you safe."

Chapter Forty-Seven

Carol Gainsbury was seated on a wicker chair on the enclosed back deck, watching Cassie run and play in the yard. Her elderly neighbor sat alongside her. One moment the sun was gracing the landscape, a picture of tranquility, and the next the light was brushed away in seconds by fast-moving dark clouds and a wind that had sprung from seemingly nowhere. A storm was brewing. She stood up and called out to Cassie through the open doorway. Her daughter had gone too far, racing beyond the yard and onto the field edged by the woods. "Cassie! Time to come in!" She sighed, realizing her daughter couldn't hear her, and as she stepped down into the yard her phone rang.

A male voice. "Mrs. Gainsbury?"

"Yes."

"I'm calling about your home insurance policy and the damage from the recent storm."

"I can't speak right now—"

"Please, hold just a moment as our manager would like to have an urgent word."

She stepped back into the doorway to shield herself from the wind, impatient, watching her daughter, conscious of the wind growing stronger and the sky darker, and then she shook her head and sucked in a deep breath as she saw Cassie run toward the trees.

The old lady beside her said, "That young rascal's gone into the woods."

Running across the yard, Carol noticed the call had dropped and she shoved the phone into the back pocket of her slacks, racing now, panicked, as she had lost sight of Cassie.

* * *

Cassie hated going to sleep because she hated the bad dreams. In the dreams, she was playing with her doll, Goldie – her sistie – when the sunlight disappeared, and in its place came a huge black cloud and then the scary monster – a great swirling tower of wind and dust, and she would wake up crying out for her mommy and her Aunt Lizzie.

As she had every afternoon since she and her mom had been staying in their neighbor's house, she was playing in the yard at the back of the property. She clutched Goldie to her chest as she ran across the yard and onto the grassy field, delighting in the bright yellow sunflowers that were spread across the ground like cute, tiny creatures.

When she looked past the side of the house and across the land, she could see her family's home in the distance. She didn't want to go back home. Not after what had happened there. She knew that the roof and one of the walls had crumbled. Her mom had told her that when the house was fixed, they'd be going back. She hadn't said anything, just sulked, because she didn't want to go but she also didn't want to make her mom sadder than she already was.

It was sunny this afternoon, as it had been for the past few days, but all of a sudden it was as though she was having the dream, even though she *knew* she wasn't asleep. The light faded and she looked up to see the great big blue sky was gone and in its place was a thick, dark tangle of clouds, stretching in every direction. She felt the wind blow hard against her tiny body, her hair whipping about her face and she squinted into the distance, terrified that another tornado was coming.

She turned toward the house, ready to run back when she heard her name being called out. The call wasn't coming from her mom at the house but from behind her, where the trees lined the grassy strip.

She turned again, scanning the forest edge and she glimpsed a figure, largely obscured by the branches and the shrubbery, a figure that reminded her of the storm man.

"I'm sorry about your Aunt Lizzie, Cassie, but the thunder beings will always keep you safe," the man said.

Cassie was motionless as she stared at the figure.

"There's a tornado coming but I don't want you to worry. I'll get you and your mom to safety."

The girl looked behind her, to the house, but the man said, "It's not safe to go back. We can get to the side road much quicker," and he pointed, "and your mom will meet us there. But we need to hurry."

Cassie threw an uncertain glance back toward the house, to see if her mom was still there, but the deep shadows that had fallen across the land made it hard to see and the wind was stronger, she could hear its wail – like the wail she heard in her bad dreams; then the man called to her again, "Hurry, Cassie. It's coming."

With Goldie pressed tightly against her, Cassie ran toward the trees.

She reached the woods. As she ran between the trees, she cast her eyes around for the storm man, but he was nowhere to be seen. She stopped in her tracks, frightened by the deep, long shadows of the forest and unsure now of whether she could keep going.

The thunder beings will keep you safe.

But who were they? Where were they?

"Hello?" she called.

Suddenly she felt a damp cloth covering her mouth, pressing against her, and before she could react, she felt sleepy, and her eyes flittered and then closed as darkness came.

Chapter Forty-Eight

Carol sprinted across the field and into the woods. "Cassie!" She pressed forward, calling her daughter's name again and again.

She could see through to the road that edged the northern aspect of the woodland and she watched with rising disbelief as a van pulled out from the roadside and sped away. Had someone taken Cassie? A heavy sense of dread descended, her heart feeling as though it was being ripped from her body, and then her phone rang. Once again, *unknown number*. Instinct told her there was more to this, more to the distracting call she'd received minutes earlier, and she answered.

The same male voice. Muffled. A disguise? "Cassie is with me."

"Oh, God…" Carol swallowed hard, her mind spinning.

"I've sent a picture to your phone."

Carol switched to her messages and opened the attachment. She gasped at the sight of her little girl curled up, asleep, in the passenger seat of a vehicle.

Her heart sank, her whole world collapsing around her. She'd lost her daughter. How? How could she have let this happen? Her voice was a croak. "Please, please, don't hurt my daughter."

"That will be up to you, Carol."

"Who are you?' she managed. "What do you want?"

"If you want to see Cassie again, then I need you to go to your car. Get onto Interstate 40 and head east to Pottawatomie County."

"Where in Pottawatomie County?"

"You'll receive further instructions on the way. Can you do that, Carol?"

"Yes."

"But there's one very important thing you need to consider. So, listen very closely." A pause. "Are you listening?"

"Yes."

"Stay on the line while you drive. Do not speak to the woman you're staying with, do not attempt to contact the police or anyone else. If you do, I can hear everything that is going on, and I can assure you that you will never see your daughter again."

Silence. A great, deep, yawning chasm of silence. Carol could not believe this was happening.

"I'm waiting for a response. Do you understand, Carol?"

"I understand." She took a long breath, holding onto the trunk of a tree for support, her knees almost giving way, and in that instant, she knew she had to steel her nerves, calm herself – *focus* – and do as she was being instructed.

I can get through this.

The phone still pressed to her ear, she hurried back over the field and across the back yard, into the house to collect her car keys, ignoring the startled expression and questioning from the woman they were staying with.

"Tell me where you are now, Carol?"

"In the house, getting my keys."

"Keep going."

Heading through the living room to the front door, Carol spied her laptop, still sitting on the living room coffee table where she'd been looking at news reports and emails earlier in the day. On an impulse, she picked it up with her free hand and then wedged it under her armpit, up against the left side of her body as she headed to her car out the front of the house. She knew she had to keep moving and do whatever it took to keep Cassie safe.

Getting into the front seat, she remembered the business card that Agent Farris had given her, and she slipped it from her pocket. She remembered the agent telling her that she could be contacted at any time, that her email account was linked to her cell phone. She flicked her own phone onto loudspeaker and placed it on the passenger seat, flipped open the laptop, and entered Farris's email address. She hurriedly tapped out a message while simultaneously switching on the car's ignition, the start-up of the engine masking, or at least she hoped it would, the tapping sound from her keystrokes.

"I need an update, Carol."

"In my car," she responded, "pulling out onto the street now."

Her hand gripped the steering wheel, her knuckles white, and she drove as he instructed, keeping to the speed limit, giving no outward signs that would attract attention.

She'd turned the volume down low on the car radio; it was tuned to a classic soft rock station when a breaking news broadcast interrupted the music. Storms were building into wild weather patterns with a high probability of tornado events in the area to which she was headed. She strained to hear the report, saw the rapidly darkening sky on the horizon, and had the strange and horrifying thought that nature was amassing its most savage forces and lying in wait for her.

But why?

Why her?

Chapter Forty-Nine

Having left The Daughters of Gaia retreat, I was behind the wheel and back on the road with the team.

We drove in silence for a while, each of us alone with our thoughts, Agnes Night Moon's words weighing heavily.

"Carson said his mother saw someone on her property," I said presently, shifting the focus away from the images that Agnes's words had conjured up, along with Zach's renewed commentary on geo-sentience. "She thought it was a worker from the neighboring farm."

Zoe nodded. "That's right."

"What if it was someone else? Someone she knew? Maybe a boyfriend?"

"Carson never mentioned his mom having a boyfriend."

"At twelve years of age, would he have known? She wouldn't necessarily have told him if she'd started seeing someone. And if she usually saw this person when Carson was at school or staying over with friends—"

"It doesn't explain what happened to her."

"It does if that friend, or boyfriend, is the killer."

"But isn't it looking like the killings didn't start until three years ago when the killer ordered the pendants?"

Zach chimed in from the back seat. "It doesn't mean he wasn't operating without pendants for years before that. But three years ago, the frequency of the killings escalated. *Something* changed."

"Zoe, is there a paper trail on the kind of work Carson's mother did?" I asked.

Zoe positioned her laptop on her knees and tapped away. "Here it is. She'd been employed for five years with a local life insurance brokerage."

"What do we know about the brokerage?"

Zoe ran a search. "Owned by a husband-and-wife team. Ron and Ellen Bennett."

"They're still there?"

"Yeah."

"Let's see if they can shed any light on Melinda Shaw's personal life."

* * *

"We were good friends with Melinda. It took us a long time to get used to not having her around." Ron Bennett rubbed his chin and considered the question I had put to him. The client meeting room in their offices was small and cozy, all comfy lounges and chairs in autumn hues and a coffee table for serving refreshments, the walls adorned with pastel paintings of rural landscapes at dawn or twilight. Ron, with his composed manner, fair skin, and red hair, was a comfortable fit for his surroundings. "Was she seeing anyone in her personal life?" He puffed out his cheeks. "I think so."

"I still think of her a lot." Ellen Bennett was a matronly woman with the smile of an angel. "I do recall her telling me and Ron there was someone she was interested in. Poor dear."

I leaned forward. "I know it's been a long time, but if you could cast your mind back. Did she give any details? A name?"

Ellen took a few minutes, her fingers tapping lightly on the arm of her chair as she let her mind roam. "It's vague but a few things are coming back. She didn't say much…"

"…wasn't the type," Ron added.

"…but I do recall her confiding that she was dating a man who was a few years younger, and she wondered if it would be a problem. She said he was a real down-to-earth, salt-of-the-earth kind of person and that he engaged in a bit of community volunteering."

"Did she say who with?"

She shook her head. "No."

"Have you heard of the Little Bear Community group?"

"Yes, we know of Little Bear…" She paused and the shift in her eyes signaled that she had remembered something. "Good God, hearing that name… that was it."

"One thing that comes to mind," Ron said, "is Melinda mentioning that this fellow had a much younger brother that he spent a bit of time with. When you mentioned

Little Bear, it brought back a memory. The younger brother spent some time there with his older sibling, and I remember Melinda saying that the young guy wanted to go into the police or the army or emergency services kind of work. Must have stuck way back in my mind 'cause I have an older brother – retired now – who was in a police rescue unit most of his working life."

"Emergency services…" I recalled Bryce's words. *I have a much older brother.'* "Does the surname Crowley ring any bells?"

Ron snapped his fingers. "I think that might have been the man's name."

A deep crease etched its way across Ellen Bennett's forehead. "But what on earth is this all about now, after all this time?"

My phone hummed and I glanced at the display. A text message from Carol Gainsbury, the last thing I was expecting right now.

Concerned, I tapped on the message and felt a sharp stab of alarm.

> *Ilona, please help. Cassie's been taken, her kidnapper has ordered me to stay on the line while I drive to Pottawatomie County.*

I was out of my chair, gesturing frantically to Zach and Zoe. "We need to go. Now."

Chapter Fifty

Carol had been driving for over half an hour. She'd reached the county and she'd been instructed to exit the interstate, driving through several rural areas and then back onto the highway. She felt as though she was going around in circles. The wind and the rain varied as she moved from one part of the county to another.

Her hands were so covered in nervous sweat that they kept slipping from the steering wheel. "What is it you want?" she asked the mystery man on the other end of the line.

"You don't need to know that. You only need to know that as long as you follow my instructions, Cassie will be safe."

"What did you do to her?"

"She is sleeping comfortably, that's all you need be concerned with."

She drove on in silence, her head starting to pound from the tension, the sheer terror of knowing her daughter was with this vile creature, when a sudden, sharp instruction came through from him. "Urgent. Take the exit to Shawnee that's coming up." A horrifying thought struck her. How did he know that? She'd been watching this whole time for a vehicle that might be following her. There hadn't been one.

How did he know precisely where she was?

* * *

"It's about another forty minutes to the county," I said as I drove. "Zoe, what have we got on Pottawatomie?"

"A sudden build-up of supercell activity. Tornado warning." Zoe's eyes were focused on her laptop screen. "It has to be our man, but what's he up to?"

"He's luring Carol Gainsford to the storm," Zach said.

"How the hell can he have reacted so quickly?" Catching Zach's eye in the rearview mirror, I added, "Don't say it." I shot a look at Zoe. "Send Carol a text. Ask whether she's reached the county yet?"

A minute later there was a reply. "She says she has." Zoe was scanning the message. "She's now been told to drive further east, to the far side of Shawnee." She navigated to her browser, tapped an instruction, and scrolled through the results. "Rough weather there. High probability of a tornado touching down."

"I think I know what he's trying to do," Zach said.

* * *

Carol was on a wide road, fields rolling off on either side, the sky an ominous dark gray, swirls of rain and mist obscuring her view, and then she felt the change in the wind power. It was suddenly stronger, buffeting the car, and on the horizon, she saw the churning spiral charging across the field toward the road. Toward her. Terror-stricken, she choked for breath, slamming on the brakes far too quickly. The car slid, careening from the right to the left side of the road as she eased off the brake and struggled to maintain control. As she steadied the vehicle, she pulled it over to the edge of the road. She needed to turn and retreat.

From the phone loudspeaker, the voice, heavy with anger, said, "I did not tell you to stop."

Her voice was ragged, breathless. "What? But–"

"If you value Cassie's life then get back on the road and drive forward. Drive! Now!"

The image of her daughter curled up on that passenger seat, innocent, vulnerable, burned into her brain. She pulled out onto the road again, gunning the accelerator, shooting forward.

The tornado was less than a quarter of a mile ahead – a screaming, seething tower thundering toward her.

"Full speed, Carol, or Cassie will be dead in seconds."

Dear God...

Her heart thumped and she could no longer draw breath. She pressed her foot down on the accelerator, the car picking up so much speed that it might have been flying, the massive, dark whirlwind of pure energy looming over her, and then it smashed into it, a head-on collision with nature's full fury.

The car was tossed like the insignificant thing it was, turning in the air – Carol's head hitting the side window – then crashing to the earth, rolling once, twice, before settling in a mist of dust, rain, and debris.

She sat, dazed, the seat belt cutting into her chest, blood flowing down her cheek from the gash on the side of her forehead. She looked through the windshield, squinting, but her vision was blurred; all she could make out were darkly fragmented shapes. She unlatched the seat belt and tried to open the door, but it didn't budge. She looked for her laptop and her phone, but they were on the floor, screens smashed.

She tried to think but her head was pounding, and she wondered what had happened. Where was she?

And then she remembered.

Cassie.

Oh, dear God, please, no… Cassie…

She lurched across to the passenger door, she was aching all over, her left arm felt as though it could be broken, but despite the pain, she pulled the handle and heaved herself against the door. It swung open and she spilled out, tumbling onto the road and then pushing herself to her feet; the wind not as powerful, but the rain drenching her.

She staggered forward and, ahead of her, a figure shrouded in the rain, the shape distorted by the blur of her vision, a bright light engulfing its head, was moving steadily toward her. Then there was the flash of a raised object. She felt the crunch of something hard against the side of her head, and the figure lunged, hands encircling her neck, fingers digging into the soft skin of her throat.

Carol was unable to breathe, her vision fading, consciousness slipping away when her attacker loosened his grip. Her knees buckled and she fell backward onto the rain-slicked road. Above her, the man was a blur, towering over her, and she caught a glimpse of his raised arm brandishing his thunderbolt, preparing to strike.

Chapter Fifty-One

The headlights were on high beam, cutting a swathe through the darkened mist of rain, illuminating a partly crumpled car by the side of the road ahead. The beam illuminated the outline of two figures beside the vehicle, one on the ground, the other with a raised weapon, about to deliver a powerful blow. I leaned on the car horn as I pulled to the road's edge and slowed, and I saw the silhouette of the upright figure turn and run across the road onto the field, only to be swallowed up by the haze.

Only minutes before, we'd received the GPS coordinates, fed through from the NOAA satellite, on the twister's trajectory. Speeding toward those coordinates we saw the tornado on the road ahead as it gyrated, shifting to the field alongside, its power and its velocity beginning to wane.

Bringing the car to a stop, Zoe, Zach, and I leaped from the vehicle and ran to the figure sprawled on the road. Kneeling, I checked Carol's pulse, saying, "She's still with us."

Zoe called emergency, barking, "Special Agent Marshall, FBI, I need an ambulance *now*."

"You two stay with her," I said to Zoe and Zach. I was back on my feet, scanning the farmland alongside the road. Hardly any visibility. Where was he? Was there a vehicle nearby, on that field?

I ran onto the grassland, offering a wider perspective of the land. Swirls of rain mixed with the debris that still trailed in the twister's wake. No sign of a running figure and I could not see a vehicle. I could run all over this farmland and achieve nothing. I ran back to the car, revved the engine, and drove onto the field, the vehicle shaking and rocking as I raced across the rough, waterlogged surface. He couldn't have gone far. Wherever he'd left his van, I should be able to spot it now that I was pursuing in my vehicle.

There were groves of trees scattered across the terrain and I saw a herd of cows. No sign of a man or a vehicle. I drove on, frustration rising. The stranger in the storm had vanished into thin air.

How?

And where was the missing little girl?

* * *

We were in the waiting room at the St. Anthony Hospital in Shawnee. I was on the phone, filling Will in on the events of the past hour. There had been no further contact made by the killer and my most pressing question, my greatest fear, was what had become of Cassie Gainsbury.

There could be no question now that Stafford would have to open the investigation up to a full range of resources but when I raised the point, I found Will tight-lipped. "For now, leave that to me," he said. I ended the call as the doctor entered the room, approaching us.

"Mrs. Gainsbury is in a stable condition," he said. "No broken bones but she has serious bruising and lacerations, and she is in shock. We'll be keeping her in for at least twenty-four hours for observation."

"Can we see her?" I asked.

"Yes, of course. I've advised her not to try and speak too much. But she has just received a phone call that she says you will need to know about."

Despite her injuries and her ordeal, Carol had a serene air about her as she lay, head propped up, in the bed. "I've had a call from the woman Cassie and I have been staying with," she said calmly as soon as we entered the room. "She found Cassie curled up and asleep on the front doorstep. She's woken now but doesn't remember a thing."

Which is what the killer intended all along, I thought. Carol Gainsbury's body to be found by the side of her tornado-wrecked car. It would be assumed she had suffered a fatal hit against the windshield and been thrown from the vehicle. And Cassie, unconscious the whole time, would be presumed to have wandered out of the woods behind their host's land, ultimately trudging around to the front door, tired and disorientated, before sitting down and falling asleep. Except nothing could be further from the truth. She'd been in her kidnapper's van and was eventually deposited back at the house.

Back in the waiting room, I discussed this intended scenario with Zach and Zoe.

Zoe pursed her lips. "But why would everyone think Carol steamed off in her car, leaving Cassie, and driving toward the nearest storm?"

"I expect," Zach offered, "it might be supposed she'd suffered a breakdown, grieving for her sister."

"And committed suicide?"

Zach shrugged, nodding. "Either way, despite the unanswered questions it would raise, it would still be seen as a tornado death. Keeping the killer's cover intact."

"He was desperate to rectify the error he made when he killed the wrong sister," I said.

"Except he's made it worse, this time exposing his actions. And now he'll know we're wise to his existence."

"Not if he believes Carol Gainsbury is dead and that the car that pulled up on the road was Joe Citizen, passing by, and he wasn't seen."

Zoe's eyes widened, her gaze fixed on me. "You want to put out a false story?"

"We need to get the police and the hospital to cooperate, and I need to discuss it with Carol. But yes. We maintain the illusion so that the killer believes no one knows he exists."

* * *

Another long, exhausting day, but not for any of the reasons I might have anticipated. The killer's brazen attempt on Carol Gainsbury's life had come as a shock.

It was late and I was back in Oklahoma City, ready to hit the pillow and certain that this time I'd be out like a light. No restlessness. No mind-wandering.

There was a hell of a lot I needed to achieve in the morning. No way was I ready to step aside and head back to Seattle. I knew Will was heading down to Oklahoma this evening and although we'd spoken in-depth earlier about this afternoon's event, I'd expected to receive another call from him tonight. Or at least I'd hoped I would have. I'd missed having him by my side, as part of the team, these past few days. And maybe I was missing him in another way. In a way I didn't want to.

Rekindling anything of the relationship we'd had over two years ago wasn't on my agenda. I'd made that clear to Will. Just as I'd convinced myself. I sensed he *did* want to revisit that earlier closeness, although he'd accepted my view on this and kept our interactions strictly professional.

So why am I hoping he calls me tonight?

A moment later, as though reading my mind and despite the late hour, my phone rang. It was the call I'd hoped for but the nature of the call, about what Will had planned for the team for the following morning, wasn't a follow-on to the attack on Carol. And it was vastly different from anything I could have anticipated.

PART THREE

Chapter Fifty-Two

Day Seven

At 7.45 a.m. Will received the confidential alert on his laptop, forwarded by the acting assistant director in DC. It had been sent to the DoJ, to all FBI SACs, and the US Marshalls Office.

Ten minutes later Marcia was on the line. "Are you seeing this?"

"I've got the CNN news feed coming through now."

Imposed over an aerial shot of several vehicles overturned on a tree-lined DC avenue, one of them the police transport vehicle, the anchor reported:

> *Breaking news. Just minutes ago, a van transporting the corrupt business tycoon, Brad Carstairs, crashed, and we can confirm that he has escaped custody. Eyewitness reports have confirmed that shots were fired, taking out tires on the lead vehicle and with another shot seriously injuring the driver. The van then careered out of control hitting other vehicles and causing a major pile-up, in which some were completely overturned.*

"Has Themis accessed the security cams at the Arrowhead Airfield?" Will asked.

"It's online now. Sending you a link."

The email icon on Will's laptop blinked.

The Arrowhead Airfield was a light aircraft takeoff and landing strip, a half-an-hour drive from the Capitol. Second-guessing the plan, Will anticipated that the transporting of Carstairs created the opportunity for his criminal contacts to intercept and crash the van on E St., NW. They would free Carstairs, and spirit him across the green expanse of the Ellipse to a waiting vehicle on 17th Street. By the time the news broke and the federal agencies were on the scene, the other vehicle would be arriving at the private airfield outside Clinton, Maryland, where a pre-approved flight plan had been lodged. Will had already checked and the commercial flight path was for a cargo haul to the south-east, but he could guess its true destination. The perfect short-term hideout, the idea subtly put in front of an unsuspecting Stafford. The last place that a national federal manhunt would have on its radar.

Ahead of his own flight, Will had phoned Ilona the night before. He informed her he'd already spoken with Detective Radner and he outlined the plan, organizing for her, Zoe, and Zach, to meet him in the morning.

He couldn't alert the FBI without concrete evidence and based on what was, to all intents and purposes, a hunch. He could have been way off the mark and throughout the night he'd begun to doubt his suspicion, getting little more than an hour's sleep in his motel room after his late-night arrival in Oklahoma City. He'd woken constantly in a cold sweat, checking the nightstand clock, primed for an event that he increasingly thought, as the hour approached, was unlikely. But if his hunch played out and he'd correctly surmised Carstairs's intention, then he was already on the spot with a plan of his own, a plan that would do more than just ensnare Carstairs, it would also expose Stafford.

Chapter Fifty-Three

From the rise of a nearby hill, Zoe and Zach adjusted their binoculars and watched the rural airfield in Pauls Valley, Oklahoma as the light aircraft descended and touched down on the tarmac. It rolled to a stop alongside a small cluster of buildings. The sky above was an uneasy mix of sundrenched pockets, surrounded by tentacles of dark clouds trailing in all directions.

They watched as the local FBI agent emerged from one of the buildings and greeted the man who was debarking from the aircraft. They had been instructed by Will to keep clear, remain safe, and observe, and then confirm if and when the arrival took place. Lowering his binoculars, Zach said, "Exactly as Will anticipated."

Zoe nodded. Raising her cell, she tapped in Will McCord's number. "He's here. And they're driving away now."

* * *

The inconspicuous, gray Ford sedan came to a stop on the driveway alongside the damaged farmhouse. The sky was bleak, and the wind howled around the splintered walls, whistling through the cracks as field office agent Vance Corey alighted from the vehicle. He moved cautiously around the exterior of the house, watching for signs of life – there were none – and then he went to the storm shelter that was just meters from the house. He lifted the ten-gauge steel door and stepped down the interior ladder to check and ensure it was empty. Returning to the top, he gestured toward the Ford.

A lone figure stepped out of the sedan and made his way across to the underground shelter. Both men then descended into the bunker.

From our hidden viewing point in the dilapidated shed behind the house, surrounded by the rubble of a ruined chicken coop and a bird aviary, Detective Radner, Will, and I emerged, pistols drawn.

Will stooped and knocked on the storm shelter door and then stood back, out of the immediate view of Corey, who opened the door and climbed out. Will then moved quickly forward, pressing the barrel of his pistol against the back of Corey's neck, speaking in a whisper. "Step out, throw your weapon on the ground and kick it away, and turn slowly, placing your hands behind your head." As he did, I fastened the outer locks on the door.

Stepping back, his pistol trained on the rogue agent, Will said, "Vance Corey, you're under arrest for aiding and abetting a fugitive and conspiring to pervert the course of justice." He proceeded to read him his Miranda rights.

It didn't surprise me that Corey had an explanation at the ready. He spoke rapidly, defensively. "What's this about? I'm here at what I'm told is a federal undercover op to contact and draw out criminal networks."

"You haven't been told anything of the kind," Will said. "We know about your past involvement with Carstairs's activities. We know you were blackmailed into helping Carstairs lay low out here."

"I had no idea, Agent McCord–" Corey looked around, sighting me and Radner with our pistols trained on him.

"You'll have every chance to plead your case in court. I don't need to tell you that you're looking at ten to twenty in a federal penitentiary. If you want me in your corner, to speak to the judge about how you cooperated in bringing down the internal network connected to Stafford, that can go a long way in reducing your sentence. But you're a special agent and you already know that, so tell me, Corey, what's it going to be?"

Corey glared back, stunned, the devastation to his career and his life registering on his otherwise bland features.

"Who enlisted you for this little exercise?" I asked.

He shook his head. "I…" He swallowed hard, unsure of his next move.

With my pistol still aimed squarely at Corey, I cupped my other hand to my ear, speaking into my comms. "This is Special Agent Farris, requesting immediate backup." I rattled off the address of the property.

"One word," Will pressed Corey. "One name. And it won't come as any surprise, we already suspect who it is, but I want to hear it from you."

* * *

Stafford glanced at his watch. He'd expected to receive the call by now to confirm that everything had gone to plan.

There was a sudden commotion outside his temporary DC office. He looked to the door as it flew open and three senior agents marched in. Their weapons weren't drawn but their bearing and facial expressions were enough to sound Stafford's inner alarm bells. "What is it?"

"Acting Assistant Director John Stafford," the lead agent announced, "you are under arrest…"

The litany of words that followed was like a deafening white noise in his head. There was disbelief and then a sudden realization that the world he knew was crashing around him.

Chapter Fifty-Four

Detective Radner was ahead of us, walking alongside the officers as they bundled Carstairs and Corey into squad cars.

I watched, my heart still thumping, the anger inside me wanting to release itself in a primal scream; anger at the fact that a corrupt agent had engineered this. I closed my eyes for a moment, letting myself succumb to the breeze that caressed my face, lifting the strands of hair from my forehead. I opened my eyes again, letting an inner calm descend, and I raised my eyes to the clouds.

Like some of the other houses further along this road, the property had once been a hobby farm but didn't appear to have had that purpose for some time now. A wide, sloping field sat at the rear of the land, blades of grass shifting in a gentle dance under a mild wind. In the distance, cornfields. The last place you would expect to intercept a fugitive and that, of course, had been the very point of it.

I turned to Will and embraced him. "Thanks."

"For what?"

"For having my back. And Marcia's. I felt abandoned last night. I should have known you'd have a game plan where Stafford was involved."

"It was a long shot. A hunch."

"Which played out."

"I suspected that Stafford had helpers within the Bureau." He shrugged, his expression displaying the disbelief he felt. "Even as it was unfolding, I could hardly believe it."

"And splitting this team diverted our focus on anything Stafford was up to, as well as being Carstairs's revenge on me, and you, for the part we played in bringing him down."

"Well, that backfired. Had the opposite effect," Will said. "I sent Marcia to covertly dig into Stafford's past. And once Marcia starts digging…"

"She's like a dog with a bone."

"Not sure she'd appreciate the analogy." We both laughed. "Stafford might not have acted for weeks, even months, he needed to find and ensure a safe hiding place – but once I made him aware of the heist gang's maps of abandoned properties with storm shelters, he had immediate access to where the shelters were and knew which one would work best."

"And he jumped on it." My eyes widened and I grinned at how Will had turned Stafford's plan against him. "What now?"

"I don't expect there'll be any problems having the UCU team revert to how it was," he said. "For the time being, anyhow. The next step for us is to stop this killer. But there's something I need to make very clear about your plan for luring him out."

"Okay."

"We won't be taking any extreme risks. If a twister starts bearing down on Courtney White's house before we've sighted or nabbed the killer, then we abort the mission on my say-so. We get out and into the shelter on the farm. Clear?"

I nodded. "We're singing from the same song sheet, Will."

* * *

Via a video link in the conference room at the local field office, Will, Radner, and I watched Carstairs and Corey being processed and led to cells at the Oklahoma City Police precinct. Commander Frank Hewson appeared on the screen. "I've had word those two will be escorted by air to DC in the morning," he said.

"Thanks for your help, Commander," Will said.

"That's what we're here for. I'm never happy, though, when it's our own kind we've had to put under lock and key."

Will agreed, exiting the link as his phone buzzed. Glancing at the display, he said to us, "The acting assistant director. This will be about Stafford's arrest." He moved out of the room as he took the call.

"I've got something I want to show you," Radner said to me. He directed my attention to his laptop screen and played a short video, taken by one of his roaming video bloggers. The video had been shot from the ground, briefly capturing the moment that a lone figure climbed the side of a building. I recognized that hooded figure and the side of that building, and my heart skipped a beat.

"This was taken here in Oklahoma City just the night before last," Radner said. "I'm certain it's the same climber we saw several times on Seattle cams, the one who talked down that suicidal young man, the one whose movements suggest the climber could be a woman."

I was cool in my response, attempting to defuse Radner's interest. "Too distant to be certain. There are similarities but at the same time hoodies and blue tracksuits are common with these climbers." I kept my focus on the screen, avoiding eye contact with the detective. Brooke had told me about Radner organizing video bloggers in several cities to take footage of the city skylines at night on random occasions. All part of his obsessive search for urban climbers, an obsession I now hoped would end with the arrest of Mark Gorton. "You think, if it is the same climber, he or she is here because of an association with Gorton?" I asked.

He shrugged. "We've questioned Gorton about that. He says he doesn't know who it is."

"And this person is clearly climbing alone," I pointed out.

Radner shrugged again, unconvinced.

"Sometimes a coincidence is just that," I said.

"Maybe."

"You've found the climber you've been searching for these past two years. I doubt there's anything further you can learn from some other, random climber out there."

"No," he conceded, "but it does leave one question mark hanging."

"What's that?"

"Why is there another climber, whom I think *is* the one we sighted many times in Seattle, also here in Oklahoma just at the same time as Gorton was?"

There was silence as I waited for him to continue.

"I can't shake the distinct impression, Ilona, that there is something else going on with that mystery climber."

"You think that he or she might know something more about Gorton?"

"It's possible. Something that might put a different spin on Sarah's fall or implicate Gorton in other crimes."

I rested my hand lightly on his shoulder. "Paul, you've found Gorton against all the odds. Maybe it's time to let this rest."

He pursed his lips but didn't respond.

Will rejoined us.

Referring to Will's call to him the evening before, Radner said, "You guys are hunting a killer that your bosses don't believe exists."

"And we could use your help with backup," I said. "The killer doesn't know it yet, but he'll be heading to a spot between Woodward and Fort Supply. And the next potential victim he's targeting out there is yours truly."

"It may not come to that." With her laptop strap slung over her shoulder, Zoe entered the room with the professor right behind her. "We know where to find the killer."

Chapter Fifty-Five

Zoe set her laptop down on the conference desk and powered it up. "The USPS was able to track Shaman's Cave as the sender of a satchel three years ago. And from those records, they gave us the name and address of the person to whom it was sent."

"And you've run a check already?" I guessed.

"They used fake ID, of course, but the PO Box was registered to an address just out of the city, in Blanchard." The ringtone on her laptop sounded at the same time and her video link to Marcia opened up.

We grouped around.

"I've established that some of the victims were members of one, in some cases, two or three associations for female entrepreneurs," Marcia advised, "but so far, no obvious connections between the women themselves."

"Take a closer look at the activities of those organizations," I said. "Did any of those women meet in person, even if only briefly, at any conventions? Any links whatsoever to suggest why and how they were on the killer's list?"

"On it," Marcia replied. "And I've done some more research on the carnivals around Oklahoma and neighboring states. They often join up with, not just market fairs, but arts festivals and local sporting events. Some make a feature of paying homage to American Indian mythology, by having locals perform."

"Arthur told us that Little Bear people often stage their pow-wows at the traveling carnivals," I reminded the others.

"Speaking of carnivals," Zoe said, "Carson told me that he once tracked down Evan Shaw, the father who deserted him, and that Shaw was a casual worker for traveling carnivals."

I thought back to our visit to Shaman's Cave. It was on the same fairground as a carnival that the market fair often partnered with. If Carson's father had been with that carnival, then he would be aware of the pendant maker's artistry.

Zoe exchanged a glance with me. I knew instinctively that her mind held the same questions that mine did. Had Evan Shaw been drawn to the legend of the thunderbird? Had he been visiting his ex-wife on that fateful day fifteen years before? Was he the man Melinda Shaw had seen outside the farmhouse?

"Okay, Marcia," Will said, "see if you can match any of those carnivals to the time and the region of the storm murders." He gestured to me and the others. "In the meantime, let's pay a visit to that Blanchard property where the pendants were sent." Locking eyes with Zoe, he added, "And while we're at it, we need to know the ownership history of the place."

* * *

Zoe and Zach remained in Radner's vehicle as Radner, Will and I approached the farmhouse. There was no answer when Will rapped on the front door and called out.

Pistols raised, we stood back as Will fired on the lock and then kicked the door in.

We held back, waiting for signs of movement or return fire, and when there were none, we swept in. It was a spacious layout. The dining, lounge, and extended living space had a natural flow with a hallway leading away to the bedrooms.

Will led the way; within a minute, we established the house was empty.

At the far end of the hallway, partly obscured by a recessed wall cavity, was a single door and when I opened it, I sighted a stairwell. "There's something back here," I whispered. And then, peering into the darkness, I called out, "FBI. You need to come out, hands in the air."

Silence.

Will was alongside me. "I'm going in first."

With the stealth of a cat, pistol at the ready, he crept down the stairwell, one slow, cautious move at a time. The sliver of light spilling from above would give him enough vision to see if it was safe. He found a light switch and flipped it as I came down the steps. Radner remained up top, keeping watch.

The basement was small, with a kitchenette and bathroom, both comparatively inconsequential against the wide bench with a desktop computer, multiple screens, and an array of connected equipment. "His own little electronics den," Will said.

Stepping up to the console, conscious of the low hum, I touched the keypad, and the screen came to life. I gazed at an icon for a computer program, sitting in the center of the screen. A lightning bolt superimposed over the image of a majestic bird with its wings folded into an X.

Beneath the icon, the name given to the program.

Thunderbird.

I clicked on the password field. *Damn.* Trying to guess passwords was never my strong suit. Maybe I could get lucky, maybe it was obvious. I typed in 'Thunderbird'.

Incorrect password.

Maybe not.

I took a moment to think this through, exchanging a glance with Will. His gaze shifted to the screen. "This is his private den. His password will be something he identifies with, something that feeds his ego."

I nodded. I said the word as I typed it in. 'Tornado.'

Incorrect password.

I took a breath. Stared hard at the icon. The lightning bolt was similar to the one on the front of the pendant. I visualized that pendant, turning it over in my mind. The image engraved on the back, the same as the one of this screen icon, underlaying the lightning bolt. Was it staring me straight in the face? The thunderbird. One of the storm gods. What was it the storm man had said to the little girl, Cassie? "The thunder beings will look after you."

Maybe we should wait for Zoe.

Instead, I typed in 'thunder beings.'

"Voila! We're in." A checkerboard display of streaming data alongside meteorological maps and live-cam footage came to life. "His private weather station setup. We need Zoe here."

While Will went up top, I sat at the console, scanning the program's icons. Dozens of them: Radar/MSLP; satellite images; forecast maps; thermodynamics; wind shear; active alerts; NOAA weather radio; GIS data; local observers; address lists.

I clicked on 'Address Lists'. Columns of data, a state-by-state arrangement of the names and addresses of his intended victims.

I recalled Zach's spirited assessment of the killer when we'd been in the back of the TTV. 'The killer may be a trickster but he's no clown, no *heyoka*. He's a reaper of death…' Agnes Night Moon's words were, 'A harvester of souls'.

Did the killer see himself, and this secret cyber program, in the same way? Harvesting thunderstorm supercell data and tornado alerts, matching them with the geographic locations of the women he'd targeted, perhaps he saw himself as a human thunderbird, reaping death under the guise of destructive storms.

I navigated back to the home screen and my eyes were drawn to one of the icons there that seemed out of context with the others.

Journal.

I clicked on it and saw journal entries grouped into months and years.

I clicked on the latest grouping. The entries were random, at times one a day for several days in a row, and at times a month or more apart.

I opened the most recent entry and, taking a deep breath, I began to read.

> *There are long stretches with no activity and then the season begins, and a match presents itself. A name. An address. A tornado prediction for that specific area. Thunderbird in action.*
> *Sooner or later all the elements fall into place and when they do, another strike is made against the evil that destroyed everything good in my life.*

I pushed back from the console, stunned by the obsession with the storms and the psychopathic intensity of this twisted mind. A journal written not just as a record of his activities but also as a justification.

I was in the lair of a man deluded into believing he was an emissary of the thunder beings, on a mission to slay some mythical serpent, but there was also something else driving this. A vein thumped in my temple as my eyes bore into the words on the screen.

Something more than an obsession with the Gods of the storm. 'Another strike against the evil that destroyed everything good in my life.' Something intensely personal.

Chapter Fifty-Six

Will came back into the basement, followed by Zoe and Zach. As they did, Zoe's tablet pinged and she stood still for a moment, scanning the data as it was delivered to her screen.

"You've got something on the ownership history?" Will asked.

It was a moment before Zoe responded and it was evident from the pause and from the expression on her face that she was startled by the contents. "It was owned by a widow – Bryce's mother, Jane Crowley. One of two properties in her will. She died sixteen years ago, and the properties passed to Bryce and his brother, Doug."

A heavy silence fell over the room. It was as though we were waiting for Zoe to say she'd been joking and then to give us the real answer.

I broke the silence. "Who was living at the house when the pendants were delivered?" I was back on my feet, pacing, arms folded, stunned by this turn of events. I was struck by the odd, out-of-place thought that I'd never seen the professor stand so still and so quiet for so long, when in fact it had been less than half a minute.

"Calling up driver's licenses and medical records for their residential history," Zoe said. While she waited for that, she took a seat at the console and her fingers flew across the keyboard as she explored the system.

Zoe could never help but be impressed by a sophisticated piece of coding, no matter what side of the law she encountered it on.

I could see that was what Zoe was looking at now.

"Tornadoes are too small to be picked up by the Doppler Radar System," Zoe told us, "but Doppler can detect powerful thunderstorms most likely to be breeding grounds for twisters. This Thunderbird program is a sophisticated piece of AI. It's compiling an hourly list of every one of those thunderstorms, along with data identifying conditions that could build into storm cells. It then divides those by geographic location, gathering real-time meteorology reports, and correlating those with eyewitness social media posts about local weather activity. And just like Themis, this system is analyzing all of this in nanoseconds and comparing it with historical data on tornado events. This is where its predictive algorithms come in, applied only to those areas immediately surrounding the addresses of the killer's targets. The programming is multi-tiered, matching thousands of data streams based on meteorological probabilities."

Zach's eyes bore into her. "Are you speaking English?"

She flashed a grin but otherwise ignored his frustration. "For example, just one of Thunderbird's data-investigative properties is to search for an isolated cell in a particular weather complex, something the weather nerds call a tail-end Charlie."

"An isolated cell?" Will queried.

"It's a rare event. A lone cell containing several air masses. Those masses are drafting up and down in loops and are far more likely to build rapidly because they're not being tempered by conflicting forces from other cells."

"So, those loops have a higher chance of producing tornadoes?"

"Yes. And I can see from its archives that this system has achieved a remarkable 70% accuracy rate in determining when a tornado is likely to form in the specified areas, often giving the killer a lead time of an hour or more."

"If this has been specially built then the killer must have enormous resources."

"Not really. This draws on all of the same elements threaded together by the NOAA, weather channels, and storm chasers. Creating this required a lot of time and a highly talented and intuitive coder. But also someone with the same kind of gut feeling that storm chasers use when they're out there in the field. Part-science, part-educated guesswork, and then, partly being on the road at the right time in the right area with the right piece of data. This is storm-chasing artificial intelligence on steroids. He'd also be accessing the system remotely while he's on the road. It's how the killer has an elevated chance of being at his target's home when a tornado is making landfall nearby. It appears to give him the supernatural abilities of a shaman or a *heyoka*." She flashed an apologetic look at the professor. "Sorry, Zach. Not what you want to hear."

Zach shrugged it off with a grin of grudging acceptance, as though this was par for the course. "The reality is, I've never expected that proof of anything supernatural would come in one, sudden, transformative moment."

"No?"

"No. I expect it will come to the human race gradually, step-by-step over the years, as we become more enlightened about the universe." Zach's delivery ebbed and flowed, as though he'd slipped into one of his college lectures. "Think of it as an evolving stream of collective consciousness. We continue to reach expanding levels of understanding far removed from what we believed a century ago, sometimes just decades ago. Take DNA as an example. It wasn't discovered until the middle of the twentieth century but by the end of that century, the human genome had been mapped." His eyes lit up, his voice rising. "Our understanding of living organisms is at a stage that would have been considered science fiction one hundred years earlier, and witchcraft in the times before that."

Zoe smiled and raised her hands in deference. "That's one way of putting it," she conceded, flashing a side-eyed grin at me and Will. "But I'm sure you'd still love that sudden, mind-blowing moment of proof that stuns the world."

He spread his hands. "It would be a thing of beauty. This AI, however, still doesn't explain how he reaches those properties as quickly as he does with his vehicle left miles away."

Zoe's tablet pinged once more, and this time Themis's voice boomed. "Information requested on the current owner of the property. The owner is Doug Crowley."

"And what about the other property?" I queried.

Zoe scanned the data. "Bryce lives on the other property, which is the one we visited when we were looking for the van he'd loaned to his nephew. Looks like the brothers each chose one of the properties as their home." She turned to me. "If this is what it appears to be, it will hit Bryce hard."

"His brother ordered those pendants," I reasoned.

Doug Crowley was older than Bryce. Fifteen years ago, Doug would have been in his late twenties, just a few years younger than Melinda Shaw. She'd expressed some concern about that to her employers and friends, the Bennetts, at the same time mentioning how the two brothers had done volunteering in their younger days out at the Little Bear community. Arthur Fire Heart remembered a boy who had gone on to join the fire and rescue services – Bryce.

Both brothers had worked on the farmlands with traditional tools. Both had been exposed to both the culture – and the legends – of the Native American thunder beings.

As a traveling machinery salesman, Doug Crowley had the freedom to visit specific farmhouses at specific times. I was reminded of a previous conversation between the members of the team. He fitted the profile.

Fifteen years ago, Doug and his younger brother had bought pendants from the Shaman's Cave at the local fair, as had others, including Melinda. If she was dating the older brother, she could very well have been with the brothers at the time of that fair visit.

It seemed that over a decade later, it was Doug who'd ordered the specially designed pendants from that same artisan.

On that fateful day fifteen years earlier, had it been Doug, and not a worker from the neighboring farm, that Melinda Shaw had seen on her property? Was it Doug she'd gone out to that day? If he was the killer, then why had he been targeting lone women ever since? And why businesswomen, unlike Melinda, who had been an employee?

"We need to find Doug Crowley," I said.

Chapter Fifty-Seven

I phoned Bryce. I had him on loudspeaker but the first question I asked wasn't one that either Zoe, Zach, or Will would have expected. "Bryce, what kind of helmets do you wear for the rescue work?"

"Our helmets? State-of-the-art firefighter issue with thermo-outer shells and retractable face shields. Why?"

"With the built-in lights for pitch-black storm or underground work?"

"Yeah. LEDs projected from an insulated band just beneath the rim."

"Does your brother Doug have one?"

"Doug? No." His chuckle came over the line. "Salesmen might be irritating but they hardly need helmets."

"Does he have access to yours?"

Hesitation. "No. But–"

"Bryce, this is important. Could he?"

"There's a shed out the back of his place. Great for storage, I have bits and pieces out there."

"Including your helmet?"

"I have all the equipment I need here at my place or back at the depot. I only keep spare items out at Doug's place."

"And do you have more than one of these helmets?"

"Sure."

"Could there be one in that shed?"

There was a moment's silence, and I could hear the wheels turning in Bryce's mind. "Actually, yes, there is a backup I stored out there, quite some time ago."

"Bryce, you told us that, like yourself, Doug always has several vehicles that he buys and fixes up."

"That's right."

"Where does he keep them?"

"There's more than one shed on his land. That's why I store a few extra items there. The second one sits right behind the first."

"And that's where those other vans are?"

"Yep."

"You've seen them?"

"Ages ago. Not certain I'd have seen what he's got out there now."

"What about Jade? Has she seen them?"

"Probably. Once again, ages ago."

I didn't need to push further on that. My memory drew on the day we'd sighted the abandoned SUV by the side of the road, not far from Millie Hargraves' farmhouse in Anadarko. Jade had said the van seemed familiar, but she couldn't place it.

I felt my heartbeat increase and I took a deep breath. *There's an ever-changing range of SUVs right here in a shed on this property. A different one could be used on each of the killer's sprees.*

I had no doubt some of those vehicles were stolen and their license plates switched. It would explain the stolen plates on the suspect van we'd sighted when we'd first surveilled road cams.

"Do you remember him dating Melinda Shaw?"

"Yeah. Carson's mom. Dreadful what happened to her."

"Was Doug her boyfriend at the time she died?"

"I don't think so, but it's too far back to be sure. Doug had lots of lady friends in those days."

"I'm at Doug's place now but he's not here. We need to speak with him on a pressing matter, Bryce. Any idea where he could be?"

"He was heading off on one of his regional sales trips either today or tomorrow. Ilona, you're worrying me. What's this all about?"

"I have to rush but I'll be in touch and fill you in later." I rang off before he could press me further.

"Little Cassie's drawing with the light coming out of a man's head," Zoe said. "It was a rescue worker's helmet."

"You didn't ask Bryce about this basement," Zach noted.

"I didn't want him to know we'd broken into the place or that Doug was now our chief suspect. Couldn't take the chance our plan could be compromised."

"You think he'd alert Doug?"

"Not intentionally, but they're brothers. So, we can't be certain he wouldn't get hold of Doug and let something slip that tipped our hand."

Zoe was furiously swiping her tablet. "Doug's usually been seen driving a Toyota Land Cruiser and that vehicle's not here. It's dark blue, and I've got Themis trawling through state road cams searching for the vehicle via license plate recognition. Once we've pinpointed it, we can get a satellite view and keep track of its movements."

Will chimed in. "The storm forecast for the area of Courtney White's home is still several hours away but as Ilona said, Crowley's already in transit."

"He'd want to be positioned at the location well in advance," Zach stated.

I felt as though I was ready to explode. "We've got to get there first."

"But you can't draw attention by having your cars outside."

"That's where your buddy comes in." My phone still on loudspeaker, I tapped in a number and Jock Harrow's gravelly tones came over the line. "Ilona?"

"How soon can you get us out to Woodward?"

"For you? Faster than the speed of light."

* * *

Fifteen minutes later, Harrow's storm-chaser vehicle pulled up outside and Radner, Will, and I clambered aboard, nodding to Jade who was beside her brother in the front.

"You two stay here and let us know when you have that trace on Crowley's Land Cruiser," I said to Zoe and Zach.

"I can do that from the TTV," Zoe protested.

"With the kind of storms forecast out there, there's no guarantee that access to the sats won't fail. You're better placed here to stay connected and keep us updated on Crowley's movements."

Zoe shrugged her understanding. "Got it."

Harrow's voice bellowed. "Buckle up."

"Where's Rowdy?" I wondered as I took my seat in the back and adjusted my seat belt.

"Not answering his phone" – Harrow was behind the wheel, pulling the van out from the curb – "which is unusual."

"That rarely happens?"

"Never happens. Rowdy's always primed to join me at a moment's notice. He's probably gone all spiritual walkabout on me after all this time." He laughed.

"We can't wait–"

Harrow stopped her mid-sentence. "No problem. Jade's with us to run the systems."

As the van hit the expressway and picked up speed, I looked out at the sky. It was strangely clear and calm here in Oklahoma City, but I knew a very different sky had been cast over the state's west.

Doug Crowley was already out there, and if he reached that farm first, we'd lose the chance to put the final phase of our trap into place. After that, we'd have no way of knowing where he might strike next.

Chapter Fifty-Eight

"So many entries," Zoe said. She was back in the basement, staring at the screen.

Zach pulled up a chair alongside her. "You want to know how all this began."

"Yeah." She wanted to understand the psychological journey that had led the killer to his hidden, murderous life. At random, she selected an early one.

> *Sometimes I relive that moment when the face appeared out of the mists after the rain stopped and the wind died. Eyes reflecting sorrow, words consoling, arms encircling me.*
>
> *Eyes. Face. Words.*
>
> *Lies.*
>
> *And I've seen it so many times since, over and over. Faces of innocence. But behind the facade is the selfishness, the cruelty, the sheer greed.*

Her attention was diverted by the ping of an incoming message from Themis. "Land Cruiser identified as that of Doug Crowley, satellite imagery located," the AI intoned.

Zoe enlarged the video feed and zoomed in, scanning the corresponding GPS coordinates as she did. She frowned, sucking in a breath. "That can't be."

"What is it?" asked Zach.

"He's on Interstate 40, headed toward the Texas Panhandle."

Zach leaned in closer to the monitor. "That doesn't make sense. Unless… are there any potential thunderbird victims near there?"

"No one on our list."

Zoe stared hard at the screen. She'd segmented the display with the sat images appearing alongside the Word document with the journal entries.

The killer's specially designed pendants had been sent to this address. Crowley's home. His basement hid a tornado-predictive AI system to rival anything used by the major weather agencies. His traveling-salesman role was perfect for hitting the road at a moment's notice. But Doug Crowley was not heading to the nearest storm and the nearest victim. Or to the epicenter of a storm. He was heading in the opposite direction.

She set the display to show a gallery of six journal entries at a time on the screen and she panned through, her eyes scanning back and forth, certain passages jumping out.

> *Sometimes I still hear the voice, calling out, screaming, but the scream becomes a whisper beneath the roar of the wind…*

Whose voice?

Zach started to say something. Zoe didn't divert her attention from the monitor but raised her palm for silence. She needed to concentrate.

Zach flinched and he cut off his words mid-sentence. He looked at her, confused but at the same time curious. Looking over her shoulder, his eyes flitted over the same passages.

Zoe sat, unmoving. Lost in thought, scanning.

> *"Keep your eyes closed, stay in the corner…" Those words were reassuring but that voice was laden with fear…*
>
> *…I still see the desolation, the fallen, shattered limbs of the great trees that I had once thought so invincible…*

The words were strangely calm but beneath that reflective tone, there was an undercurrent, something simmering beneath the surface. At what point did that hidden, savage side break out? When he was out in the storms, closing in on his targets?

She navigated back to the main screen, surveying the other folders – dozens and dozens of icons, most tornado-related – and spied another folder that differed from the others, simply titled 'Tools'.

She clicked on the icon and opened a PDF file headed Fire Rescue Tools. One page contained pictures and descriptions of the emergency-worker helmets. Another page contained diagrams of an item described as a combination ax with a hammer and fire hook. A multiple-tool-in-one, the retail description cited it as ideal for firefighters and emergency workers, for forced entry, chopping through doors and walls, and search-and-rescue tasks. It was a sleek, sharp, curved ax-head attached to a fiberglass handle, with the neck forming a hammerhead on its opposite side, and a curved, all-purpose hook at the base of the long handle. She could see how the subtle zigzag effect this created on each end might be perceived as a lightning bolt in Cassie Gainsbury's stick-like drawing.

Where was Bryce Crowley when Ilona had phoned him earlier?

"I'm calling Bryce Crowley back," Zoe said to Zach.

He nodded but remained silent, waiting.

"Bryce, this is Zoe Marshall."

"Zoe, thank God."

She could hear both relief and anxiety in his voice.

"Is Ilona with you? I'm going nuts wondering what's going on."

"Ilona called from your brother's house—"

"I know."

"But what she didn't tell you is that we were inside."

"What?"

Zach raised an eyebrow at Zoe's approach, but her focus was on the call.

"There's a hall leading to a back area. A partially self-contained living space with a basement directly underneath," she continued.

Bryce's voice had gone cold, and he spoke slowly. Clearly unnerved. "You need to tell me what's going on. Has something happened to Doug?"

"Hear me out," said Zoe. "The basement is full of some very sophisticated electronic equipment."

"What kind of equipment?"

"Weather-related artificial intelligence systems. You need to tell me what you know about the basement, Bryce."

"Doug spends a lot of time away, on the road. He's rented out that back area for years."

Zoe swallowed hard. Her grip on the phone tightened so much that her knuckles hurt. "Rented it to whom?"

* * *

Zoe stood motionless, phone still in hand.

Zach shot her a concerned stare. "Are you okay?"

There was a buzz from her laptop. Themis's voice. "Urgent weather update, Zoe."

Zach's eyes followed her as, shaken out of her trance-like moment of shock, she went to where the laptop sat on a side bench.

"I can't believe this." Her eyes were glued to the screen as she furiously tapped and scrolled.

Zach came alongside her. "What now?"

"A derecho. The weather forecasters are going berserk."

"A derecho?" Zach combed his memory. A Spanish term. "Hurricane-force storms that can last for days."

"We were expecting supercell activity and tornadoes but *this*… this is rare. Derechos are widespread and hundreds of miles in length, moving at rapid speeds, causing multiple twisters and torrential downpours. This one formed north of Amarillo and now it's two hundred miles long and rolling across the border toward Woodward. Ilona, Will, and Radner need to turn back, it's too dangerous." She was on her phone, getting no response, redialing the number over and over. "Damn…"

Zach checked the news feed on his phone. "Stay-at-home warnings issued for northeastern Texas and northern Oklahoma. It's taken out a section of the electricity grid. Over thirty thousand homes in Texas have lost power." He glanced at Zoe. "Phone networks will be affected."

"And the killer's not who we think."

"What did you find out from Bryce?"

"I'll tell you on the way." Zoe grabbed her jacket as she headed for the exit.

"The way where?"

"The place I stayed when I was fostered. Vema's old house…"

Zach screwed up his face. "What?"

"We need to get over there. Now."

Chapter Fifty-Nine

At the rear of Courtney White's farmhouse, positioned to its southern end, was a large double garage and work area. It featured a windowed loft and by stationing themselves at opposite ends of that upper landing, Will and Radner each had a view over the tops of the trees, of the long driveway, and the surrounding tracts of land. If the killer followed his MO, by leaving his van somewhere out of view and approaching on foot, they would see him – either coming over the fields or, failing that, when he emerged through the treeline as he advanced to the house.

Harrow and Jade had dropped them at the farmhouse and driven to a spot no more than a few minutes along the road, where it was out of sight.

When the killer approached, he needed to believe that the farmhouse was empty except for the woman he expected to find.

Will's phone pinged with a call from Harrow. "Will, our tornado alerts are telling us there's a derecho – a couple of hundred miles of supercell activity with dozens of twisters touching down, headed our way. If any of them get too close, then even if you catch this guy we're likely going to have to hole up in the shelter."

"I understand."

Radner had picked up on fragments of the conversation. "Trouble?"

"In spades." Will looked out at the darkening sky and the billowing, threatening clouds. The rainstorm deepened. He bit his lip in anticipation. Where was the killer?

Chapter Sixty

It hadn't taken long for Zoe and Zach to drive over to the house where Zoe had briefly lived with Vema Coulston all those years ago. Zoe had a hurried conversation with Vema's daughter while Zach looked on. With Zach now standing beside her, Vema's daughter stood on the wraparound porch, watching, and then waving at Zoe, who drove the old van, the Coulstons' secondary vehicle, out of the shed.

"Thanks for helping us," Zach said.

"No problem." The young woman brushed away a strand of hair. "We always thought the world of Zoe and my mom would have been so proud of her. I don't know what this is all about, but if it helps the FBI, then I can tell you one thing, my mother would have loved that, absolutely loved it."

As instructed by Zoe, Zach refrained from revealing that the man they were after was responsible for Vema's death. He walked over to where Zoe had stopped the van.

She stuck her head out the window. "You take the hired car back to Doug Crowley's place. I created a backdoor in Thunderbird. Send the link I've coded to Marcia, and she'll be able to access it remotely."

Zach shook his head, showing surprise. "Zoe, I'm coming with you."

"Zach, listen. Thunderbird has the precise coordinates of Courtney White's farmhouse, and the system uses its own backdoor to access the NOAA satellites. I need to get to Ilona and the others and warn them. But just as importantly, I need you and Marcia manning Thunderbird as my eyes and ears, keeping me updated on exactly what the storms are doing. I'll need a constant overview of the whole area."

"I should be with you."

"I won't be in danger except from tornadoes. I'm way better off having you here on Thunderbird, alerting me to those."

"What if I can't raise you? We haven't been able to call Ilona."

Zoe held her phone aloft. "I've linked this to Thunderbird. Even if the phone lines aren't getting through, either you or Marcia should be able to transmit a message via the web or by satellite."

"Are you pulling rank on me?" he teased.

"Zach, I would never pull rank on you. But I am telling you what the hell I need you to do."

"Same thing."

"I need you to trust me on this."

He shrugged, unsure. "If you're certain."

"Dead certain."

Before she pulled out onto the street, she took a moment to glance back at the house with its colonial-style wraparound porch, large windows, sandstone walls, and ornate eaves. This had been an urgent, rushed visit – no time to stop and reflect on the past, to open up to the nostalgia of an earlier, simpler time; to the ethereal, almost melancholic sensation of reliving something that was gone. Perhaps another time. She shrugged off the sentiment, turned the wheel, and pressed down on the accelerator.

* * *

Returning to the basement in Doug Crowley's house, Zach activated the link Zoe had installed on the PC and Marcia appeared in the video frame. "Do you have full access?" he asked.

"Sure do. Thunderbird's dashboard in all its glory. I'm issuing a command now for live-sat feeds of Woodward County."

246

Zach revealed to Marcia what Zoe had told him about the rental of Doug Crowley's basement.

There was a momentary silence and then Marcia said, "I'm not usually lost for words…"

"Zoe will try and phone Ilona about this, but we need to as well. We should be patched through to Ilona's, Zoe's, and Will's comms through Themis."

"I'm trying those but not getting through. Lots of interference."

"Marcia, after Zoe left and I was on my way over here I was struck by something else. Some thoughts about Doug Crowley. Did some research on my cell and he has some real estate investments of his own. If he's not headed toward a twister, then where's he going?"

"Go on."

"He's got a property in Texas, and I've looked up the details."

"Okay. What's this about?"

"The property is similar to the one here. Roughly the same acreage. And it has more than one large shed at the rear."

"And?"

Zach hesitated. He turned in the chair.

He'd heard something. A door closing in the residence above. Footsteps.

"Zach, what's going on?"

Glancing back at the monitor, Zach placed his right forefinger to his lips in a shooshing motion.

He moved to the foot of the basement stairs. Paused, looking up. The footsteps grew louder. *Who the hell is in the house?*

And then he saw the feet at the top of the stairs, and they began to descend.

Chapter Sixty-One

Zoe had been on the road for forty-five minutes and it was as though she'd passed into another realm given the sudden change in the weather – the winds howling, heavy rain beating against the windshield, the wipers zipping back and forth, struggling to cope. The car radio was tuned to a local station, and Zoe felt her heartbeat drumming in her ears every time a news update was broadcast.

> *Damaging thunderstorms that began firing up across northern Texas have formed into a derecho, currently estimated to be two-hundred miles long and growing, with hail as large in some areas as three and a half inches in diameter. The National Weather Service has received over a thousand reports of storm damage and residents across the northern region of the Texas Panhandle, Oklahoma, and southern Nebraska are cautioned to remain indoors unless in an emergency.*

Her phone, in the car's holder, had been on constant redial to Ilona, Will, and Harrow's numbers. No answer. Over and over. And then, a breakthrough.

Will's voice. "Zoe?"

"Thank God." She turned down the radio volume and hurriedly told him what they'd learned about Crowley's movements. "He's not the killer, but I know who rents that basement…"

There was a massive crack of thunder, a lightning bolt sizzling overhead, causing her to swerve, and the line fell out.

"Damn."

* * *

My right hand cupped my comms as Will told me what he'd learned from Zoe about the surveillance of Doug Crowley. "Seems we've misjudged Crowley's movements."

"That doesn't make sense."

"No. And Zoe says he rents out the back of that house."

"What? To whom?"

"Didn't get that, the line died. Anyway, Crowley's not headed here, there's no sign of anyone else, and there's dozens of twisters – a derecho –closing in. We're going to abort and get clear of the area. I'll call Harrow to pick us up. See you outside."

I was about to retrace my steps to the back part of the farmhouse and exit the way I came in, when I heard a sound like footsteps on gravel out the front. I paused and listened. From my position in the living area, I was far enough back from the window to be obscured from view but angled so that I could see the outside area. No vehicles had approached the house.

I waited, tensing up. The wind was loud. Was it just the wind?

All of a sudden, there was a loud rapping on the front door.

What the hell?

I moved forward, senses on high alert. How could there possibly be anyone out there? We'd cased the immediate area. The shelter was clear. Will and Radner had eyes on the road and the long driveway. I activated my comms but could only hear weak static. No answer from Will.

Another loud rapping and then a raised, distressed, male voice, distorted by the wind. "Anyone here? Can you help?"

I was at the door. "Who is it?"

"I'm… hurt. Can you…" The voice faded, and then there was a coughing fit. "Oh, God…"

Whipping my pistol out from its holster, I unlocked and partially opened the door, peering out.

A lone figure was standing back from the entrance, head tilted downwards. Helmet. Goggles. Rescue flak jacket with the collar pulled up and framing the edges of the obscured face. "Sorry, ma'am, but I smashed my car." His voice was fading in and out under the howl of the wind.

I opened the door wide and moved back, raising my Glock and taking aim at the man. "No sudden moves. Put your hands behind your head and move into the house. Slowly. I'm FBI and you are under arrest." In that instant, I realized that this man, forlorn demeanor, feigning injury, had one arm trailing his side, the other behind his back, holding something.

In a flash of blurred movement, the man swayed to the side, raised his arm, and swung a firefighter's ax in a high, wide arc. The hard edge of the hammerhead was forged behind the blade at its neck, slamming into my shoulder even as I pivoted to avoid it. I cried out and my pistol flew from my grasp and clattered to the floor.

The storm man moved swiftly. He was through the front doorway, another 180-degree sweep of the hammer-ax cutting through the air, the tip of the blade just inches from my face as I swiveled, moving further back. My gun was within clear view but out of reach. The killer advanced again, the long handle of the hammer-ax swinging effortlessly as though it was a natural biological extension of his arm.

I grabbed hold of the leg of a chair and pulled it into position over my body as the blade struck, splitting the piece of furniture in two as I scampered to the side. Springing to my feet, still holding onto one of the severed pieces of the chair, I jammed it into the blur that was the lower half of the killer's face. He sprang back, momentarily

stunned, and then raised the ax again. That split moment
was all I needed to dive sideways and pick up my pistol,
pivoting as I did so to avoid the ax as it swung. Once
again, the blade missed but the handle edge connected,
lower down this time, on my right side. I fired the Glock
as I tumbled backward, the bullet going wild, whizzing past
the killer and embedding itself in the far wall.

Before I could take another shot or jump to my feet,
the man was gone, flying out the front door and slamming
it behind him.

Will and Radner had heard the shot and came charging
in from the back. "Ilona!" Will reached me but I scrambled
to my feet and was running for the front.

"He's here, Will." I flung the door open, stepping to
the side to protect myself in case the killer was waiting to
strike. There was no sign of him.

The three of us raced out the front and cast our eyes
around. The fierce wind stung our eyes. The grounds were
clear. Radner moved to the south end to scrutinize the
grounds there, while Will and I took the northern and
eastern aspects.

Thrusting through the low-hanging foliage of the
treeline, the wind growing in strength and smashing
against me, I spotted the killer away in the distance. He'd
run across the sloping northern aspect, hidden from the
house by the grove of trees, to where his transport waited
– not his van – but something else, small and light and
painted in camouflage-like grass green, and on which he
now sped toward the heavily misted horizon as dark
clouds rolled overhead, punctuated by sheets of lightning.

Chapter Sixty-Two

I squinted, focusing on his disappearing figure and the machine that carried him, the rumble of its engine drowned out by the howl of the wind.

A dirt bike was easily transported in the back of any of the vans he used. It was compact enough to be unseen, or seen only as a speck from a distance, when he used it to traverse fields from his van to the farmhouses he'd targeted; its motor always obscured on approach by storm winds or the thunderous roar of a tornado. It was easily hidden behind treelines or deep inclines or sheds, just out of sight of the houses.

He was garbed in first-responder gear and helmeted with an in-built flashlight. The ax held in the hand that trailed behind him was something that, even if glimpsed, would not raise concern; it was a standard firefighting, rescue emergency worker's tool. Knocking and calling out, telling of how he'd crashed and been injured, he was not a threatening figure. Rather he was someone to whom any of the women alone on a tornado-threatened property would open their doors and offer help. As Liz Markus had done. As Vema Coulston had done.

Just a glimpse had been enough for me to see that the killer had strapped his weapon across the bike's crossbars. There was nothing he hadn't simply but ingeniously allowed for.

A reaper of souls.

Riding the storm.

I swung around, pushed back through the tree foliage. We needed to intercept him before he reached his van. We needed Harrow's TTV. I called out for Will and Radner.

The sight of the killer's distant figure atop that dirt bike, hurtling across the farmland as the storm winds swirled, was an image that wouldn't shift. And it brought forth my memory of Zoe's photo of herself and Carson on their bikes, childhood buddies for a brief time, Vema alongside them. Carson Shaw, a meteorology student turned part-time weather-channel reporter and part-time freelancer, at one time a storm-chasing contemporary of Harrow and Rowdy. He'd been on the spot, chasing a story when we'd been at Beth Willard's farmhouse in Hays. He was a semi-professional dirt-bike racer who'd traveled the race circuit. Was he somehow involved? But that wouldn't make sense, it was his mother who'd originally died at the hands of this killer.

As Will and Radner came into my view, so did Harrow's TTV as it screamed to a halt in the driveway. Harrow jumped down from the cabin as I pointed back through the trees and hurriedly told the men what I'd seen.

"Can your rig catch that bike?" I asked.

"Yeah, but I wouldn't be able to follow him onto narrow trails."

"Then we follow as far as we can."

"And then?"

"I continue on foot."

"You kidding me? You'd never catch him."

"He'll be hampered by this weather, he won't be able to speed, he'll be in danger of getting bogged. It's an option." I threw a glance at Will and Radner. "If Jock can get us close enough, there's another option. We shoot out the bike's tires."

"We'll damn well try," said Will.

Harrow was already climbing back into his cabin. "Then let's get this show on the road."

But even as he did, I heard the rumble of an engine and a van I didn't recognize screeched to a stop behind the TTV, crunching gravel.

Zoe leaped from the van. "Ilona!" She rushed forward, eyes wide, her springy curls whipping about her forehead. "Doug Crowley isn't the killer."

"Carson?" I was barely able to believe I was saying his name.

Zoe recoiled. "He's already been here?"

"The killer attacked Ilona–" Will began.

I gestured. "He's halfway across the field, on a dirt bike."

"I saw his van on the adjoining road," Zoe said quickly. "He won't be going anywhere in that. I popped the tires."

"Then we can catch him in the van."

"If he reaches the van first and sees the tires…" Zoe paused, and bent forward, gripping her knees, as she caught her breath "…he'll take to the hills, scouting for trails your rig can't follow." She ran back to the Coulstons' van, flung open the back door, and pulled an electric-blue dirt bike from the back. "An old friend." She began strapping on a bike helmet. "If you can't head him off, then I'll be on his trail, at least we'll know where he's headed."

"Too dangerous–" Will began.

Zoe didn't let him finish, she was in the seat and gunning the engine. "I'll keep my distance."

"The derecho–"

"We should still have a bit of time."

"I'll ride with you," I said.

"That'll just slow us, tip us off balance. There's another bike as a backup – Vema's – but no time to show you…"

Shooting a glance at McCord that meant 'I've got this', I pulled the second bike from the van and pushed it alongside Zoe, mounting it. The ignition sparked the engine into life. "Fast learner," I said, "and I've ridden a motorbike before." I donned the other helmet from the van's rear, watching as Will slid into the back of Harrow's van alongside Radner.

Although I knew that Will had heard my rushed exchange with Zoe, I'd also seen his stunned expression. I knew his mind, like mine, would be reeling, coming to terms with the fact that it was Carson Shaw who was out there and whom we had to intercept.

I recalled Marcia's research on traveling carnivals. They often partnered with local market fairs, like the one Shaman's Cave was part of, and with arts festivals and sporting events, of which championship dirt-bike racing was one. It would explain how Carson came to see the pendant designer's work.

Those thoughts were pushed from my mind as Zoe's voice sounded over the comms that linked me with the others. "Don't focus on speed," she said. "Twisting the throttle and accelerating fast is easy, but keeping the bike from overturning or crashing isn't. The key is in the braking."

Zoe jumped her bike forward and demonstrated first the rear foot pedal for braking, and then the front lever, for either slowing or stopping safely, accelerating again with deft touches of the throttle. "There's no chance of catching him if you keep crashing and that's going to be made even harder to avoid in this wind," she added. "But no matter how experienced he is, Carson faces the same conditions."

Conditions that Carson relishes, I thought, recalling the words in the journal – his fascination for tornadoes.

Zoe added, "If a twister appears in our path, then we get out of its way. Fast. Apart from that, watch me closely, follow my lead, and keep shifting your weight to keep the bike balanced."

"Zoe, if you do catch him up, just keep him in sight until we've got backup."

Zoe signaled her understanding as her bike sped onto the field.

* * *

At first, I was certain I'd quickly got the hang of riding the dirt bike safely but swiftly, despite the heavy buffeting from the wind and the lashes of rain. The dark green sky and even darker clouds restricted the daylight. I'd lost sight of our prey, but Zoe was clearly in my sights and as I sped forward, I pushed the crushing thoughts of our discovery from my mind.

Focus.

Booming cracks of thunder, the sky darkening further. My comms were live and I spoke Zach's name, and then Marcia's – no response, an undercurrent of static. Then I raised my voice, "Will? You there?" but the silence was even louder than the static or the crashing sounds of the thunder.

I slowly increased my speed to close the gap that was widening between me and Zoe when suddenly I hit a patch of sunken ground; there was a savage gust, and I lost control, skidding, swaying, and braking too fast. The bike twisted, lurched, and I was briefly airborne, before crashing to the ground.

Chapter Sixty-Three

I braced myself as my body hit the earth and slid with the metal of the bike pressing into me. The bike and I came to a stop and for a moment I lay still, gasping for breath, hurting all over, but the pain was nothing compared to my anger and frustration.

I shifted the bike and rose, first to my knees, stabilizing myself, and then to my feet. No broken bones, just one hell of a series of bruises. Thank God for the helmet. I checked my comms and there were still blasts of static, so I had to assume it was in working order.

Beyond the farmland's border, there were sweeping hills, dotted by thick scrub with narrow, winding tracts of land, perfect for the killer's escape.

He knows the area, must have studied it from sat images, maybe he's been here before and scouted it out.

The lost time from coming off my bike created a greater gap between me and the fast-moving Zoe, and of course the storm killer.

Carson.

Applying his name to this killer jarred me. Mentally, emotionally, I hadn't reconciled myself to being on the trail of Zoe's reporter friend. I still perceived myself as being in pursuit of a stranger. I wondered how Zoe was dealing with this revelation. There'd been no time to reflect or exchange notes on what we'd learned with events exploding suddenly, and now everything was happening at lightning pace.

Upright again, I fired up the engine and the machine sprung forward. Going slower and keeping an even balance – staying the course – meant I had a better chance of keeping Zoe within sight. I *knew* that, and I had to make certain I managed it. I steeled myself against the buffeting crosswinds that slammed me from every side.

Deep breaths. Focus.

I skidded, almost toppled again, but using my feet, tapping the ground on and off to retain stability, easing the throttle back, and then forward in evenly distributed strokes, I avoided another crash and pushed on.

Momentarily I lost sight of Zoe, the darkness from the heavy, fast-shifting cloud cover swallowing up the light. The sheets of rain coming in fits and starts, and the mist drifting, were obscuring the landscape. And then Zoe was there again, no longer directly in my line of sight but off to the east on what appeared to be a deeper slope, then vanishing again into the folds of the undulating land.

Heading away from the direction in which the killer's van would be on the distant road. Glancing in that direction, I saw the heavy smudge in the sky, and then the resulting whirlwind that hit like a detonation.

Blocking the killer's path to his van.

Don't panic. Focus on the balance, on easing the throttle, on maintaining pace. I cannot lose sight of Zoe. Shoulders hunched, my body leaning into the sway of the bike, I negotiated the rough ground, the sudden rises and dips, and the destabilizing wind. My eyes didn't stray from the ground ahead, but my mind was a spinning kaleidoscope of thoughts. Should I have grabbed Zoe by the shoulders and physically restrained her from taking off after the killer?

I can't let Zoe come to harm.

I'd prayed Will and Radner would reach the van with its slashed tires ahead of Carson and be lying in wait. But the tornado had crossed the killer's path, forcing him to divert to the hills where I could see it would be increasingly difficult to apprehend him, especially with the storm showing no signs of a letup, and with the derecho heading toward us with a line of successive twisters. Harrow's TTV would not be able to follow this path.

The one thing Carson could not have anticipated, though, was that he'd be pursued by two agents on dirt bikes, tracking him into a maze of ridges, slopes, and scattered shrubland. Clever, clued-up Zoe, anticipating various outcomes, had stacked the Coulstons' bikes into one of that family's vans, a backup in the event of a scenario like this. Why? Because she'd figured out the killer's ruse.

But what was his plan now?

I activated my earpiece again, to check with Will on his location, and to touch base with Zach's and Marcia's satellite monitoring of the area but the line was dead. Even the grating static was gone.

Chapter Sixty-Four

Zach stepped back, his body rigid, wracked with tension, as a man came down the basement stairs. Zach recoiled, but then his nerves calmed as the light fell across the other man's face. "Rowdy?"

"Sorry if I startled you."

"What are you doing here?"

"Came to see Doug."

"Jock was trying to get hold of you. He's on the road with Ilona and Will."

"I was at the city precinct."

Zach frowned. "The precinct?"

"I heard about the arrest of Billy Joe Garrick, I remembered him from high school, same class as me and Bryce, and it triggered an odd memory."

"Odd?"

"Yeah. For a short while, Billy Joe hung out with me and Bryce. And although Bryce's brother, Doug, was several years older than us, we sometimes got together with him for a drink, or to play some sport. Doug seemed to hit it off with Billy Joe, kind of took him under his wing. He treated him like he did Bryce, like a younger brother."

"So?"

"Years later, Bryce, Doug, and Billy Joe joined me on one of my sabbaticals with The Daughters of Gaia."

"Rowdy, I don't have time for this—"

Rowdy raised his palm. "Hear me out. After the sabbatical, Bryce had to get back to work, and Doug was off on a sales trip, and on the spur of the moment, Billy Joe and I joined him. We rambled across Okie and into

Texas and we stayed overnight at a property Doug had bought there."

Zach's ears pricked at this. One of Doug Crowley's properties. He bit down on his lip but said nothing.

"Doug was fixing a meal and I wandered out the back. I guess I was a little curious. There was a locked shed, but I remember looking through one of the tiny windows around the side. There was a whole stack of household stuff. Furniture. Electrical items." He shrugged. "I didn't think anything of it at the time, and I heard later on that Billy Joe had run-ins with the law. Bryce and I hadn't seen or heard of him in ages. I had no idea that all these years later he might have still had contact with Doug. When I heard about this current arrest, and that he knew Doug's son, Nathan—"

Zach's interest was piqued. "Rowdy, why did you go to the cops?"

"When I told them what I was thinking, they decided they wanted a word with Doug. Detective Dan Walker's with me." Rowdy pointed overhead. "The door was unlocked, and I figured Doug might be back here and couldn't hear me, so I came on through while the detective went to scout out the area around the back."

Zach heard more footsteps on the level above, moving quickly, and then Walker appeared, coming down the stairs.

"Hey, Zach."

"Hey."

"Didn't expect to find you down here."

"FBI business."

Walker gestured. "What's all this?"

"Some pretty sophisticated tech."

Walker stared at the GPS satellite imaging of a vehicle, showing in a micro-window in the top left-hand side of the large monitor. "I gather you guys are also looking for Crowley. You know where he is?"

"We're tracking his Land Cruiser."

"Then we need to follow."

They were interrupted by Marcia's voice, calling out from the video screen. "Zach, update on the derecho, and it's not good."

Chapter Sixty-Five

It was years since Zoe had last ridden a dirt bike. But from the moment she heard the engine growl and felt the machine rumble, the know-how came flooding back.

Her eyes were fixed on the distance and the rapidly disappearing murderer. And that was the only way she could perceive the man she chased. A killer. A stranger. Not her old friend. Not the boy she'd once known, nor the ambitious, eager-to-please weather-channel reporter that he'd become. Another part of her railed against these thoughts, certain there had been a mistake, that there had to be some explanation. *Something...*

Sheets of rain swept in. The ground was softening but still hard enough, enabling the bike to feel light beneath her as it skimmed across the farmland.

But the meadow was uneven, the wind harsh, and she bounced around, muscles straining, nerves taut, constantly adjusting her frame to flow with the bike's trajectory, all the little techniques she'd once learned, dredged from the recesses of her mind.

And then a sudden drop, and an unexpected steep hillock before the field gave way to the steeper rise of the hills. Her wheels spun as the wind slammed and then the bike was in the air, turning before it crashed and slid.

She felt as though the earth was swallowing her up. But then she quickly shifted her body from under the bike, brushing away clumps of grass and soil as she stood, willing herself to ignore the spreading pain, squinting her eyes against the grit in the wild wind.

She pulled the bike up and pushed it forward as she clambered back on. No time to stare off into the distance to try and calculate the widening gap between her and Carson. She couldn't hope to match his speed or his riding prowess, he'd been racing dirt bikes for years. Her most important task was to keep him within sight so that she could tell the others the direction he'd taken.

One fleeting glance behind her and she saw that Ilona, though far behind, was still in the chase. *Thank God.* But she couldn't dwell on how Ilona was faring, or where Will, Radner, and Harrow might be now that intercepting the killer at his roadside van was impossible.

She gunned the engine and with its front wheel angled skyward, the bike jumped forward and she sped on, eyes scanning the misted distance for that fast-moving speck.

Even with every muscle primed to keep the bike moving, a part of her brain was doing its own thing, reflecting, analyzing, trying as she always did to make sense of everything she encountered.

She knew the answers were in the killer's journal.

Carson's journal.

> *Sometimes I still hear the voice, calling out, screaming…*

The thoughts that had tumbled about in her mind when she'd first read that entry came into sharper focus now. Whose voice? The only screams Carson would write about were his mother's. Melinda Shaw. But how could young Carson have heard her calling out from down in the basement of their house with the thunderous torrent of the wind outside?

Because Carson wasn't in the basement.

Sometimes there is a blinding moment when realization dawns, blurred outlines of what you think you know snapping into a different shape. For Zoe, this was that moment.

He lied to me, just as he lied fifteen years ago to the first responders, and to Collette Rayburn, when they found him wandering in the ruins after the storm.

Maybe Carson believed his imagined story, perhaps he'd brainwashed himself into seeing it as truth. But the only possibility was that he'd been a short distance away from their house, in their neighbor Collette Rayburn's storm shelter.

His mother died, trapped outside, a victim of the tornado, just as he'd relived it in his journal:

> *I wondered if the shelter's door was heavy enough and fastened as securely as it needed to be to… "Keep your eyes closed, stay in the corner and hold on tight." Those words were reassuring but that voice was laden with fear and why was there no action…*

What had happened in that shelter?

Over a decade after Melinda Shaw's death, Collette Rayburn was believed to have been killed the same way, in a tornado, but she'd died at the hands of that boy, now a man. A killer who believed he was on a mission for the thunder beings to rid the world of the evil of the serpent.

> *There is nothing as intoxicating as taking to the wind… another dark soul erased.*

Zach's voice crackled over her comms. "Zoe?"

"I'm here."

"Marcia and I have been trying to raise you guys."

"The storms are disrupting everything. Ilona and I are on the dirt bikes, she's following me and we're tracking Carson northwest of the farmhouse."

"Marcia accessed regional zoning maps. There is a steep hill ahead."

"Already on it."

"There's a flat area beyond that, with a huge construction site for a retail and office complex–"

"Then he'd know. He's hoping to steal a work vehicle–"

"Zoe, the derecho is less than a hundred miles southwest and the NOAA is predicting several of the twisters are EF3s and there's a potential EF4. They're headed straight for that area. The site manager's office is the only safe place if the twisters hit head-on. Look for a prefabricated, modular hut, two-stories. It's built from galvanized steel and plasterboard so the ground level will provide the best protection, except–"

She cut across him. "Carson will be there."

Marcia chimed in. "Zoe, we're still trying to raise Will and Ilona, but when you get to that office, if the killer comes at you…"

"I'm armed, Marcia."

"How far behind is Ilona?" Zach asked.

"She'll make it," Zoe began but there was a sonic boom type of thunderclap, and contact was lost in an ear-splitting surge of static. With the news that the derecho was advancing at hyper-speed and the comms being constantly knocked out, she suddenly felt incredibly alone.

Chapter Sixty-Six

The rise of the hill was not as steep as Zoe had expected but the trails between the scattered shrubs were winding and narrow, slowing her. She pressed on, determined to remain upright, and after what seemed an interminable length of time she crossed the crest of the rise, applying the brakes in short spurts to ensure she didn't hurtle too fast and tumble on the downward side.

On a stretch of level ground beyond the base of the slope was the construction site, the wire fence surrounding it torn in places and felled in others by the violent gusts. Half-finished walls of varying heights had partly crumbled, steel rods littered the ground, and the raised metal walkways and ladders had been ripped from their fixtures, crumbling and swinging furiously.

In the site's darker recesses Zoe spied what she believed to be the site manager's office, and in the flashing shafts of half-light, she caught a glimpse of Carson's bike sliding to a stop there.

She brought her bike to a halt at the base of the slope, aware of the danger from flying objects, the whole worksite ahead of her unstable. It was then that she saw another twister. Beyond the site and swirling across the horizon. And then a second and a third, each a mile or so apart – a haphazard line streaking toward her, sooner than she had anticipated. She sucked in a deep, ragged breath.

Good God.

The beginning of the derecho had cut a path of destruction across Texas and now Oklahoma – hundreds of miles of tornadoes: savage winds of up to two hundred miles per hour, picking up and propelling machinery, vehicles, fencing, and parts of buildings, with flash floods erupting, and visibility erased by torrential rain.

There was no way to keep clear of Carson. Not with the sheltered space on the construction site being the only option to shield her from the derecho.

Cupping her comms, she tried to speak to Ilona but there was nothing but static. She looked back but could no longer see far behind.

Even if she tried to retrace her movements to find Ilona, warn her, guide her to the site office, there was only a scant chance she would be able to locate her.

She'd keep trying to raise Ilona and the others, but for now she turned, abandoned the bike, and ran to the enclosure.

* * *

The office was a large room, cloaked in darkness. Powerful, relentless shafts of wind had smashed the windows, spraying the interior. Cabinets and chairs had been overturned and scattered, and water flowed in thin streams from the corners of the roof.

Carson was in the far corner – looking every inch the thunderbird after which he'd named his storm software – positioned against the wall for the best shielding from the elements, brandishing his hammer-ax. A dark sentinel with his helmet flashlight casting a spectral glow.

Zoe inched along the wall by the entrance to afford herself as much shelter as she could and then she paused, catching her breath, her eyes remaining fixed the whole time on the figure at the far diagonal. She might as well have been glaring at a man she had never met or even seen before.

Neither spoke. Seconds passed but it felt like a protracted passage of time. Outside, the thunderous boom of the twister bearing down on the site was a nightmarish cacophony, like banshees wailing. Zoe unholstered her Glock and aimed at him.

When he broke the silence, he had to shout to be heard. "Back at that farmhouse. It was a trap."

"We traced the pendant order, Carson," she shouted back. "We found the basement you rent. We found Thunderbird." She gripped the pistol so tight that she thought the bones of her knuckles might burst through her skin. "You come at me with that ax, and you'll be on the ground with a bullet in your chest before you get halfway."

"You think I would do that? To you?"

"I think we both know the answer."

"You're wrong. This has nothing to do with you. With us."

"Us?" The word came out in a spit.

"Old friends."

"You're a murderer."

He gestured to the tempest outside and responded in an oddly philosophical tone. "The storm won't let me be taken, Zoe. It's here to help. It's far, far more than you could believe."

"You think you're some kind of *heyoka*?"

"If you knew the full story, you would understand."

"The full story?"

"Of how the spirits guided me to the Little Bear people."

Her voice rose, her anger flashing. "You killed Vema Coulston, the woman who fostered me when I was living here. She posed for a photo with the two of us."

"Vema–?"

"You killed her without making that connection, without knowing anything about her."

"The Serpent–"

"If The Serpent possessed Vema, then it's done the same to me. Are you going to kill me, Carson?"

He didn't answer, his eyes behind the visor clouded with confusion, the line of his mouth hardening. "The one thing I missed was the real reason you and your FBI friends were here. I bought into the whole idea that you were here because of those damn storm looters. Meeting you on the Nebraska border seemed to fit that narrative, but I should have sensed what was really going on…"

"You were watching us at the Little Bear pow-wow."

"I wanted to be certain. Once again, I figured that was part of your search for the looters." He screwed his mouth in frustration and Zoe could see he was conflicted as to why the spirits hadn't made it clear to him.

The room rocked as the wind blasts intensified and the cracks of thunder boomed louder and deeper. Zoe felt the chill in her bones. She needed to cut through Carson's delusion and make him see reason. "The FBI knows who you are. Other agents are on their way. There's no going back to your old life."

"Then the thunder beings will lead me to a new one."

"If you still see me as an old friend, Carson, then believe what I'm telling you. You're sick, and for your sake and the sake of all your victims you need to give yourself up and get help."

"The Serpent has to be stopped. I know what it did to my mother."

"I know you weren't down in your mother's basement that day. So, what happened, Carson?"

"We didn't have a storm cellar but there was one alongside our neighbor's farmhouse."

"Collette Rayburn's." The force of the wind lessened suddenly, its roar decreasing, and Zoe knew that meant the twister had shifted direction, veering away from a direct hit.

Carson's head tilted, aware of the change, but he kept speaking, watching Zoe closely. "Yeah. And ever since she'd been a little girl, my mother and her parents had been able to use the Rayburns' shelter in the event of a tornado. Our houses were close together, on either side of the border fence…" His speech became robotic, almost trance-like, as though he'd disassociated himself from the storm and was reliving that earlier life. Was this a state he lapsed into when he was writing in his journal?

Zoe wondered if Ilona was okay and if she was close. She needed time and realized she could buy it by keeping Carson in this stupor. Keep him talking. "What happened?"

"Collette had a niece, Amy, who visited her aunt a lot, and we played games."

"You were in that shelter?"

"Playing hide and seek. I'd sneaked into the shelter and climbed into a great big wicker basket in the corner. Best hiding place ever, I thought. But I was only twelve and I must have been tired because after a while I started to doze and then I heard Collette and Amy clambering down the ladder; I heard the wind, and Amy said, 'But Mommy, I don't know where Carson is.' The door clanged shut and Collette told Amy to go into the other corner and pull a blanket over herself, close her eyes and put her fingers in her ears."

"They never knew you were in the basket?"

"No."

"And *your* mom?" Zoe prompted.

"Outside, banging on the door, calling out to Collette to let her in, asking if I was with them."

"Collette didn't let her in."

"My mom was desperate but then her shouts began to fade – the tornado was getting louder, hurling objects, and I remember wondering what Collette was doing, why was it taking so long, and I was about to step out of the basket when I heard my mother's scream – like no other sound I'd ever heard. Then in a matter of seconds, the roar of the tornado was gone. I heard Collette tell Amy, 'It's okay, it's passed.'

"I was frozen with shock. Looking back, I can see now that my twelve-year-old self sensed I was in danger if I revealed myself, because Collette had deliberately shut my mother out. Even then I hoped, maybe even expected, that my mom would be okay, that she would have found a way to protect herself."

Carson's voice was muddied with the anguish he'd carried all these years, and Zoe was momentarily stunned into forgetting everything else that was going on around them.

"They found her body a mile away. I went to live with the Little Bear community until foster parents were found because once he'd sold off my inheritance, my father disappeared. Little Bear taught me about their culture. I learned how the Great Spirits control the weather. How it can be used both for the good of the earth and for justice. I knew then that it was those spirits I heard calling me when I came out of the shelter."

"Why didn't Collette let your mother in?" Even as she asked, Zoe guessed the reason.

"She was a ruthless businesswoman obsessed with building a farming empire. She'd wanted to buy our property for a long time, but my mom wouldn't sell. That old farm was our home."

"So, Collette Rayburn got what she wanted. But that's no reason to go out and murder every single woman who runs a business."

Carson snapped out of his reverie, his eyes probing Zoe's, his voice pitched in contempt. "Collette was an example of how the Devil does his work, playing to their greed. She lied to everyone about what happened that day and she fooled everyone with her fake sincerity. Her business tripled in size, and she began investing in other farming ventures." His voice rose higher in anger. "She was planning to run for Mayor. To lift her profile, she created an association for small businesswomen."

Realization dawned on Zoe. That was the organization to which several of the victims had belonged. That was where Carson had first begun to collect the names of the other female business owners.

Carson clenched his fists, his body shaking. "I'm the perfect instrument to make certain no other land-owning businesswoman with a storm shelter could be manipulated."

Zoe recalled the words in the journal.

> *I've seen it so many times… Faces of innocence. But behind the façade… the sheer greed…*

He tapped his temple. "Mankind's obsessed with creating AI that outthinks us at impossible-to-conceive speeds. I developed tornado predictive software that does exactly that. Three years ago, Thunderbird was ready."

Three years ago, not before, thought Zoe. That was when these killings began. "You've got it all mixed up in your head, Carson. Every time you use your system and strike those women you think you're striking Collette. But those other women are just victims like your mom."

"No, they're not."

"Carson, this isn't rational thinking. You need help."

If he heard her response, he didn't show it. "The twister's gone."

Another stretch of silence, it was as though the two of them existed in a vacuum. Then, without uttering another word or moving forward, Carson hurled the ax, and it caught Zoe off-guard, glancing off her outstretched arm. Zoe's pistol flew from her grasp as she recoiled in pain.

Carson charged, barreling his body into hers and sending her crashing to the rain-swept floor. Moving at blinding speed, he grabbed hold of one of the fallen cabinets, tilted it on its side, slid it, and then slammed it down onto Zoe's legs. She was pinned to the floor, wedged against the wall. She cried out and tried to raise herself but her battered legs were trapped under the weight.

He scooped up his ax as he dashed through the exit.

"Carson, you won't make it. There're more twisters…"

"They're out there to stop you, not me, not a *heyoka*."

Zoe caught a glimpse of him strapping the ax to the bike, and then he was on his machine; its engine rumbled, and he took off.

He doesn't know Ilona was behind me. But where is she?

Chapter Sixty-Seven

My bike was sliding more than riding down the steep, slippery, water-logged slope, hindered by the near-dark and the shrubs. I could see a construction site, and my breath caught in my throat as I watched a figure in a long rescue jacket run from the opening of the small enclosure, climb on his dirt bike and speed off. I stifled a sigh of frustration. I couldn't give chase, as there was no sign of Zoe and I had to make sure she was okay. I saw Zoe's bike ahead. Was she harmed?

Minutes later I brought the bike to a stop and ran into the manager's hut, my heart almost stopping when I saw her sprawled on the floor, pinned by the cabinet.

It was heavy but I managed to lift it just enough for Zoe to pull her legs free.

"Are you okay?"

Zoe ignored my concern as she rubbed her bruised muscles. "Carson's taken off…"

"Will you be okay while I follow?"

Zoe shook her head. "Ilona, there's a whole crazy conga-line of twisters coming. You need to stay here."

"Carson knows how to avoid them, and I can't let him escape." Standing up, I turned to the exit. "Hang tight, keep your comms open…"

"Ilona!"

* * *

Scanning the direction that Carson had taken, I sighted him starting up the slope – not back the way we'd come but further along the foot of the hill and angling northwest, heading toward a thick grove of trees. He hadn't covered as much ground as I expected – perhaps because of the crosswinds. Heartened by this, I upped my speed over the grassland, determined to catch him. I was exhausted by the relentless thrust of the wind – which ebbed and flowed, pushed and pulled – and the pain pounding my body, but my adrenaline was pumping like never before and I almost felt as though I was harnessing the wind's power as I rode, just as I imagined Carson must have felt.

I reached the same point from which he'd turned onto the hill. I was speeding up the slope, when a sudden powerful wave of wind struck the hillside, lifting and projecting both our bikes through the air as though swept up by a tidal wave, throwing us from our seats. We crashed to the ground, rolling as we hit, the bikes smashing down alongside us, crumpled and useless.

I pulled my body in tight to absorb the impact as I hit. I gasped for breath, feeling as though I was glued to the ground by the wind, struggling to move against its sheer force. I glanced around. Where was Carson?

An even greater, deeper darkness descended, and I looked up at a thick black column of fury that was spiraling right toward the hill. It rotated westward as it scoured the earth, churning up massive chunks of dirt and grass, missing the construction site but its tailwinds ripped apart what remained of the wire fencing, sending it sailing along with a heavy spray of steel bolts, metal casings, and rods.

And in its immediate wake, another tornado, its column wider and darker, and within its whorling mass I saw what looked like the head of a hissing, writhing reptile. This twister thundered toward me, traveling in an unrelenting straight line with an ear-splitting boom. It was a sound to match that of a detonated skyscraper, smashing down with hundreds of tons of granite and steel pulverizing the ground.

And just as in that scenario, there was nowhere to hide and no way to outrun it.

Between me and the twister was a section of the sprawling construction site. As I pushed myself to a kneeling position, I saw Carson further down, on his feet, running against the wind, forcing himself forward as the wind pushed against him, vying to reach the site in search of shelter.

I sucked in a deep breath of air, braced, and then rising to my feet I began to run in that same direction, every nerve and muscle primed, pushing forward with a strength I never imagined possible.

My eyes widened in terror as one of the site's cranes came tumbling awkwardly past the perimeter of the building zone. Seconds later, it was airborne as though lifted by invisible hands, and came smashing down on the ground just a few feet in front of me. I weaved to the side, narrowly avoiding its metal cabin, shards of glass and steel coils raining down over me.

I plastered myself to the ground, but felt my body being viciously tugged, then lifted, as the wind intensified – the twister drawing up into its funnel anything that wasn't secured to the earth. In desperation, I flung my arms out, reaching, grabbing hold of the door handle to the crane's cabin.

Fighting the turbulence, I slowly managed to bring my other arm around to grasp the other end of the handle as my feet were whipped up above me and I strained with every fiber against its seemingly magnetic pull.

I yanked at the door, once, twice, a third time. It budged, and I yanked again with both arms, and then the door swung out. Stretched vertically and being wrenched with greater and greater force, I strained to pull my body closer to the opening, managing to get one hand inside and take hold of the gearshift, thrusting and twisting to get my head and shoulders inside, and then…

My fingers, covered in sweat, slipped off the lever and my upper body was pulled outside again. My other hand still clutched the outer handle but the pain in my fingers and knuckles was so overpowering, the tornado so strong, that I knew I couldn't hold on. My remaining grip was loosening and then the crane itself shifted and began lifting off the ground.

The crane was several feet in the air when it dropped back, abandoned by the vortex as the core of the tornado passed and stormed away. I lost my grip and was tossed like a rag doll, spinning and then crashing down onto the hillside.

Chapter Sixty-Eight

I lay motionless, legs and arms askew, afraid to try and move in case I couldn't, intense pain radiating through my body, my vision blurred. The rain eased and the wind died down as the roar of the tornado faded into the distance.

An eerie calm descended.

Minutes earlier I'd been in the epicenter of a fury that was impossible to comprehend unless you'd been in its midst.

How many more of these damn things are coming?

My heart was pounding, my breathing too rapid, and I took long, slow, deep, calming breaths. I wiggled my fingers, stretched my arms, and my thoughts erupted and began crowding in. Where was Carson? Had Zoe been protected in that hut when the twister smashed it head-on?

It took me three attempts to push myself to my feet and regain my equilibrium. Nothing seemed to be broken but my body must have been a mass of bruises.

I was at the foot of the hill. I staggered across the meadow to the corner of the building site where the office stood. The site was unrecognizable – rubble strewn everywhere, the air thick with floating, falling debris.

Carson was up ahead of me. He'd made it to the doorway of the office enclosure which had afforded him enough shelter and something to take hold of, so that he hadn't been sucked up into the tornado. Now he was atop Zoe's dirt bike, which had been pulled into the hut to protect it – whether by Carson or Zoe I didn't know – and he fired up the engine and sped off.

There was no way for me to follow.

As I watched the bike recede into the distance, the wind strengthened, and the freight-train-sounding roar of another twister assaulted my ears. I braced as the wind whipped around me, knocking me from my feet. I detected from its push that it was blowing in from a different angle, and then I saw it, on a trajectory that would miss the building zone, a half-mile to its west, zigzagging, turning, and I gasped in horror and disbelief. It was tearing straight toward the point where the low-lying meadow skirted the hillside, and Carson was in its direct path.

I was helpless to do anything but watch. The swirling torrent swept through groves of trees, snapping the trunks. Carson was ripped from his seat, his body and the bike swallowed up by the churning tower – toy things savaged by a monstrous force of nature. Like his mother so many years before, his broken and misshapen body, somewhere miles distant, would be slammed at two hundred miles an hour into the earth below.

Chapter Sixty-Nine

Zoe was at the doorway to the ruins of the office as I staggered over, reaching her. Exhausted, acknowledging each other's survival with a nod, we embraced. "I know this wasn't the result you envisaged," I said.

Zoe didn't respond straight away. She held on tight to me, calming herself with slow, measured breaths. "The killings have stopped, that's the main thing."

"Someone you thought was a friend was everything you're committed to fighting against."

Zoe cleared her throat, tears filling her eyes. "I don't know how any of this was possible."

I nodded.

After a while, we hobbled around the perimeter of the building zone to the access road on the far side. From there, we stood on the curb, watching as Jock Harrow's TTV rolled to a stop. Will, Harrow, and Radner jumped out.

Will sprinted over, hugging Zoe close, and said, "Thank God you're both okay. Carson–?"

"He didn't make it." It was all Zoe needed to say. Will nodded his understanding, and then he turned and embraced me. No words. It was as though the easy, invisible language we'd once shared when we'd been a couple had resurfaced. When he loosened his hold, allowing a fraction of breathing space between us, our eyes met and held. His were moist, and in them, I read that whatever restraints and good intentions he'd harbored since I'd joined this team, they were cast aside at that moment. I sensed he might take my chin in the palm of his hand and kiss me on the lips. I hoped he wouldn't – but then an unexpected emotion shifted within me, and I hoped he would. I knew instinctively that I would kiss him back and that I would not regret it.

The moment passed but it was as though there had been a subtle connection of another kind, the thought passing between us.

He swallowed, and I saw the relief in his expression that I had not come to any lasting harm. "It could have been you."

"It could have been any of us," I said.

* * *

As the others settled into the seats in the back of the TTV, Jade said, "I'm not sure how this came about, but Rowdy's over the Texas border with Zach, and with that cop you guys know from the OPD. Seems they've had some sleuthing of their own going on."

"Sleuthing?" Harrow echoed. "Rowdy?"

"What is it?" Will asked.

Jade activated the computer. "Take a look."

A news broadcast played on the monitor. Brooke Goodman was on camera, mic in hand. And both Zach and Rowdy, along with Detective Dan Walker, were in the background.

> *Less than forty-eight hours ago, the Oklahoma Police Department arrested several men on charges of having looted storm-damaged homes over the past few years. And in further breaking news, the same undercover officer responsible for those arrests has arrested a man believed to be the kingpin behind a string of these gangs in several states. I'm on the scene of acreage in the Texas Panhandle, where the proceeds of many raids were being hoarded in a shed on one of the properties owned by the man. This is where the alleged kingpin – traveling salesman Doug Crowley – was intercepted. Police allege that Crowley used his knowledge of properties that contained storm shelters, not just for post-storm looting raids, but also for another arm to his criminal enterprises – harboring fugitives from the law for profit.*

"It looks like goods were continually being moved to various properties for local distribution," I said. I sensed that between them, Walker, Rowdy, and Zach had guessed what Doug Crowley was up to, and tracking his movements, had been able to intercept him.

"We were right that something criminal was going on with Doug Crowley," Zoe observed, shaking her head in amazement. "Just not what we thought."

I watched a shudder ripple through my friend. Another unwelcome reminder that nothing was as it seemed, that the world around us exhibited two faces, the one it wanted us to see, and the one hidden beneath.

Chapter Seventy

Aftermath

The following day

The SUV pulled up alongside the deserted racetrack.

"Thanks for driving me out here," Zoe said.

Zach was solemn. He hadn't been his usually effervescent self since he'd reunited with her and Ilona and Will. They were all still processing the kaleidoscopic events of the past twenty-four hours. "When I heard from Marcia about how many twisters were converging on that spot… and we hadn't been able to raise you… I felt I should have been out there with you," he said.

"I'm glad you weren't. Ilona and I were lucky enough to survive as it was. Even so, Prof, I'm sorry for coming off so strong back at the Coulstons' place, barking orders at you like you were some kind of underling."

"You were doing exactly what you were trained to do. Taking charge in the field, making the right calls."

"Thanks."

"You sure you don't want me to walk over there with you?"

Zoe shook her head. "I just need to do this… for myself."

He gave an understanding nod. "A kind of closure?"

"Maybe."

Even though Zach was several years her senior, and had once been her college lecturer, Zoe couldn't help but notice that he'd adopted something of a hang-dog expression when she'd first met up with her childhood friend, Carson, after they arrived in Oklahoma. It was endearing, and she liked Zach, she always had, but she'd never envisioned their relationship as anything other than friends and colleagues. She wondered if he felt differently. Better if not, she told herself. Most likely he was simply being overly protective of her, like a well-meaning older brother. "I'll tell you what, I could sure use one humdinger of a smooth Scotch when we get home."

"Double shot?"

"Maybe triple."

He grinned.

She stepped out of the vehicle and walked across the grassy entry arc, past the auditorium seating, into a modest sports stadium with a vast expanse of dusty, winding tracks, set against a panoramic backdrop of forested hills.

Zoe looked over the track where she and Carson had once ridden. Every Saturday. Six months of fun and laughter. Those fond memories were fractured now. She would never again be able to reflect on them with the comfort of happy childhood remembrance.

Who was that boy she used to ride with? What had happened to him?

Had the tragic events that followed those carefree days changed him into a different person? Delusional. Vengeful. Or had that always been a part of him, locked inside, waiting to break free and worm its way into every corner of his psyche?

She would never know. The question would always be hanging in the air, unsolvable, and that was the thought that lodged in her mind and haunted her more than any other.

After a while, she turned and walked, with a limp, back across the open ground to where Zach waited. In the morning, she and the others had a flight to catch. Today had been a day intended for rest and recovery but was a fitful one for her. She hoped that the sheer exhaustion she felt would be enough to ensure she fell into a deep and peaceful sleep tonight, despite the pain of her bruised legs.

It was dusk and in those woods beyond the track, as the night began to make its move, the piping sounds of the common nighthawk could be heard in short bursts, rising higher as dozens of the birds joined the chorus. Vema Coulston had once pointed out those birds to her. They were slender creatures with long, pointed wings, their mottled plumage of grays and whites providing the perfect camouflage.

Vema told her that those creatures held the answers to all the world's mysteries. Zoe couldn't see the nighthawks as they flew among the treetops, but as they winged away, the chorus faded, whisking their secrets away with them.

A kind of closure.

She felt that if she gave in to the temptation, she could have been lured into the darkness in search of those birds and their arcane knowledge.

Chapter Seventy-One

One week later

I was perched on the corner of a rooftop that afforded me a bird's eye view of several tree-lined streets. A raft-shaped cloud drifted across the moon. The tension in my muscles was blunted and I allowed the tranquility of the night sky to instill in me its reflective tones.

Breathe in, breathe out.

I felt like a different person when I was climbing. Free. Unfettered. Facing a challenge like no other.

Beholden to no one.

When my feet were on the ground and I was in agent-mode, I was practical and professional. Relentless but cautious. Except for what I believed had been rare moments when I pushed the boundaries too far, endangering my safety. I expected that was a glimmer of my urban-climbing self breaking through, something I couldn't allow to happen again.

I'd been forced to rest for seven days now, as my bruises healed, but today I'd felt reinvigorated. Brimming with restlessness.

Breathe in, breathe out.

Night had settled over the city of Seattle. No rain. I knew I still had to take it very carefully, but this was an easy climb, a quiet office block, deserted after-hours, with plenty of handholds, turrets, and ridges.

Just the previous day I'd received a call from Carol Gainsbury, thanking me for saving her life on the road in Shawnee. Carol told me how much she appreciated the simple sense of calm and comfort she felt in knowing that whatever the future held, she and her daughter, Cassie, were together, and safe. Ultimately, that's what all this was about, I thought.

The reason I do this.

And it underlined the importance of a system like Themis that enabled us to zero in on cases that might otherwise remain unsolved, or threats that would go unseen and unknown.

At times when I was in this state of mind, and on one of these climbs, I pondered the double life I was living. Two faces, one I showed to the world, one I kept hidden. A duality that I knew couldn't continue. Especially not if a time came when Will and I considered giving our relationship another chance.

When I'd joined the UCU, I'd made it clear that wasn't an option, convincing myself it was the last thing I would ever want, but that was hardly the truth. It was a stance I'd adopted, a necessary one for my emotional protection, but also because it struck me as the most professional way forward. I'd buried my feelings for Will as deep down as I could but as much as it irritated me, I knew they still simmered.

Far below I heard a siren, growing louder, then fading slowly into the distance.

A whoosh of wings and a crow came to rest on the turret at the opposite end of the roof's edge. The bird's piercing black eyes seemed to bore into me with an otherworldly intensity, as though probing my thoughts.

I stared back, wondering at the creature's thoughts. A part of me envied the bird's gift of flight, its freedom to sweep across the rooftops, at one with nature, with a majestic view stretching to the horizon.

I'd often witnessed crows during my climbs, and they fascinated me. During my Quantico days, I'd read up on these birds, learning about their problem-solving skills, and how when one of them died, others in its group, known as a murder of crows, gathered around it, not just to mourn but to determine its cause of death. Banding together, they then hunted down and chased the predators. Something with which an FBI agent could identify.

The crow gave out a harsh caw, and I couldn't shake the impression it was calling for me to follow. It flapped its wings and rose. I watched as it glided above the city, turning in a wide arc and then soaring away.

THE END

If you enjoyed this book, please let others know by leaving
a quick review on Amazon. Also, if you spot anything
untoward in the paperback, get in touch. We strive for the
best quality and appreciate reader feedback.

editor@thebookfolks.com

www.thebookfolks.com

Also in this series

THE PIPER'S CHILDREN (Book 1)

A boy is found wandering in the woods, dressed in medieval clothes and speaking a strange language. When another child turns up, it doesn't shed any more light on the mystery for FBI agent Ilona Farris. Only by digging into her own past will she begin to work out what is going on, and who these children are, seemingly lost in time.

THE WHISTLER'S OMEN (Book 2)

Special FBI agent Ilona Farris faces a problem when a man is murdered in Seattle: the victim was meant to have died in a plane crash twenty years previously. Worse, spotted by the scene is a man dressed in a straw hat and long coat who rumor claims is the legendary El Silbón, a lost soul who stalks the living. Finding out the truth will be tough and perilous.

THE DEVIL'S ARTIST (Book 4)

When a wreck on the interstate kills several people, a mural in Seattle that seems to glorify the disaster creates outcry. However, upon discovering that the painting was created days before the event, criminal investigators are baffled. Are they dealing with a psychic artist, or someone who played a role in the incident? Soon other murals appear, and the race is on to stop further tragedy.

FREE with Kindle Unlimited and available in paperback!

More fiction by Iain Henn

DEAD SET ON MURDER

Eighteen years after disappearing without a trace, Jennifer's husband's body turns up, yards from her home. Apparently without aging one bit. She knows something is seriously amiss. Fortunately homicide detective Neil Lachlan shares her concerns. But when the case overlaps with a manhunt for a serial killer, it will put Jennifer's life on the line.

THE GREATEST BETRAYAL

Liz Carter is the proud owner of a successful advertising business when she begins a whirlwind romance with handsome airline pilot Callan McKenzie. Yet after his estranged ex contacts him, he disappears without a trace. Liz resolves to move on with her life, but a chain of events has been set in motion that threatens all she holds dear.

FREE with Kindle Unlimited and available in paperback!

Other titles of interest

THE IDEAL COUPLE
by Anna Willett

Detective Veronika Pope turns up at an old mining town in Western Australia, tasked with solving the cold case of a couple who went missing there some years ago. The townsfolk are not welcoming and everyone seems to be hiding something. Out on a limb and in the middle of nowhere, Pope is in danger and will need to make a friend to stay alive.

FREE with Kindle Unlimited and available in paperback!

**OUTCAST SISTER
by James Davidson**

London detective Eleanor Rose is lured back to her home city of Liverpool by Daniel, an ex-boyfriend and colleague who's in danger. But when she retraces his steps to a grim housing estate, he's nowhere to be found. Has she walked into some kind of trap? Is Rose ready to confront the demons she finds there?

FREE with Kindle Unlimited and available in paperback!

Sign up to our mailing list to find out about new releases and special offers!

www.thebookfolks.com